A HEART FULL OF STARS

A Collection of Futuristic and Fantasy Erotic Romance

ISBN-10:1-940078-35-0
ISBN-13:978-1-940078-35-9

Cover by: Chaos
Cover art photo credit: **bestdesigns**

Also by Megan Hart

Tear You Apart
The Favor
The Darkest Embrace
Precious and Fragile Things
Exit Light
Beneath the Veil
Reawakened Passions
Hot and Haunted
Collide
Dirty
Broken
Tempted
Stranger
Deeper
Naked
The Space Between Us
Pleasure and Purpose
Switch
Stranger
Vanilla
Perfectly Reckless
Hold Me Close
The Resurrected
Lovely Wild
Precious and Fragile Things
Clearwater
All Fall Down

Foreword

I'm pleased to present to you this collection of futuristic and fantasy erotic romance novellas. If you've read these stories before and have decided to add these updated versions to your digital bookshelf, thank you! If these stories are new to you, I hope you enjoy them as much as I enjoyed writing them.

Amidst A Crowd of Stars is one of my favorite stories of all time. Even now, years after first writing it, I cried a little when I read it. It was released on its own as well as reprinted in the back of a paperback version of another of my futuristic erotic romances, Passion Model, but while it takes place in the same overall "universe," those stories weren't related. Marrin and Keane's story can be read all by itself.

Anything You Want was so much fun to write! Also set in the same universe as Amidst A Crowd of Stars (and Passion Model and its sequel, Driven) Milla and Jarden are an unlikely pair of lovers...but then, aren't they all? Take a cruise through the stars with them on their way to passion and love.

Everything Counts takes place in Somnus Keep, where Elspeth Valerin must learn to harness the innate gifts she carries inside her, or remain alone forever. When her past returns to haunt her, love will save her.

A Dream Upon Waking, also set in Somnus Keep, is about Noa, a young woman in search of her *ahavatera* — true love. Riordan de Cimmerian does not fancy himself the man to fulfill her destiny, but Noa is convinced otherwise.

Trial by Fire continues Noa and Riordan's story. All three Somnus Keep tales are connected to several other fantasy romances, Neither the Sea Nor the Stars, The Clear Cold Light of Morning and A Siege of Herons, all currently in production. So if you like the world of the thrall, there are more stories on their way!

Read in bed!

—M

Dedication

Once upon a time, a wolf and a unicorn fell in love…
This is for my wolf, who keeps me moving always forward.

AMIDST A CROWD OF STARS

To anyone who's ever loved through the years.

Chapter 1

Today

The medica was young, perhaps just out of the training academy. She still wore her uniform crisp and pressed, her blue hair slicked back from her forehead and held in place by the woven band marked with the symbols of her profession. She gave the man at the patient's bedside a warm grin and patted his shoulder.

"How nice of you to stay with your grandma all night."

The man was handsome enough to make her flutter her eyes. His dark hair, streaked by the harsh Lujawedan sun, fell to his shoulders in sheaves that made her fingers itch to run through it.

His hair might show the effects of the sun, but his face showed no sign of weathering. He smiled, his hand in the patient's, thumb stroking the paper-thin skin of her hand over and over.

"This is my wife," the man said without any condemnation at her assumption, for which the medica was grateful.

"Oh, I beg your pardon."

He looked back to the woman in the bed, her eyes closed and face pale. He leaned forward to stroke her hair, long and lush and bleached white the way the sun bleached everything on this planet. His hand caressed her cheek for a moment, and in the presence of such admiration, the medica blushed and left the room.

Chapter 2

Yesterday

Marrin woke to the feeling of kisses on her bare stomach. She kept her eyes closed, but smiled as her husband trailed his lips along her skin to the slope of her hip. She waited, breath held, for him to continue, and he didn't disappoint.

He never did.

"Good morning," he whispered against her skin, teeth nipping in a way that made her sigh. "The sun is shining again."

This made her laugh, as it always did, for on Lujawed, the sun almost always shone. "Good morning."

She cracked open an eye to look down at him, settled between her thighs as though he had no place else to be for the rest of the day. He laid his cheek on her thigh and let his hand stroke along her side. Her hand came down to rest on his hair, the glorious length of it that time and the sun could burnish but not diminish.

"I love you, Keane." The words slipped out without effort. She stroked his hair, like silk against her fingers.

"I love you, Marrin." He turned his lips to kiss the skin beneath his cheek, then grinned. "I would love you better."

She parted her thighs in reply, her eyes already going half-lidded in anticipation of the pleasure he would bring her. She heard his chuckle and felt the hot puff of his breath on her clit a bare micron before his lips kissed her there. She sighed, shifting. His hands curved around her hips to hold her to him while he began to make love to her with his mouth.

He kissed and licked her gently no matter how much she squirmed, taking his time. He always did. It was one of his charms, this constant ability to give his full attention to any task he performed, as though he had all the time in the world to complete it.

Because he does, she thought, lifting her hips as his mouth teased her flesh. To a Seveeran whose lifespan was limited only by accident or choice, anything worth doing was worth taking time for.

Her breath caught as his tongue fluttered against her folds. He nuzzled her, then parted her with his fingers to taste her. His low noise of arousal urged her own, and she answered with a gasp.

"Keane!"

He didn't answer with words. He slid a finger inside her to stroke in time with his tongue. He'd found the pace she adored. Smooth, steady, alternating patterns of light tongue flicks and harder licks. He slid another finger inside her love-slick passage, filling her.

She wanted more, but he wouldn't give it, her deviously sensual husband. No. Keane teased her, adding a twist to his hand that had her crying aloud and clutching the bedclothes as her hips rocked upward. He pressed his mouth to her clit, not moving lips or teeth or tongue. Letting her get off by rubbing herself against him. Letting her dictate the pace and pressure. Giving over to her control…until she was on the edge and ready to soar over. Then he pulled back, hand stilling, and blew repeated puffs of air against her pulsing clit and would not touch her with more than that no matter how she begged.

When she calmed, he withdrew his hand micron by terrible, exquisite micron, and slid up her body to kiss her mouth. His cock nudged her opening, and though she was so wet for him she felt the sheets damp beneath her, he did not enter her.

"I love you," he murmured in her ear, sending shivers to perk her nipples into peaks as hard as *lliwrock*. "One hundred rotations I've loved you, Marrin, and I would have a thousand more."

She opened her eyes and linked her hands behind his neck to pull him back to her mouth. "I'd give them to you if I could."

He made no more talk but slipped inside her with the practiced ease of long experience. He paused when he'd filled her and she marveled anew at how well they fit together. Like pieces of a puzzle carved by Adonai's own hand. He moved, his face pressed to the curve of her shoulder. Slow, long strokes, his stomach pressing her clit with every movement until she was back on the edge again.

She clutched him, fingers drawing trails down his back to cup his muscled buttocks. She pulled him closer. They melded, joined, moved as one. He withdrew and slid in again, the tip of his cock extending to nudge the entrance to her womb. Out again and his penis contracted. In, and it lengthened.

The dual sensation of his external and internal stroking never failed to send her to heights of pleasure she'd have said were impossible if she hadn't lived with them for so long.

"I love the way you take all of me inside you." Keane moved faster. His hand found hers. Their fingers linked. He lifted his head to look into her eyes, and the love shining in his gaze lifted her up and up, all the way to the sky.

Her orgasm fluttered at first, then rippled and at last exploded through her. She gasped and cried his name, pleasure making her mindless for a moment. Her body tensed and relaxed.

He gasped and shuddered, his back arching as he thrust into her one last time. She loved seeing him this way, perfect features creased with ecstasy. His body slowly ceased to jerk and shiver, and he lay down on top of her to nuzzle against her neck.

"Good morning," she said after a moment. "It's always a good morning when you wake me like that."

He laughed, the sound as rich as cream dribbled over fresh-picked berries. He got up on one elbow to look at her. "Are you sure I can't convince you to come with me today?"

"Not a chance, sport." She settled herself on the pillows as he shifted his weight off her. Now that the lovemaking was over, her hip had flared into the same dull ache that always plagued her. They didn't speak of it, but he knew and was careful of it.

"No?" He kissed her beneath her ear. "I've heard the silk merchants will be showing off their new fashions."

She laughed and pushed at his shoulder to let her up. "Where do I ever go that I'd need something like that?"

"It's not a question of need, but want."

She glanced over her shoulder at him still sprawled in their bed and looking so handsome it made her throat close with emotion. "You go and have a good time."

He stretched out. Still sinewy and firm, still looking as he had the day she'd met him in the starport. Nothing had changed about him. No wrinkles, no lines, no bulge or bumps of age.

And she… Marrin caught a glimpse of herself in the mirror over the dresser. When had she gotten so old?

She got out of bed, her throat still closed and her breath short. She went to the window and drew back the outer curtains, but left the inner set alone. They were sheer enough to let in the light but keep out the sun's harshest rays. In the daylight she could see every blotch and bump on her skin, every imperfection.

"Marrin?"

And then she turned from the sight of her own face, not needing to see anything but how she looked reflected in Keane's gaze. "Yes, sweetheart?"

"Are you all right?" He'd sat up and was looking concerned. "You look pale."

She nodded, her hand going to her throat to try and ease some of the pressure there. She tried to catch her breath, but could not. She tried to speak, but could say nothing. She reached for him, and his face was the last thing she saw as her knees crumpled and dropped her to the floor.

Chapter 3

Forty rotations ago

"What will you do tomorrow?"

Marrin turned to look at her assistant. Former assistant, she corrected herself. As of this moment, Marrin Levy no longer had an assistant, or needed one. It had taken a full two rotations to get all the details sorted out, but now that everything had been taken care of, she was more than ready to let go.

"Sleep as late as I want, for one thing." She smiled at Darlin. "Have a leisurely lunch in the courtyard. Perhaps go shopping in the afternoon for the girls' birthdays."

"Sounds perfect." Darlin's bright grin shone against the dark skin of his face. "I'm envious."

"You know you're always welcome to visit us."

He reached out to her for a hug. "We'll all miss you, Marrin."

"It's long past time for me to step down." She returned his hug without even a sentimental tear at the thought of leaving the position she'd had for the past eighty rotations. "Time for me to spend some time with my husband."

"Keane will keep you busy." Darlin laughed and squeezed her again.

"I'm sure he will."

And Keane, it seemed, intended to start keeping her busy the moment she returned home that evening. Marrin saw the glow as she walked up the curving stone path leading to the house she shared with Keane. She paused, looking over the low-slung white building nestled into the red Lujawedan earth. He'd lit candles in every window.

More candles illuminated the entryway and made a path through the smoothly curving halls toward their sleeping room. She followed the flickering light. By the time she got to the bedroom, her heart had already started to beat faster.

"Keane?"

More candles beckoned her toward the bath chamber. Smiling, she followed them and found her husband waiting for her. He looked up as she entered, glancing over his shoulder, and she caught her breath as she still did so often when she looked at him, even after all this time.

"You're late," he said gently, turning. The candle glow lit his bare skin with a loving touch, hiding scars and making shadows turn every glimpse into seductive temptation.

"They had a party for me," she explained. "I had to say goodbye to everyone."

He smiled and held out his hand. "Everyone will miss you."

She went to him and took it. "I'm ready to give it up. Ready to be home with you all day long."

He bent his head to brush his lips along hers. "I'm ready to have you here."

So many rotations, and still that simple first kiss upon meeting after being apart never failed to send a shiver of desire through her. Marrin tilted her head as Keane's hand cupped the back of her neck. His fingers massaged the two small spots at the base of her skull, eliciting an immediate response.

Her moan made him laugh. "You're still tensed up."

"I'm starting to feel much better." She pressed herself against him, and the heat of his skin seeped through her *nawe*.

The hand not on her neck slid to her hip and began inching the floor-length garment upward with his fingertips. Cooler air, blown through vents in the bath chamber floor, caressed her feet and ankles, then her thighs as he gathered the thin cloth and exposed her skin.

Keane kissed her, lips parted. She opened her mouth wider beneath his to let his tongue stroke her. His hand slipped around from her waist to cup her between the legs. The heel of his palm pressed her clit while he used his fingers to nudge aside the filmy barrier of her panties. He stroked along her folds.

"You're so wet for me."

"Always." The word came out low, throaty.

He pulled her closer, the hand on her neck sliding down to palm her buttocks and gather more of her *nawe*. In another few moments he'd pulled the garment up to her hips, then over her ribs and head. He tossed it to the floor.

"You won't need to wear that again." He bent back to kiss her again, both hands on her ass, holding her close to his thickening erection.

She laughed. "No? I do if I intend to ever go anyplace other than this compound."

He nipped her jaw, urging her with his teeth and lips to tilt her head back so he could slide his tongue along her throat. "I intend to keep you here with me...naked."

"All the time?" Her giggle became a gasp as he bit the tender spot between her neck and shoulder. His hands rubbed her buttocks, dipping between her legs to brush her folds from behind before sliding up again along the ridge of her spine.

"All the time."

Marrin put her hands flat on his chest. His heart thumped under palm. She traced the indent running from his throat to the place his navel would have been had he been Earther like her. It was sensitive, that thin place in his skin where once he'd been connected to the artificial womb in which he'd been grown, and her touch made him shiver.

She didn't bother arguing with his impractical suggestion she never wear clothes again. At that moment, the thought appealed to her so greatly, she was more than willing to believe in it. She kissed his chest and tasted his warmth. Keane's arms closed around her, cradling her.

"I love you," she said, emotion all at once hitting her harder than she'd expected. "I would never have been what I am today if not for you."

He kissed the top of her head. "I love you too, Marrin."

His fingers traced lazy circles on her bare back. She looked to the sunken tub set into the tiled floor and smiled. He'd filled it with steaming water and floated gillyflower petals on top. She breathed their scent and tilted her head back again to look up at him.

"Are you going to join me in there?"

He smiled, revealing bright, white and shining teeth. That same happy grin had been the first thing she'd noticed about him all those years ago. "Of course."

She needed help getting into the steaming water, but Keane held both her elbow and hip in such a way she was able to slide into the tub in what seemed an effortless motion. He knew how her joints, especially her hips and knees, pained her. He was always there to lift and carry for her, to open doors, to help her with stairs. He never made it seem as though she couldn't do it on her own. Always, every assistance came as though it sprang naturally forth from everything else he did to care for her—everything he had done for years.

Marrin settled into the water with a sigh and breathed in the scent of the flowers. He'd added oil to the water too, and it glided along her skin.

"Such luxury," she teased. "An entire tub full of water, just for me?"

"That's why I have to share it," her husband said.

The water slopped over the sides of the tub when he got in, and they both laughed. She slid into his arms, her back against his front, and he cradled her.

"I can remember when there was no water for bathing like this. When we washed once a week and used the bathwater for irrigation."

"We still do," he reminded. "Only now it goes out through a drain and into the earth, instead of being poured by hand from the tub."

She laughed again, the sound a little rougher this time. Against her back, his cock lengthened and grew hard. Marrin nestled closer. Keane's hands came around to cup her breasts.

Her nipples tightened instantly beneath his skilled fingers. He pinched them lightly between his thumb and forefingers, tugging gently. Pull, release, and again, followed by a circling motion.

Her clit pulsed in time to his treatment of her nipples and she parted her legs. The hot, slick water washed over her like a tongue, licking. Marrin shuddered and let out a small moan.

Keane slid one hand down her side, over her hip, then between her legs. His fingertip unerringly found her swelling clit. He stroked it, dipping low to caress her folds before moving back up to place a steady pressure on the bundle of nerves.

The fingers on her nipple pulled and released without ever letting go. In a moment, the fingers on her clit did the same. Tug, then release in small, steady movements that nonetheless caused the sensation to build up and up until she became mindless with it.

She writhed, back arching, legs spreading to allow him free access to wherever he wished to touch her. "Keane—"

He murmured words of love in his native language she didn't need to understand to know their meaning. He lifted her in the water, the hand on her clit leaving for a moment to slide beneath her buttocks. His other hand came down to grip his cock and guide it inside her. Keane seated her on him, facing away, her head tilted back to rest upon his shoulder and her breasts pushed upward, out of the water.

He moved her, letting the water aid him. Keane thrust inside her with exquisite slowness. His fingers went back to circling on her clit.

The shallow thrusts rubbed her just behind her pubic bone and made her moan and shift, seeking to thrust herself further down on his shaft. Wanting to fill herself with him. His cry as she succeeded forced an answering one from her throat.

She rocked herself against him, losing herself in the pleasure washing over her. The slap of the water against her only aided the sensation of his hands on her. It rushed over her clit and breasts and belly, caressing her in every place his hands were not and in other places when his fingers found those.

His cock extended and contracted inside her as he neared his climax. Knowing he was so close made Marrin's orgasm tumble toward her like rocks rolling down a hill. A flurry and rumble of sensation built inside her, gathering together, gaining speed, centered in her clit, but drawing sensation from all the rest of her body.

He gave her what she wanted. Hard, solid thrusts deep inside her. Hard enough to lift her from the water. Marrin didn't care. She arched to create a better angle. Keane's lips found her temple. Her hand came around to run her fingers through his hair.

They both spoke but what words came out, Marrin could not have said. Words of pleasure, senseless. Lovetalk, Keane called it. An outpouring of emotion echoing the outpouring of sensation in their bodies.

Keane no longer rubbed her clitoris. He put his palm over it. His thrusts moved her against his hand, the stimulation more subtle, but no less perfect.

Marrin's orgasm rippled through her. Her fingers tightened in his hair. She cried out. Her tunnel clenched his cock, earning her a cry of pleasure from his lips.

It sent another wave of climax over her. She tensed, relaxed, tensed again when he thrust once more and held her hips hard enough to hurt if she hadn't been so filled with ecstasy.

"Marrin," he whispered.

The water ceased its sloshing and rippled gently. The scent of gillyflowers covered them. Marrin floated in her husband's arms, replete.

Chapter 4

Forty-two rotations ago

"You're going to wear a hole in the floor."

Keane's calm bemusement was usually enough to defuse her, but not this time. Marrin looked up at him but had to blink hard, twice, to get her eyes to focus on his familiar beauty. He reached out a hand, and she took it.

"Aliya will be fine," he told her. "She has the best medica. The best care. And she's stronger than you think, Marrin."

Marrin linked her fingers in his. "She's been in labor for more than a day. If she doesn't have the baby soon—"

"They will take care of her," he soothed. "And Sarn is with her. He will let us know when something happens."

Marrin nodded, knowing Keane was right. She gave him a grateful smile. "Now is the time when you remind me it's time for me to let go. Again."

He pulled her into his embrace with a gentle laugh and nuzzled her neck. "Aliya is with her husband, doing what mothers have done for hundreds of rotations. What you did, without benefit of such fine facilities, I might add. And you survived it."

Marrin looked around at the pale blue walls, the soothing art, the soft and comfortable furniture meant to cradle those waiting for news of their loved ones. "I gave birth to Hadassah in my own bed with the *vadid* howling in my ears and Raluti telling me the wind meant good fortune for births. What she really meant was it was fortunate for those outside the hut because they wouldn't have to listen to me screaming."

"But you did it," he reminded. "In a place you didn't know, with people who weren't yours."

She squeezed his hand. "So much has changed since then. There were no medicas. No town, really. No paved roads."

He nodded and smiled and hugged her closer against him. "Aliya will be fine. She'll have this baby in a few more hours, and you'll be a grandmother."

Marrin made a small groan. "I don't know if I'm ready to be a grandmother."

"Well, I'm ready to be a grandfather." Keane ran his hands down her back. "I look forward to cradling a small one."

Marrin tightened her arms around him. "Are you sorry you never had any of your own?"

"I have three of my own. Just because they didn't spring from my seed makes them no less mine."

She tilted her head to look at him. How lucky she had been the day he walked off the freighter with her letter in his hand.

"I love you."

He kissed her forehead. "I love you too."

The hours passed. The baby was brought forth. The mother and father were congratulated and the infant admired, and the family expanded by one.

Marrin held her tiny newborn grandson in her arms and sought signs of Aliya's father Seth in the tiny boy's face. She found it in the crinkle of his forehead as he frowned, and she wept, kissing the spot and wetting his little face with her tears.

At home, when she and Keane had left the new parents to rest, Marrin stayed quiet. Thinking. Lujawed had rotated past its sun a multitude of times since she'd arrived as a young woman with two small daughters and an idealistic, unrealistic husband set on changing their lives.

Their lives had changed all right. Seth had found the plot of land granted them by the Interstellar Homestead Act didn't quite live up to the photos in the brochure he'd shown her. If they wanted green grass and a tidy little cottage, they'd have to work on it. Work hard.

Lujawed in those days was habitable only by sweat and effort. By hauling water up from wells dug so deep they needed to be lined with *lliwrock* to keep them from collapsing. By erecting buildings that could stand up to the *vadid*, the ever-present desert wind that howled and bit and ground away at the surface of everything, leaving it pitted and scarred.

They'd had help from the natives, grateful to trade their labor for the luxuries brought in on the Homestead Freighters. Nomads, the Lujawedi had no use for permanent dwellings. They didn't understand the need for roads, for sanitation facilities, for hospitals.

Goggles that kept the sand from their eyes and water pouches that kept their beverages cold were welcomed and coveted. So long as the Homesteaders kept to their own sections of the planet, the Lujawedi didn't care what the newcomers did with it.

And amazingly, Lujawed remained amicably split between its nomadic natives and the newcomers who'd come seeking a better life. Unlike many of the other homesteaded planets, Lujawed had been settled without war. Marrin could take pride in being one of the original colonists. Every rotation they honored her at a city council dinner—but it had been several rotations since she'd been asked to sit upon the council.

That was the way it went, she supposed, turning from the window where she'd been staring. Out with the old and in with the new. Only she didn't *feel* old, damn it. On a planet that rotated twice as fast around its central sun, her years were doubled, but not her lifespan. She was a grandmother who felt like she ought to still be that young mother digging in the sand.

It was largely due in part to Keane, who aged so slowly he seemed not to. Now Marrin watched him at his meditation in front of the small burning candle. The scent of the powder he burned tickled her nose, and she sneezed. He opened his eyes with a smile, unfolded himself from the floor and came toward her with long strides.

"Time for bed," he said.

She turned to leaned back against him, and his arms came around to hold her close. He put his cheek to hers as they both looked out the window to the land that seemed only yesterday to have been barren and brown and now shone with soft green grass and vibrant desert flowers.

"So much has changed." Marrin sighed. "Keane, where has the time gone?"

He turned her in the circle of his arms and kissed her forehead. "Time goes. It's what happens to it. What's wrong?"

She tilted her head back to look up at him. "Nothing's wrong. We have a grandson."

"We do." Keane smiled and brushed the hair from her forehead with his thumb, then let his hand come down to caress her cheek. "And look at all you've accomplished."

"All we've accomplished," she corrected. "I'd never have made this estate what it is today if not for your help. I'd never have been able to manage the irrigation systems that let us grow that first crop of *udeji* melons. And now look at us. Landowners. Largest supplier of fresh *udeji* melons in the entire colony."

He smiled again and kissed her, letting his lips linger on hers. "You should think about retiring, Marrin. You've worked hard. Take some time to enjoy your new grandson."

She laughed and squeezed his bum. "You just want me to sit around here with you, getting fat and lazy."

"I beg your pardon." Keane made a show of sounding affronted. "Lazy I'll give you, but am I fat?"

She ran her hands over his hips, then up his taut belly and firm chest to link her fingers behind his neck. "Most definitely not."

Keane reached down and swept her up into his arms. He walked her to the bed and laid her down, stretching out along her body. "Not too heavy for you?"

She laughed and pulled him down on top of her. "No. Never."

Then he began kissing her, and she didn't think about melons or the desert or anything else but his hands on her. He lifted the hem of her gown to her thighs, then higher to expose her belly. Keane kissed the scars there. Her badges of honor, he'd always called them, the signs of her pregnancies. They'd always made her feel self-conscious before him, but to Keane they represented something so miraculous and glorious he never failed to make her find them as beautiful as he did.

Seveerans didn't reproduce with their own bodies any longer. Science had replaced childbirth. Seveerans procreated solely via artificially inseminated and cultivated embryos in a *crèche* system. To Keane, the fact Marrin had carried her own children inside her body and given birth to them seemed like something out of a fairy tale.

He gave only a moment to her marks, though, instead moving lower across her belly to the area between her thighs. She sighed when his breath fluttered across her clitoris. She gasped when he used his tongue to stroke it. Marrin closed her eyes and leaned back into the pillows, giving herself up to him.

Keane slid his hands beneath her buttocks to hold her closer to him. His lips and tongue began a familiar pattern. He knew so well how to please her. He knew just where and how to touch her. How hard or soft, fast or slow, how she needed him.

It wasn't instinctive, but rather years of experience that had given him such talent. Experience and enthusiasm. But most of all, love. Love allowed him to find the right spots to send her soaring, let him discover new places to make her gasp his name and arch her back under his caress.

Keane slid a finger inside her, pressing upward while he pressed down on her clit with his tongue. The dual sensation was exquisite. She shivered. Bright sparks of pleasure radiated outward from her center, up her belly, spiking her nipples and parting her lips in a breathy sigh.

"I love when you make that noise." He paused in licking her to look up. "It makes me so hard."

She smiled down at him. "And I love it when you get hard."

His answering grin made her heart pound. He bent back to her clit, nuzzling it lightly before beginning to lick again. He had her on the edge in another minute, earning a moan of regret when he pulled away to tease her. Keane loved to tease her to the brink and hold her off, bringing her close and refusing to give her release until she exploded under a breath or a whisper.

Tonight, Marrin had no patience for that. Her body craved him. She twined her fingers in his hair and pulled upward. Keane followed willingly, kissing her. The taste of her arousal made another low moan leak out of her. He thrust his tongue inside her mouth, mimicking the way she wanted him to push his cock inside her.

"Make love to me," she whispered against his mouth, her fingers moving again and again through the dark silken length of his hair.

She didn't have to ask him twice. Keane slid inside her slickness without effort, all the way to the hilt. He filled her completely. He moved in slow, smooth strokes, angling his body in such a way that he rubbed her clit with his every thrust. It drove her half-crazy, the way he did it, the stimulation not direct enough to send her over the edge, but tantalizing enough to keep her hovering on the verge of orgasm.

He buried his face in the curve of her shoulder. His teeth stung her. The small pain was enough to jolt her entire body upward. He thrust harder. She wrapped her legs around the back of his thighs, pulling him closer while her hands made furrows in the smooth skin of his back.

His low cry sent another wave of ecstasy through her. Sweat slicked their bodies as they moved. Keane moved harder inside her, hard enough to move the bed against the wall, which made her smile and laugh a bit, breathless, even as she moaned in pre-orgasmic splendor.

If her sudden vocal appreciation of his skills surprised him, Keane didn't show it. He responded by moving faster. Harder. Marrin's orgasm began in a thunder of beating heart and shouts.

A second one followed on the edge of the first with no more than a heartbeat between them. Keane kissed her as his body shuddered in its own release. He collapsed against her, though even in his pleasure he remembered to hold himself up on his arms so he didn't crush her.

They breathed together. In. Out. Completely in time with each other. Then he propped himself up and looked into her face. He kissed her. "Will you at least think about staying home with me?"

The seriousness in of his question surprised her into sitting up. "You mean it?"

Keane rolled onto his back, one lean arm behind his head to support it. "I do."

"Keane, my work—"

"Your daughters and their spouses have taken over the company. You have shareholders and a board and secretaries and volunteers." He looked up at her, his dark eyes shifting color as they did when emotion moved him. "You've worked hard to get where you are. But now, can't you consider taking a rest?"

"I've worked hard and you've been behind me every step of the way. You've worked as hard as I have. And you've always refused any sort of official position in the company."

He smiled. "Those who matter know my place at your side. Those who don't will always assume I'm just your Seveeran houseboy. Pretty to look at."

She reached to caress his face. "It's been a long time since anyone accused you of being that."

"What I'm saying is, Marrin, why not let it be true? Retire. Stay home with me every day. I'll be your houseboy and make it worth your while."

She laughed and leaned down to kiss him. "You're wooing me."

His grin remained as charming as it had always been. "I am."

"Stop working?" Marrin leaned back against the headboard, thinking. "I'm not sure I'd know what to do with myself all day."

"Lounge in the garden, breakfast on the terrace, make love in the afternoon."

"Be lazy is what you're asking me to do, Keane."

"Take your reward," he corrected gently. "And let go so your children can also have a chance to prove their value with hard work."

She sighed. "You want me to let go of something I've spent half my life working to build."

"And I want you to spend the other half enjoying the fruits of it." Keane linked his fingers through hers. "I want you to spend the time with me."

And that, she decided as she looked down upon him, was reason enough to do as he asked, because Keane had never asked her for anything before.

Chapter 5

Fifty-two rotations ago

The door opened and Marrin looked up, her mouth full of pins. "Sarai, good, you're here."

Her middle daughter, the fairest one, closed the door behind her and set down the bouquet of *udeji* melon flowers Hadassah had insisted on carrying for her wedding.

"You look gorgeous, Dassah." Sarai gave her younger sister an admiring look. "Jaron will faint when he sees you."

"I hope not." Marrin slid another pin into Hadassah's trailing hem. "We don't need any fainting going on."

Hadassah took a deep, shaky breath. "Ma, do I look all right?"

Marrin stood and looked into her daughter's face. Her baby, the child she'd borne in the desert, the one of her daughters who'd known no other world than Lujawed.

"Gorgeous." She smoothed Hadassah's dark curls over her shoulder. Of the three girls, Hadassah looked the most like Seth, who'd never even had the chance to see her. Marrin hugged Hadassah tight, not caring that she crumpled the gown of fine Lujawedi flaxene. "Absolutely beautiful."

The door opened again, this time for Aliya. "Are you ready?"

Hadassah lifted her chin and took a deep breath. "I'm ready."

Marrin looked at her children—the three bright, shining lights she had produced—and her throat closed with emotion. "Your father would be so proud."

Her girls hugged her then, and the four of them clung to each other in the circle they'd always made.

The door opened a third time, this time to Keane, who held back for a moment upon seeing the clustered femininity that had left him flustered and left out on occasion in the past. "We're ready whenever you are, Dassah."

Hadassah, who had never known another father, had nonetheless been the one who'd clashed most fiercely with Keane over the years. Marrin would walk Hadassah to the wedding canopy alone. Now Keane looked discomfited, and Marrin knew her husband well enough to know he didn't want to be accused of interfering.

"Keane…" Hadassah stepped free of her sisters' and mother's embrace. She reached for his hand and he took it with a look of surprise. Her voice clear and unclogged by tears she said, "I know I've been an awful brat to you in the past. And I know you've always been patient with me, even when I didn't deserve it. I appreciate more than you can ever know how you agreed to my wishes about this wedding…but I've been stupid and stubborn, and I've changed my mind. I'd be honored if you'd walk with me to the canopy."

Marrin watched as his eyes changed from black to blue to green, expressing his shifting emotions.

He nodded and squeezed Hadassah's hand. "I'd be so honored to walk with you. If that's what you really want."

"You're the only father I've ever had." Hadassah's voice broke at last. "And I know I haven't often shown it, but I love you."

Then they all cried except for Keane, whose eyes didn't shed tears, and they hugged and kissed, and then it was time for Hadassah Levy to become Hadassah Levy Curani.

No bride had ever looked lovelier, no mother had beamed brighter with pride, and no father had ever given away a daughter so tenderly. It had been a perfect day, with food and family and friends. At the end of it, exhaustion claimed Marrin, and she tumbled onto her bed face down before rolling onto her back with a sigh. Keane laughed gently from the doorway.

"The last to go," he said, shedding his formal jacket. "And now, we're alone. The whole house to ourselves. We've never had that."

Marrin watched him undress, her eyes lingering on his body in constant appreciation. "Have you ever wished it had been different when you came? That we'd had the chance for a honeymoon like most married people get?"

He turned from the dresser where he'd been placing his watch and the interlocked chain he wore around his wrist. "Do I wish I'd been able to spend a week with you at an overpriced tourist resort indulging in decadent sex and overeating bad food? No, Marrin."

She laughed. "I mean do you wish we'd had the chance to be a couple before we were a family?"

Again, he shook his head and stepped out of his trousers, hanging them with the same neat efficiency he always did. At last fully naked, he moved toward her and stretched out on the bed beside her.

"The moment I stepped off that freighter and saw those three little faces, I was in love," Keane said. "Falling in love with you came later and was a pleasant side benefit."

She nudged him with a frown, but his answer pleased her. "You don't think it would have been easier without the girls?"

"Easier? Undoubtedly." He put his hand flat on her belly, fingers splayed. "Would I wish it had happened differently? Never."

He leaned down to kiss her, his tongue urging her lips to open. His breath was sweet from ceremonial wine. She licked his lips, tasting.

"It would've been easier to make love to you at the beginning without three little ones always underfoot," he whispered as his hand began a lazy ascent toward her breasts. "But maybe we can make up for it now."

"Pretend this is the first time?" she teased.

"If you like." His hand cupped her breast.

Her nipple rose beneath his palm. Keane rubbed his thumb across it. The barrier of her dress blunted the sensation but made it no less delightful.

"I was so nervous that first time. I don't think I'd want to repeat that."

"You were nervous?" He laughed. "I was afraid I wouldn't please you and you'd send me back."

"Keane, you weren't!"

He paused in kissing her to look into her eyes. "I was."

She'd never known he'd been afraid, too, the first time they had made love. The admission touched her. She put her hand to his face.

"I couldn't have sent you back," she said. "I loved you too much to live without you."

His tender kiss hadn't changed in all the years they'd been together. Familiarity couldn't steal the sweetness of it, or quench the fire he always created when he put his mouth on hers. No matter how many times they joined, each time was as exciting and fresh as the first time.

"You're not naked," he whispered in her ear. "And I am."

She remedied that by sitting up and tugging her dress off over her head. "We can't have that."

His low chuckle parted her thighs. His hand stroked the curls there, finding the already upright button of her clit and pinching it lightly. He rolled it between his thumb and forefinger before moving his hand down lower to slide a finger through her folds.

Slickness, begun at the sight of him undressing, already coated her. He brought some of it up to coat her clit, making it slippery. He rubbed her in small, tight circles interspersed with an occasional up and down stroke that had her whimpering in short order.

He kissed her mouth, her cheek, her jaw, down to her collarbone where he nibbled along the ridge and smoothed his tongue across her skin. He moved lower to suckle her nipples, one then the other, while his hand continued to work between her legs. Marrin looked down to see him stroking himself too, the thickness of his cock appearing and disappearing into his fist as he pumped it.

"Come here." She reached for him.

He shifted on the bed so she could reach his erection. He kissed her hipbone. She angled her head just a bit, and took him into her mouth.

His low, strangled moan sent a pulse of pleasure through her that she could so affect him. Marrin slid his cock down the back of her throat as far as she could until her lips touched his belly.

His hand stuttered in its movement against her clitoris as she sucked him harder. The break in his rhythm only gave her more pleasure, brought her closer to orgasm faster. Her clit throbbed and her hips moved as she slid her mouth up again, then down.

"Marrin, I love it when you take me all the way in your mouth."

His throaty words made her body tingle. She loved that about him, his ability to tell her exactly how he was feeling at all times during their lovemaking. What he liked, what he wanted, how to please him.

Before Keane, Marrin had never spoken during sex. Orgasms were like buried treasure. "X" marks the spot. Find the map, follow clues, and maybe you'll hit the jackpot.

Keane had shown her the freedom of speech, of telling her partner exactly how she liked to be touched and where, exactly what would work to get her off.

"I want to be inside you," he murmured, even as he pushed himself deeper into her mouth.

She gave him one final, loving suck and then let him go. She got onto her hands and knees to look down at him, his eyes gone yellow in his arousal. He licked his lips, and before she could move, Keane got behind her and slid inside.

A moan escaped her as he filled her. Her ass tipped upward as she put her forehead to the bed, her hands on either side of her head, bracing herself. In this position he could grip her hips to move her, use a hand to slide around in front and tweak her clit while he thrust. He could go deeper, harder, and she gasped out in pleasure as he did.

"You're so beautiful," he told her, as his hands rubbed circles on her buttocks and the small dimples on either side of her lower spine. His fingers traced the jut of her shoulder blades, the line of her backbone and the cleft of her ass. He thrust inside her slowly as his hands caressed her body.

Climax stole her words. She pushed herself backward against him, needing him to thrust harder. To fill her. He groaned. She answered. Their pace quickened.

His erection stretched her. She settled her legs wider, pushing upward on her elbows. Keane reached around to press his fingertips to her swollen clit, and Marrin cried out. She pushed herself harder against him, each movement dragging his fingers along her erect button and stabbing his cock into her core.

They moved together in perfect time. The dual sensations of his erection inside her and the pressure of his hand on her clitoris was enough, at last, to send her over the edge.

"I want to hear you come," he said. "Nobody will hear you but me."

He was right. They were alone. After all the years in a house filled with children, they were at last alone. She screamed out her ecstasy, voice hoarse and her breath leaving her in great gasps as her orgasm pounded through her. Nobody to hear them, not now. Not with the girls all grown with families of their own. The time of quiet, furtive lovemaking had passed. Now there was no need to be silent in their passion, and the thought of it made her open her mouth and cry out, simply because she could.

He thrust harder, and she bent forward to open herself to him, to take him deeper. She cried out again, another burst of climax filling her. She tensed, relaxed and tensed again. Keane cupped his hand over her, easing off the direct pressure that made her body jerk in the aftermath of her climax.

His thrusts became ragged. He cried out as she had, a wordless sound of joy. His cock pulsed. His fingers tightened on her hip.

A third time her body contracted around him, a smaller and gentler orgasm that made her moan and push back against him hard as he thrust forward one last time and shivered in his climax.

He stayed inside her for another breath, another heartbeat, and as she felt him begin to soften, he pulled out of her and lay down on the bed, pulling her into his arms to spoon her as they both caught their breath.

"Who needs a honeymoon?" she said when she could speak again. "This is much better."

He kissed her between the shoulder blades. "It is."

And they slept.

Chapter 6

Eighty rotations ago

Only ten rotations ago, there had been no school auditorium in which ceremonies like this could be held. Students had taken classes in a building much like the one-room schoolhouses of their ancestral Earth. Like everything else in the colony, hard work had provided the new building with its bright, airy classrooms and the large auditorium in which they all now sat.

Sarai's class was the first to graduate from the new school. Marrin watched her middle daughter march down the aisle with the rest of her classmates, her fair hair bleached blonder now by the harsh sun that lightened everything over time. Today there were fifty students, an unbelievable number when she thought about the first few families that had come to Lujawed. Marrin had never have imagined one day she'd sit in an air-cooled room and see her daughter receive a degree for an education as adequate as any she'd have received on Earth.

Seth had been the one to dream of this, the one to look beyond the barren desert and blinding sun to imagine green fields and a thriving town. This had been Seth's dream, not hers.

Keane's fingers linked through Marrin's and squeezed, and she gave him a grateful glance. Sarai's graduation had hit her harder than Aliya's, though she wasn't sure why. Maybe because her oldest daughter had always been the one to make the milestones and seeing Sarai make another only emphasized to Marrin how much time had passed in her own life. In another four years rotations Hadassah would finish her primary education. By that time, the university would likely be finished, and she could attend an actual university instead of taking correspondence lessons.

Her babies weren't babies any longer, and though Marrin didn't want to hold them back, part of her mourned the loss of her role as young mother. They didn't need her any longer. Not like they had.

She half-listened to the speeches, her mind on the company she'd finally turned into a success. Ashco had turned its first profit this year. A year of good weather and an unusually plentiful rain season had allowed her to siphon some of the expense she'd normally have spent on irrigation into finishing up the climate-controlled warehouses and implement the distribution system that allowed the crop to reach all parts of the colony before it spoiled.

Luck had been with them this year, no doubt about it. It meant money and security, and the realization of a dream and the success of the business contented her in ways she'd never expected. Marrin Levy, a businesswoman? She'd have laughed at the thought. Now, she couldn't imagine herself as anything less.

Keane's arm rested along the back of her chair, and she stole a look him. Without him, she'd never have made it to this place. The fever that stole her first husband had left she and her daughters bereft, alone in a harsh land that was not home. A young mother of two, with a third growing in her belly, struggling to plant and harvest a brown and bleached scrap of land without the man who'd brought them there... There had been so many times she'd come close to giving up. If she'd had the money she'd have taken her children and gone home, but he hadn't left them even with that.

Three rotations of struggle, of poverty, of hunger and backbreaking labor had finally forced Marrin to send away for what the Homesteaders called a "field-husband." A man to work her fields and help take care of things.

Love hadn't been meant to enter into it. She looked at Keane's face, his eyes trained on the stage where there were more speeches being made. His lovely, dear face, which hadn't changed since the day she'd first seen him.

He turned to look at her and they shared a secret smile. The speechmakers stopped talking. The audience rose to clap and cheer for the graduates, and Marrin turned from the sight of her husband, the man who'd come to tend her fields, but who'd ended up tending her heart, and found Sarai's beaming smile.

The colony was still small enough to support group celebrations like this one. The tables had been set with flowers and pretty cloths. A band hired to provide music. Food, laid out in a bounty that proved to any who doubted how prosperous they'd all become.

Marrin watched Sarai chattering with her friends. Her other daughters, Aliya and Hadassah, had also abandoned the dull company of their parents to seek their companions. Marrin had a plate of salad and a glass of iced water, but wasn't doing much beyond looking around in amazed pride.

"You're Sarai's mother, aren't you?"

Marrin turned at the question to see a woman of about her own age she faintly recognized. "Yes. I'm Marrin Levy."

"Arlene Simpson. I'm Jack's mom."

Marrin didn't know Jack, but she smiled and nodded anyway. Keane came up beside her and put his arm around her shoulders, squeezing gently before stepping away to take the plate from her hands and begin finishing the salad.

"Hi," he greeted Arlene.

The other woman's eyes widened slightly. "Hello. I'm Jack's mom." Her smile thinned as she looked at Marrin.

Keane smiled and shrugged, more honest in his reply than Marrin had been. "Sorry, I don't know Jack."

"Jack Simpson?" Arlene's tone clearly said Keane ought to know him. "He might be a year or two behind you."

Keane paused with the fork halfway to his mouth, an eyebrow raised. "Sorry?"

Marrin tensed, her gut twisting. It wasn't the first time their apparent age difference had been brought up in casual conversation, but it had been quite a while. Anyone who knew them knew Keane wasn't as young as his Seveeran genetics made him appear.

"My son," Arlene said patiently, as though Keane were an idiot. "He graduated today with your girlfriend."

"My girlfriend?" Keane's face showed an amusement Marrin envied, but didn't feel. He looked around the room, clearly biting back a laugh.

"Well, yes...you're Sarai's boyfriend, aren't you? I just guessed you—"

"You guessed because I was here with Marrin and behaving in such a familiar manner that I must somehow be related to her, and you assumed for some reason I was here because of her daughter, who graduated today with your son." His smile remained pleasant, his voice light, but he'd set down his plate and put an arm around Marrin's shoulders.

Arlene looked confused, from Keane to Marrin and back again. "Well, yes."

"Marrin is my wife," said Keane without changing his tone.

If the woman's face could have blushed any more crimson, Marrin didn't see how. Arlene Simpson stammered and stuttered and backed away like Keane had somehow insulted her when really, she was the one who'd put her foot in her mouth.

It made Marrin feel no better to watch the other woman's distress. Much of the time she could forget her husband was of a different race that didn't age the same way Earthers did. She aged every day. Keane did not.

"Don't let her bother you," he murmured in her ear, his arm tightening around her waist that she was proud hadn't thickened in their years together. "She had no idea."

"I know."

Marrin put on a smile, talking with the rest of the parents and well-wishers, but by the time the day was over she had a pounding headache from gritting her jaw. Tears stung her eyes as she sought the privacy of her bath chamber and splashed cold water on her temples. Sarai had gone to a graduation celebration, taking her sisters with her, and the quiet house was a balm to Marrin's strained nerves.

The sound of a whistling teakettle caught her attention and she lifted her head. She was too far from the kitchen to smell the *udeji* blossom tea, but she knew that's what Keane would be preparing. She went to the kitchen and found her husband. He'd set the table with her favorite mug, the teapot with steam curling from the ceramic top, and a plate of cookies. He'd included a vase with a flower plucked from Sarai's congratulations bouquet.

This simple act of caring moved her to tears. More emotion after a long, emotional day. The best part of it was she didn't need to explain herself to him. All she had to do was look into his eyes, and Keane knew just what to do to make it all better.

Or if not better, at least bearable. He took her in his arms and pressed his lips to her temple as he stroked her back. His fingers tangled in the hair falling over her shoulders—which she now noted with some distress was streaked even further with white. That the bleaching came from the sun and not just her age didn't help. They might all live on Lujawed, but most of them had come from Earth originally, and standards of beauty were the same.

"I thought it didn't bother me anymore."

His lips curved against her. "It shouldn't. It's only misconception."

"I know."

"I'm seven rotations older than you."

"I know that," she said, swatting him. "But you don't look it."

"And I never will," Keane said gently. "But that doesn't mean anything. Did you fall in love with me because of what I look like?"

"No," Marrin said, "but that you're gorgeous helped a lot."

He laughed and hugged her, rocking her in arms still strong from long hours working in the fields, although he no longer needed to labor that way. "I could say the same. The first time I laid my eyes on you, you took my breath away."

She scoffed. "I was covered in dust and had three screaming children circling me like satellites."

"A pearl covered in mud is still a pearl."

She tipped her head back to look up at him. "I love you."

"I love you too."

His hands slid up and down her sides, resting at last on her hips. He shifted her around until she was snugged up against him. Heat flared in her belly at the feeling of his erection already straining the front of his loose trousers.

"We're alone," he reminded her. "The girls won't be home until tomorrow."

"However shall we occupy our time?"

Keane smiled. "I think I can imagine."

The kitchen table was just the right height for him to slide inside her while as he stood between her legs while and she sat on the table. The curved plazglass table warmed to her skin, bared in only moments when he lifted her skirt and tugged down her panties. One hand cupped the back of her neck and the other anchored her hip as he moved inside her. Marrin locked her ankles around his hips, pulling him closer, holding him tighter.

Sometimes they made love slowly, taking hours. Sometimes, like now, they came together hard and fast, with nothing more than a glance to serve as foreplay. It didn't matter. She was as ready for him now as if he'd spent half a day caressing her.

The teacups rattled in their saucers as his thrusts rocked the table, and Marrin let her head tip back, back, laughing and gasping her pleasure as he filled her.

"Touch yourself," Keane said, his voice hoarse. "I want you to come with me."

With Keane supporting her she had no need to hold herself up, and it was easy to slip a hand between them to stroke her clit in time to his thrusts. She cried out as she rolled the small button under her forefinger. Keane stretched and filled her, in and out, while she rubbed.

He kissed her, mouths open, tongues darting and becoming desperate as their mutual climax approached. Marrin heard a clatter and a crack but took no time to see if they'd at last made the cups fall over. She lost herself in her husband's kiss, in the pleasure of his magnificent, unique cock as it moved inside her, in the sensation of her own hand between her legs.

He gathered her closer, his grip tightening. Her face pressed against his chest. She found his skin with her teeth and tongue, tasted the salt and spice of his sweat and of their passion, and he groaned when she nipped him.

"Come with me, Marrin."

She already was. Bright sparks of joy filled her. Her body jerked. Keane thrust inside her, sending another burst of ecstasy exploding through her. She cried out, riding him, digging her nails into his shoulders hard enough to bruise him.

He thrust again, this time hard enough to move the table. His back arched. He shuddered, then relaxed against her, panting.

Marrin heard a slow dripping and turned her head to see they had, indeed, spilled the tea. It had made quite a mess on the floor, too, but at that moment, she couldn't rouse herself enough to care.

"You wear this old man out," Keane whispered into her ear, nuzzling and nipping before hugging her tightly.

"Never," she replied.

"You can try," came his teasing reply.

"I can try," Marrin agreed and put her arms around the man she loved.

41

Chapter 7

Ninety-nine rotations ago

"Hurry, Keane! Hurry! It's starting!"

Aliya danced, holding her pot with both small hands. Sarai joined her sister, a mug in each of hers. The baby, Hadassah, no longer such a baby, but a girl of nine rotations, held a mixing bowl up toward the darkening sky.

Keane, his long, dark hair tied at the nape of his neck, stepped through the glass doors at the back of the house and onto the slate patio. He'd put on the shirt she'd made for him, Marrin saw, and although she tried to pretend the sight didn't make her heart leap, it did.

"Keane, it's starting!"

"All right." He laughed and reached for the mug Sarai handed him. He tipped his face toward the sky. A drop of rain splatted him between the eyes and he laughed again, spreading out his arms as more water came from the clouds.

The girls squealed and held up their containers, trying to catch the still slow-falling raindrops. They danced in their festival dresses, their small faces bright with excitement. Marrin's heart hurt to look at their joy, so fierce and overwhelming was her love.

"Look, *Ima*, look! Flowers!"

And indeed, what had been moments before a brown and barren yard had now begun to bloom. More rain pattered down, soaking instantly into the parched ground. Green tendrils that had been dormant an entire season now sprang up from the ground so fast they could see them growing. Flowers, red, purple, white and yellow, bloomed on vines and stalks. The smell of them filled the air, and Marrin breathed deeply, astounded as always by the annual miracle.

The blessing of rain. Lujawed was a desert planet, its water held so deep within its embrace it took the deepest wells to reach it. Yet once a year, thankfully without fail, clouds gathered. The skies opened. And water, the gift without which they couldn't survive here, poured forth in torrents. Sometimes four days. Sometimes two weeks. Glorious, fresh, sweet and life-giving water.

The Lujawedi called it *idvad*, and so the colonists had taken on the term, adopted the holiday festival when all work ceased and every attention was given to collecting and appreciating the sky's bounty.

Watching her daughters' dance, Marrin's throat closed with emotion. She held her face up to the sky, letting the rain hide the tears suddenly sliding down her cheeks. She blinked rapidly and her gaze fell on Keane, who looked up at her from where he bent, laughing, to help Aliya empty her pot of water into one of the rain barrels.

One full rotation had passed since the day she had gone to Bosie Starport to pick up the man who had answered her ad. One Lujawed rotation, one round of seasons, one passage of time, and yet so much more.

He stood, his dark eyes flaring briefly blue in the way he had that she'd found so disconcerting at first. Seveeran eyes changed color with emotion, unlike Earther eyes that always stayed the same. And now, not for the first time, Marrin wondered what other differences his race had from hers.

She blamed her shiver on the chill rain, but knew it had nothing to do with that and everything to do with this man she'd taken as her field-husband. Keane Delacore.

Though they wanted to, the children couldn't stay up all night. When true night fell, Marrin dried them off, dressed them in warm clothes and tucked them into beds to be soothed to sleep by the unfamiliar sound of rain pattering on the roof. They fell asleep in moments, and she took the time to touch their faces, each one so precious to her she could scarcely bear it.

Her girls, Earth-age nine, seven and four. Growing so fast and so beautiful. She tucked the blankets around them and left their room, closing the door behind her.

The rain had grown heavier. It slashed the windows and sliced at the grass that had grown up in the past few hours. Marrin slid the glass doors open and went outside, water soaking her instantly to the skin.

Baths were a luxury. She wanted to spend as much time as she could with water on her skin. She let it wash over her as she walked into the garden that hadn't been there earlier.

And she found him. Standing, arms outspread again, face tipped up to the downpour, eyes closed, mouth open to drink.

It seemed somehow too intimate to see him this way, in this ecstasy. She had shared a home with him for a rotation. Taken meals together. Argued and been kind, laughed and wept, labored with him side by side in the melon fields that were only now beginning to take full root.

She had spent a rotation with this man, who was no longer a stranger to her, but she had never seen him lose himself in such joy. She made to back away, to find her own place to stand and take in the rain, but Keane, at that moment, turned his head and saw her.

He turned slowly to face her, his arms going down. The shirt she had made for him of white flaxene and red embroidered flowers had gone sheer, showing every ridge and muscle of his chest. It made her knees feel as though they would not hold her; she stumbled at the sudden, unexpected sensuality of seeing Keane wet and outlined by red thread she had sewn with her own hands. She had seen him stripped bare to the waist many times, but this was somehow all at once more and too much.

She took a step back on the tiles made slick with rain. She stepped onto grass and soft earth, smelled the scent of flowers she crushed beneath her bare heel. Her hair clung to her as her gown did, molding itself to her body as his shirt hugged him, and she realized his eyes were roaming over her as hungrily as she was certain hers had over him.

She had seen his eyes go blue and green and only once, red with anger. Now they were tinged with amber and gold as he blinked. He'd taken away the tie in and his hair and it fell over his shoulders and halfway down his back.

She took another step back. Keane moved fast, smooth, with agile grace she'd always admired. His hand caught her by the upper arms just as she teetered with uncertain steps on the mushy ground. She gasped at his touch, for other than an occasional brush of fingers when they passed each other something, Keane had touched her only once before.

He had never taken advantage of the rights granted a field-husband, never called on the contract they'd both signed that granted him conjugal rights in exchange for his labor. Keane had never pushed her, and she'd always been grateful...until now.

Now he slanted his head to hers without asking for permission. His kiss seared her, and Marrin opened her mouth to taste him. Her arms went around his neck. His went around her back, pulling her close. His tongue darted inside her mouth and she groaned.

She had almost forgotten desire. She had pushed it away for so long, since Seth's death from a native virus, that she'd been certain she'd never feel it again. Now it crashed over her, blooming inside her like the flowers had bloomed all around them, brought to life by the rain, and by Keane's hands on her.

He pulled at her dress, tugging it upward over her thighs. His hands trailed along her heated skin and she shuddered when his fingers reached the spot between her legs. He pressed against her and she cried out, the noise muffled inside his mouth, still kissing.

He lay her down on a bed of soft grasses and flowers and left her mouth to pull off his shirt. He took her hand and put it over his heart, which thumped so hard it moved her fingers against his skin.

"Do you want this?" he asked, voice hoarse. "Marrin, I have to know if you want this. If you want…me."

She nodded. "I want you, Keane."

Had he been afraid she would say no? He closed his eyes for a moment and his shoulders heaved, but when he opened his eyes again, he smiled. He stretched out along her to kiss her again. He put her hand on the bulge in his trousers and groaned when she curled her fingers around it.

Wet clothes were difficult to remove. They fumbled with desperate fingers, both laughing and kissing and shivering in the rain, but at last they were naked together and Marrin looked over his body in wonder. To see that his erection was basically the same shape and girth and functioned in the same manner was more of a relief, and she couldn't help reaching to touch him as he knelt next to her.

"You're perfect," she told him, cupping her fingers around his length. His erection throbbed at her touch, and she smiled. Not so different.

Her touch had made him shudder, but he still smiled. "Glad you think so."

"I wasn't sure—"

"You've heard stories?"

She nodded. Keane bent down to kiss her, his body covering and warming her. "Yes. It does extend and retract during lovemaking, but not enough to hurt you."

She let out a breathless giggle. "Good to know."

His hand smoothed away the hair from her forehead, then slid over her cheek, down her neck to her shoulder, further down to cup her breast. "You're sure you want this?"

To answer him, she brought him back to her mouth to kiss her again. He tasted so good, so sweet and fresh. It made her stomach leap and jump and her clit follow suit. He was smooth and firm and fully masculine. He was kind and a hard worker and good to her children. She wanted him for all those reasons, but also for one more.

She loved him. The knowledge of it, of realizing what she must have known for months but ignored, made her gasp aloud. Her eyes opened and she stared into his.

"Marrin?"

She shook her head, not wanting to speak or ruin this moment they had taken so long to reach. Keane searched her gaze, but said no more. He bent back to kiss her throat. His mouth slid down as his hand had, and he suckled at her breasts one at a time until she gasped and put her hand on the back of his head.

His lips moved further down her ribs, to her belly, and she tensed. Hard exercise had kept her fit and poverty had kept her trim, but three children had changed her body in ways that would never recover. She bore scars. His lips traced them slowly, kissing each silver line as she tensed in mingled self-consciousness and desire.

"I've never seen such beauty," he murmured. "My people have nothing like this. No birth. You've done such a blessed thing, Marrin."

She had no time to reply because he had slipped lower. He parted her thighs and nuzzled her. She cried out, wordless, and put her hand over her face. Her pelvis bumped up against his mouth and he put his hands on her to hold her still. Her reaction should have embarrassed her, the enthusiasm of it made her blush, but it felt too damn good. His tongue found her clit and he licked her while she wiggled.

Whatever difference their races had, Keane knew how to make love to her. He used his mouth to bring her to the edge, then moved aside. He slid a hand under her buttocks and tilted her toward the sky. He parted her folds, exposed her to the beating spatter of the rain.

She'd gone mindless with pleasure. His tongue had made her throb, but this, this was unbelievable and unbearable. The rain, so rare and precious, pattered against her swollen flesh. Marrin broke, shattered, and exploded into shards of bright, shining desire.

He slid inside her while she was still pulsing. She climaxed again at once from the feeling of his cock inside her. She had gone so long without love, without touch. Now, as the skies had opened up, so did her body open to Keane.

He moved inside her, his face buried against her neck. Marrin put her arms around him, her fingers sliding along his wet skin to clutch his buttocks and urge him to move.

She didn't think herself capable of another orgasm. The two she'd already experienced had left her wrung out and drained. She would concentrate on Keane's pleasure now, but to her surprise, her body began to respond again as he made love to her.

He pushed inside her, pelvis to pelvis, but then to her astonishment, his cock kept moving inside her. It grew. It nudged her cervix, which should have been painful but wasn't. When he pulled out, she lost the sensation of anything different. In again, and the feeling of his penis moving deeper into her made her tunnel spasm around him.

He groaned. "Oh, you feel so good."

He moved faster, riding her. The ground had churned to mud beneath them. Slippery grass allowed their bodies to slide with every thrust. Desire puddled between her legs and in the pit of her belly again.

He moved faster, panting. She joined him. He gave a low cry and so did she. They moved in unison, giving and taking, each move as orchestrated as a dance they'd practiced for hours instead of performing for the first time.

He lifted himself onto his hands to thrust harder inside her, and to look down into her face. His eyes met hers. His face contorted as his climax approached. The sight of him in such bliss made her own fill her again.

She climaxed a third time, a small fluttering that didn't match the intensity of the first two, but was still enough to make her gasp aloud. Keane smiled when she did, eyes showing pleased surprise. In the next moment, they closed and his face contorted again.

He thrust inside her again, hard. His body tensed and he shuddered. Then he collapsed on top of her.

Marrin put her arms around him, holding him tight to her. Warmth filled her. She started to cry.

Keane got up on one arm to look at her. His body shielded her face from the rain. Concern filled his eyes. "Marrin?"

She shook her head, her emotion making her feel foolish and awkward in a way their lovemaking had not. Keane caressed her cheek. He smiled and bent to kiss her.

"I love you too," he said into her ear.

And there in the garden, in the mud and rain with the smell of flowers blooming and going to rot, Marrin kissed the man who was no longer her field-husband, but her husband entirely.

Chapter 8

One hundred rotations ago

Where was he? Marrin kept a firm grip on Hadassah's hand, no matter how hard the little girl tried to get away. Sarai and Aliya were running in circles around her, trying her already thin patience. Marrin searched the crowd exiting the starport, many of them greeting colonists who'd come out to meet them. Some carried the bags and bore the pale skin of new colonists as yet unburned by the harsh Lujawed sun.

She didn't see the man she sought anyplace. Tall, he had written. Dark hair to his shoulders. He'd be wearing a blue jumpsuit with white piping, and carrying a black leather bag.

His name was Keane Delacore. He was forty Earth years old, though Seveerans aged differently than Earthers and she shouldn't be surprised if he looked younger. He looked forward to meeting her in person, and her daughters.

If he didn't show up, she'd take her children and go back to the homestead. She would feed them and put them to bed, and maybe she'd go decadent and fill the washtub for a bath. If he didn't show up, she'd be no worse off than she already was—and maybe she'd be better.

If he didn't show up, she would somehow find a way to pay a labor crew to help her in the fields. How, she didn't know. She had no cash and, as yet, no crop to count on. She had nothing to barter, nothing to sell.

Seth had left her with nothing but three children and debt. In the three years since his death, Marrin had watched everything they had brought with them from home be sold off or break down in the harsh desert atmosphere.

Her husband had been a good man with a wonderful dream, and it had not been his fault the immunizations against native viruses hadn't worked for him. It happened in .0001 percent of the population, a risk so miniscule even Seth, who calculated everything, had been willing to take it. It wasn't his fault the *idvad* had been scarcer than usual their first two years on Lujawed. And it wasn't his fault he'd taken sick as their first crops failed, or when he died, but though none of those things were Seth's fault, there were days, many of them, when Marrin blamed her husband bitterly for her current situation.

The crowd of exiting passengers had trickled to nothing. Marrin kept her back straight, her eyes dry, her grip firm on Hadassah's straining hand. He wasn't coming.

"Come on, girls," she said at last, when the only person remaining in the starport station was the elderly Lujawedi sweeping the floors. "Let's go home."

As she turned, one last figure appeared in the starport doors. A tall man with dark hair to his shoulders, wearing a blue jumpsuit with white piping.

He stepped cautiously through the doors and looked around. His eyes fell on their little group and he smiled, stepping forward, the look on his face one of a man greeting long-lost friends. He looked overjoyed to see them, and Marrin stepped back at the sight of Keane Delacore's smile. He didn't look forty. He looked even younger than her twenty-six years.

"Marrin Levy, I greet you," he said.

The formality of his speech took her aback for a second, but then she nodded. He spoke in Universal, in which she was competent, but not fluent. Perhaps he wasn't either.

"Welcome to Lujawed." Her voice sounded strained and brisk even to herself. She cleared her throat and held out the hand not holding Hadassah's. The little girl had shrunk behind her mother, watching from around Marrin's hip. "You must be Keane."

"I answer to that, yes."

He had an easy grin that tried to make her mouth twitch upward in response, but it had been so long since Marrin had smiled that the effort failed. His faded a bit when she nodded at him instead. He turned his attention to Sarai and Aliya, who had ceased their running and now stared with wide eyes at the stranger their mother had agreed to bring home with them.

"You must be Aliya." Keane pulled something from his pocket and held it out to the oldest girl, who reached out a trusting hand.

Instinct almost made Marrin intercept him, but she resisted. This man had passed every test the Association for Interplanetary Spousal Provision had given him. He'd scored higher in morality, work ethic and intelligence than the other ten applicants Marrin's own analysis had matched her with. She was already technically married to him, and had been since the moment she'd signed the plazscreen at the agency office three months ago. So she stayed her hand and waited to see what he had brought.

"Thank you!" Aliya looked stunned and happy. She took the chocolate—a full bar, still sealed, and held it to her chest. "Oh, thank you!"

"And Sarai," said Keane, pulling another bar from his pocket. He had to bend farther for her, but she took the present with no less enthusiasm than had her older sister.

"Thank you!" the girl cried, and added a spontaneous hug. Sarai had always been the most affectionate one.

Keane's eyes met Marrin's over the top of Sarai's head. He looked away in a moment and focused on Hadassah, still clinging to Marrin's leg, though the bounty of chocolate had drawn her out.

"And Hadassah." Keane straightened, hand pulling out a third chocolate bar and handing it toward her.

Hadassah grabbed it and kicked Keane solidly in the shin.

"Hadassah!" Marrin's shocked cry echoed throughout the empty starport. "Oh, I'm so sorry—"

Keane shook his head, standing upright and giving a far kindlier smile to Hadassah than Marrin would have. "It's all right."

She cleared her throat uncomfortably. "She's usually not—"

"Marrin." Keane shook his head. "It's fine. Really."

Marrin nodded. "Shall we go?"

"Lead the way." Keane lifted his bag. "They told me the rest would be shipped out to your place once it goes through decontamination."

"Yes. I've brought the truck. It's outside."

The colony of Bosie couldn't be called thriving, but it had grown quite a bit since she and Seth had arrived six rotations before. Seeing it now and imagining what it must look like through Keane's eyes, pride and dismay warred inside her. To an outsider it didn't look like much, but to one of the original hundred and forty colonists, it was a metropolis built of love and sweat.

"You're seeing it at a great time," she told him as she hefted the too-big-to-be-carried Hadassah onto her hip and walked toward the truck. "Just after the *idvad*, when everything's in bloom. In a month, this will all be gone."

She indicated the flowers on vines covering most of the buildings.

Keane nodded. "I've read everything I could find about Lujawed. The holos are amazing, but not even close to seeing it for real."

That earned him a smile. She settled the girls into their seats and harnesses, then climbed behind the wheel as Keane took the passenger seat.

"It makes it all worthwhile," she admitted. "Knowing that for a few weeks out of the year, it's all beautiful."

By the time they got from town to the ranch, Keane had fascinated two of her daughters with tales of his journey.

Hadassah had always been the most stubborn one, the most spoiled and petted and cosseted, having essentially three mothers instead of only one. She glared at Keane the whole way home. She slammed the door in his face when they got to the house, and she stuck her tongue out him.

Marrin sent her to her room for that last insult and apologized once more to Keane, who smiled and shrugged, holding out his hands.

"It takes time," was all he said. "For everyone."

That first night, she offered him the choice of sides of the bed and lay stiff as iron when he climbed in beside her. Their contract stated there would be conjugal benefits included in exchange for his work. Seth was the last man who had touched her. Aside from her children, he was the last person to have touched her in any other than the most casual ways.

She waited, eyes wide in the darkness, for the slide of a hand along her skin, for a mouth to seek hers. She listened for a shift in his breathing, for the rustle of clothes.

"I'm sorry," Keane said at last, his voice a richness dissolving into the darkness like honey dripped into tea. "I'm really tired from the journey. Would you mind if I just went to sleep?"

"No, of course not. Not at all."

And so he went to sleep, while she lay beside him for a long time, unable to do the same.

Keane worked hard by her side, and cheerfully, doing whatever task she set for him. He was vocal in his appreciation of her skills in the field, and of the meals she cooked, and of the way she washed his clothes. He never failed to thank her no matter what she did for him.

He won over Sarai and Aliya with his gentle manner, and he tolerated Hadassah's constant sassiness with patience and bemusement. Day after day he made himself a part of their family. Night after night he slept beside her in their bed, and night after night he made no move to make love to her.

"Good night, Marrin," he always said, and her answer returned, "Good night, Keane."

Months passed and she found herself laughing with him over after-dinner tea, and discussing the girls' schooling, the crop, the repairs they needed to make to the house, and the sad state of their now mutual bank account. She found herself remembering how he liked his breakfast prepared and making sure his clothes were mended and clean. She discovered herself staring at his hair as it fell over his broad shoulders and down his muscled back, now tanned by the sun.

She watched him when she thought he wasn't watching her.

When he'd said Seveerans aged differently than Earthers, he had meant their lifespans were longer. Once they reached maturity, they did not appear to age. They'd removed themselves almost entirely from the birth process. Genetics and specialized breeding had found a way to stop aging but not death; there was no fading away as there was in Earthers, no gradual decay and decline in quality of life as joints began to ache and vision faded, or memories began to disintegrate. If accident didn't claim their lives, Seveerans simply reached a time when they no longer wished to live, and then they no longer did.

It bothered her that he looked younger. When they went into Bosie, the people who saw them assumed Marrin Levy's field-husband was good for more than planting and harvesting. That she'd hired herself a young lover as well as a laborer.

Why it should bother her so much she couldn't say, since essentially, for all intents and purposes, that was what she had done. Bought a man to replace the one who'd died. What nobody else knew was that she and Keane weren't lovers. More like partners. And it wasn't any of anyone's business, was it?

"I think I'll go into town today," she said one morning.

Keane looked up from his newsform. "I'll go with you."

"No need."

He smiled easily. "I'd like to."

"I think I'd rather go by myself." Her words sounded stiff without reason, angry without reason, and she saw confusion in his eyes. She lifted her chin.

How could she explain that she didn't want to walk down the street and listen to the whispers that followed them? Especially when they weren't true.

He got up from the table. "Marrin, did I do something wrong?"

"No, of course not."

He frowned, an expression that rarely crossed his face, and moved closer. "You look angry."

"Well, I'm not, okay?"

Fuming, she crossed to the sink and ran the water, hard, though it wasted it. She splashed the dishes and slapped them with the sponge until he came over and twisted the faucet closed. He looked at her. "Tell me what's wrong."

"I just want to spend some time by myself," she snapped. "Is that so much to ask? Do we have to spend every moment together? Can't I just have some time to myself for once?"

She couldn't look at him. Shame turned her face away so she wouldn't have to see his look of hurt. She wiped her hands and started to move away.

He reached out and grabbed her upper arm. It was the first time he'd ever touched her deliberately. His grip was strong. It would leave bruises if she tried to yank her arm from his fingers. She didn't try.

"If I've done something—"

"You haven't."

"Marrin." Keane's gentle voice made her want to cry. "Look at me."

She did then because she couldn't help it. She kept her expression neutral. "What?"

"Are you going to send me back? Release me from our contract?"

His question surprised her. "No."

He nodded. "Good. Because I don't want to go back."

He released her and she stepped away. "Why not?"

She'd never asked him his reasons for agreeing to become a field-husband, for traveling light years from home to scratch out an existence on a planet as despairing as Lujawed. He'd never offered an explanation. She knew he wasn't a criminal because the agency had done a thorough background check. But beyond that, he'd never spoken of home or family.

She assumed his answer had something to do with some trauma on Seveer. A falling out with his family maybe. Or debts he couldn't pay. What other reason could he have had for coming here, and not wanting to go back?

He didn't answer her question, but posed another one of his own. "Do you wish you'd never sent for me? Or that I was someone different?"

"Yes," she said, though she didn't know why.

She turned her back and left the kitchen and Keane, and she went to town alone where she spent the day looking in shop windows at items she didn't need and still could not afford.

When she got home, she found the house quiet. The girls slept in their room and Keane in a chair by the window, a newsform on his lap. A covered plate in the coolbox made tears spring to her eyes again. She crept from the kitchen to stand in the living room doorway, watching him.

Then she went to his chair and stood. He opened his eyes.

"Because I'd miss you and the girls," he whispered in answer to her earlier question.

"We'd miss you too," Marrin whispered back. "Come to bed."

She went to the bedroom and got into bed, and Keane got in beside her. They lay in silence for a few minutes.

"I'm sorry I'm not what you expected me to be," he said at last.

"I'm sorry I expected something different."

She heard him shift, felt the bed dip as he turned toward her. She waited for him to touch her, but all he said was, "Good night, Marrin."

"Good night, Keane."

Chapter 9

Today

"Good morning, sir!" the medica chirped as she opened the blinds to let in the sun.

The poor man had fallen asleep by his wife's bedside, holding her hand. The medica smiled and moved closer to put her hand on his shoulder. She drew it back immediately with a small cry of surprise.

"Oh, my," she said as she ran for someone to come and help her.

Another medica joined her a moment later. "What's wrong, Pimmie?"

She gestured. "They're gone."

"Both of them?"

She nodded. "Yes. She was ailing, but the young man seemed fine yesterday."

The other medica moved closer. "She was his grandma?"

Pimmie shook her head, remembering the conversation of the day before. "Oh, no. She was his wife."

The other medica looked more closely at the man's face. "But he's Seveeran. They don't just die. They have to choose—"

"And he chose," said Pimmie, tears sliding down her cheeks. "He chose to go. When she did."

She smiled through the tears. "He didn't want to be without her."

"Well, now they're both in the stars," said the other medica. "Together."

And as she turned to leave the room, Pimmie thought she heard a whisper, but when she turned back to listen, it had gone.

Good night, Marrin.
Good night, Keane. I love you.
I love you, too.

ANYTHING YOU WANT

Megan Hart

Chapter 1

It was the biggest cock Milla Sulay had ever seen. A full ten inches long, three inches wide and made of clear, bendable plaz-foam, it hung next to a neighbor of similar width and girth. That one had an attached, realistically detailed scrotum designed to hold the battery powered motor that provided the unit's patented *thrust-n-grind* motion.

"Take them away," she said to the SRV-S 327 that had shown her to the stateroom. Milla tried to sound bored instead of appalled—or worse, intimidated—by the immense "amenities."

The servbot couldn't have cared less. Programmed to obey simple commands to the letter and with an extremely limited intuitive function, the SRV-S 327 would turn down her bed, hang up her clothes or draw her a bath, but it would perform all of those functions because that was its purpose, and not from desire. It certainly wouldn't make judgments about her bedroom habits, no matter what they were. Or weren't.

"As you please, miss," said the servbot in an accent straight out of Olden England. It bobbed its squat metallic body in a parody of a curtsey. "Will there be anything else, miss? Warm bath? Vibro-masturbatory massage? Shall I ring for a Pleasurebot to service you?"

The warm bath sounded good, but Milla wasn't interested in being vibrated to orgasm by a faceless, rolling torso made of metal and plaz-glass. The Pleasurebot, on the other hand, was a possibility. "Nothing right now. Thank you."

The servbot didn't require thanks any more than it had required an explanation. Its internal circuits whirred faintly and it bobbed again on hidden springs, then turned on the gear wheel it had in place of feet and left the room. Milla closed the door and leaned against it with a sigh before looking around the cabin with a grin so wide it tickled her earlobes.

Her first night in her very own cabin, with an entire week ahead of her. A full seven Old Earth-measured days to do whatever she wanted. Milla caught sight of the empty hooks where the gigantic phalluses had hung. Nothing she had planned included self-pleasure. She'd have time enough for that when she got to Selkca and her homesteader's plot. Years of time, in fact, to make herself come. It would probably be her only choice.

This week, Milla was going to spend every minute she wasn't eating expensive pastries being seduced, caressed and aroused as often as possible. She intended to make enough memories to last her for the rest of her long, possibly lonely life.

Chapter 2

Jarden could ignore the flashing red light indicating a cabin in need of service, but there was no way to ignore the whoop-whoop of the bell. With a groan, he rolled onto his back, the hard bunk protesting with every movement. He stabbed at the button on the wall.

"Your turn, buddy," he said with a jerk of his thumb toward Peter. "C'mon, you go and let me get some sleep."

Peter, a fully equipped COK-275, looked up from the holo-bloid he was watching. "Huh?"

Jarden sat, hunching so as not to hit his head on the bottom of the bunk. "Your turn."

Peter shook his blond head. "Oh, no. I am on break."

Jarden sighed. "Fella, you don't need a break. Right? You can go all night, isn't that the slogan?"

"COKs never quit!" Peter beamed, proud, but didn't trigger off the holo-bloid.

Jarden reached over to do it for him. The high-pitched voice of the chanteuse currently embroiled in some sort of chastity scandal cut off in mid-croon. Peter blinked, but made no move to turn the holo-bloid back on. That was one good thing about that unit's lack of brain power. Peter didn't usually resist suggestion, whether subtly worded or strongly enforced.

Of course, there was always a first time.

"Cabin 378 needs service, Pete. Go on and get it."

Again, frustratingly, Peter shook his head. At six-two, with a fused-alloy frame and muscles built from the highest quality components, he wasn't easily pushed physically, even if his mental status made him easily influenced. Jarden couldn't make the 'bot get up and go by force. He had to find a way to convince Peter he wanted to go.

"Think of that hot, wet pussy waiting for you, Peter." Jarden watched the front of Peter's thin briefs tent, just a little. "Yeah, see? Think about fucking some sweet, hot piece of snatch, right?"

Peter's hand went to his crotch and massaged. "I like to fuck."

"I know you do, fella." Jarden himself liked to fuck, quite a bit. The problem was, unlike Peter, Jarden wasn't a COK, a DIK or a

STUD of any model year. He was as human as any man could be, aside from the sixty-seven percent of him that had been recreated from artificial materials. The artificial systems regulating his circulation meant he could keep an erection more than twice as long as a so-called normal man, and climax more than once during a fuck-session, but damn it, he still needed to sleep once in a while. With the Pleasure Princess at full capacity and several of the Pleasurebots who'd normally be providing the sexual services the passengers required out of operation for repairs, Jarden had been pulling double shifts.

"I'm tired, Peter," Jarden explained simply, because Peter couldn't understand anything much more complex. "I need a few hours of shut-eye. Okay?"

Peter's hand had, by this time, stroked himself to full erection. Jarden had seen it before. Impressive and aesthetically pleasing, Peter's prick was top-of-the line. Now it nudged its way from Peter's stick-seam fly, and Peter shuddered a little.

"Peter." Jarden pointed at the flashing light on the wall. "Cabin 378. Hot pussy."

Peter stopped stroking his cock and blinked. "I'm on break. I'm on break."

Fuck. "Peter."

Peter's big blue eyes, fringed with thick black lashes, didn't blink this time. "I'm on break."

Shit. "Okay, hold on, fella. We'll get you to the servshop. Okay?"

Peter's erection wilted in his hand and he stared at it, the mouth that had been built for kissing opening in feeble surprise. "I'm on break?"

"You're broken, fella," said Jarden. "No question about that."

Which meant that Jarden wasn't going to get that nap after all.

Chapter 3

Milla had bathed and slipped into a sleek toss-away of sheer pink. She'd fastened the stickseam all the way to her throat, where the high collar tickled her chin. The gown itself, meant to be worn but once, swung around the tops of her thighs. Bare beneath, her skin tingled from the application of Arous-All lotion she'd slicked onto her bath-damp flesh after getting out of the tub. She'd paid extra for real water.

God-of-Choice only knew how long she'd have to go without real water to drink, much less bathe in. Selkca was a desert planet. Its native population had the ability to produce H_2O via some internal synthesis, but the Homesteading Council's information had informed Milla all 'steaders on Selkca had to rely on monthly deliveries of imported, artificial water.

When the knock came at her cabin door, she'd just put down the bottle of Arous-All lotion. The cabin had been fully stocked with the entire line of Arous-All products, guaranteed to "Get you ready!" As if she needed help. She'd been ready practically from the moment she'd signed the travel contract.

She opened the door, already tilting her head in anticipation. She'd ordered a COK-275 from the extensive room service menu, and those 'bots were always tall. The one standing in front of her, however, was taller even than she'd expected.

"Miss Sulay?"

She nodded and stepped back to let him into the cabin. "I was beginning to think I'd have to call again."

"Sorry for the delay. I've been authorized to give you an hour's credit for the time you had to wait." The man flashed perfect white teeth unblemished by jewels or etchings.

Correction—not a man, Milla reminded herself. The perfect abs and biceps, the sultry smile and eyes the color of the space outside her cabin window belonged to a mandroid. A Pleasurebot. A creature built for the sole purpose of providing sexual pleasure. She looked him up and down, admiring him, and he put his hands on his hips with another grin as the front of his thin toss-away briefs bulged.

"You're wearing Arous-All," he said.

Milla nodded. He had dark hair cut short in the back and falling long over one dark eye. Tawny skin. Nipples like arti-chocolate discs. "Turn around."

He did. The view from the back was as impressive as from the front. He had a tight, rounded ass and long legs. Milla moved closer and cupped his rear with both her hands. He didn't move, not an inch, as she rubbed her fingertips along the line of his spine and stepped back.

She moved in front of him to study his face, noting the brightness of his eyes, the moistness of his lips…and something else. The faint lines of weariness around his bright eyes and moist lips. He hid it well, but he was tired. Pleasurebots didn't tire.

"You're not a COK," she said.

He shook his head. "No, miss. I'm sorry, but all of the COKs were in use. I can provide all the same functions, though. And give you an additional hour of credit to your account for the inconvenience."

"Two credit hours?" Milla crossed her arms, still staring at him. "What's your name?"

"Jarden."

His voice, low and sexy, peaked her nipples beneath the sheer toss-away. Did it matter he wasn't exactly what she'd ordered? Milla shifted her weight from foot to foot. Her thighs rubbed together. The Arous-All lotion had seeped into her pores and gone straight to the pleasure center of her brain. She was ready to fuck and come. Did it matter if he wasn't a COK?

"You're not a 'bot," she said in a low voice.

Jarden's expression didn't change. He didn't blink, didn't lick his mouth, didn't even let out a sigh. "No, ma'am. I'm not."

Milla had expected him to lie, and it impressed her that he didn't. She studied him. "Isn't that…illegal?"

Jarden shook his head. "The Pleasure Princess qualifies for entertainment exemptions under the Interstellar Transport Act."

"Oh." Milla had an idea of what that meant. Something to do with slaves. She felt suddenly ridiculous in her flimsy toss-away in front of a real man. "I was expecting a 'bot."

Jarden took her in his arms before she had time to squeak. "I promise you, I can make you just as happy as any 'bot can."

Pressed up against him that way, Milla had to tip her head back extra far to see his face. He was still smiling, but it didn't reach his eyes. Not the way it would have on a COK or a DIK, whose emotional triggers were genuine and unfakeable. The fullness in his briefs, however, felt real and substantial. She ran her hands up his bulging biceps to rest on his shoulders.

"I have to be honest with you," she said. "I really wanted a 'bot."

She waited for his answer. Jarden pulled her slowly closer, his big hands resting on her rear. "I promise you, I can do anything you want."

He bent to nuzzle her neck, and Milla closed her eyes as she let him. His mouth and tongue felt no different on her skin than a 'bot's would have. His hands were rougher, but that wasn't a bad thing. In fact, those rough hands excited her. Maybe it was because of the Arous-All, but the more he kissed and sucked and nibbled at her neck, the hotter Milla got.

"All right," she breathed, voice hoarse, when he slid a hand beneath the hem of her toss-away. "But I'm warning, you, I expect to be completely satisfied, and I'm not interested in working too hard for it."

Jarden pulled away to look at her face, and something in his gaze made Milla wish she'd been a little kinder. "It's what I'm here for, miss."

A 'bot wouldn't have said even that. A 'bot wouldn't have looked at her like that, as if she were not the first horny, arrogant woman to demand service with nothing in return. It was the reason she wanted a Pleasurebot and not a man, so she didn't have to feel guilty about being selfish. Pleasurebots got off as a matter of course and didn't need emotional connection.

Both of Jarden's big hands had slipped beneath the toss-away now. His fingertips skimmed the curve of her waist and dipped low in the back to cover her bare flesh with his palms. His fingers curved around her buttocks to stroke the ticklish crease, and Milla parted her legs. Jarden teased her ready pussy from behind, with just a whisper of a touch.

Her nipples poked the sheer fabric of her gown. When Jarden bent to take first one and then the other into his mouth, her lips parted in a silent gasp. He mouthed her breasts, wetting her toss-away, while his hands kept up their tour of her body.

He murmured against her breasts, "I'm here for your pleasure, miss. Anything you want."

God-of-choice, his simple statement weakened her knees so much she had to clutch his shoulder to keep from sagging. That was what she wanted. Someone to give her pleasure, whatever she wanted. However she wanted it.

"Get on your knees for me," she whispered. She'd never said such a thing before, though she'd thought it many times.

Jarden did at once. His mouth traveled her body as he lowered himself to the floor in front of her. Even on his knees, he was tall. His face was level now with her belly, but she wanted it lower.

"Push up my gown." The words came with effort, from a mouth so dry she had to swallow hard to speak.

Slowly, slowly, Jarden put a hand on each of Milla's thighs and slid them upward, pushing the toss-away up as he did. The cabin's climate was automatically regulated based on the body temperature, and now a cool gust of air breezed across her bared, heated skin.

Milla had fully depilated in the bath, every hair on her body from the neck down. The smoothness of her skin without hair had made it even easier for the aphrodisiac lotion to infiltrate her blood and turn her on, but even if she hadn't rubbed herself with it, she'd have been aroused.

"Lick me," she said, then louder. "Lick my pussy, Jarden."

Jarden put his mouth on her immediately. His tongue slipped along the seam of her cunt and lapped the bead of her clit. He circled it gently before using the flat of his tongue to stroke. His hands held her steady. Milla put her hand on top of his head, her fingers twining in the silk of his hair.

She muttered something incoherent. Her crotch pushed forward, seeking the further heat of Jarden's lips and tongue. He held tight to her ass and kept her still while he licked and sucked gently on her clit.

It felt so good she wanted to come right then. Hard. She wanted him to keep fucking her with his tongue until she exploded. Instead, she tightened her fingers in his hair and tugged, not terribly gently, until Jarden left off feasting on her pussy and looked up at her.

His eyes gleamed and he swiped his tongue along glistening lips. "Tell me what you want."

The hitch in his voice and the rise and fall of his shoulders as he breathed hard made her want to believe that eating her cunt had turned him on. Without question it would have aroused a COK or a DIK, but despite Jarden's expert prowess between her legs, she couldn't manage to forget he was a man who might not even find her attractive. One who might be faking because it was his job.

She licked her own mouth, her knees weak and stomach knotted with arousal. Her body had no problems with the man on his knees before her. If only her stupid brain would cease its endless musings.

She stepped away from him. His prick had filled the front of his briefs, at least she could see that. His cheeks had flushed, too, as well as the smooth column of his throat.

"Take off your briefs." She'd tried to sound confidant, but it came out sounding like a plea.

Jarden stood, up and up, and thumbed his toss-aways down muscular thighs. He stepped out of them and stood in front of her, his hips pushed slightly forward. His cock thickened, getting straighter as she watched, but he didn't touch himself.

He was waiting for her to tell him what to do.

"What do you think about to get yourself hard?" The question slipped out before she knew it, and, once spoken, it was too late to take it back.

If he'd smiled, she would have sent him from the room at once, but Jarden only licked his mouth again. "Tasting you got me hard, miss."

"Do I…taste good?" Oh, the question was difficult to say, but impossible not to ask.

Jarden nodded. His fingers flexed, as though he meant to touch his cock, but he kept his hands at his sides. Waiting for permission, she realized, and the thought sent bolts of pleasure straight to her clit.

Her fingers went to the stick-seam at her throat. She eased it apart, micron by micron, and folded open the flimsy material. The cool air drifted across her breasts, peaking her nipples into tighter, throbbing points. Between her legs, she was a furnace. Each time she shifted, Milla could feel the slickness coating her there. Could feel the swollen folds of her pussy and the hard bump of her clitoris under which her heartbeat pulsed.

Jarden's gaze took her in from face to feet. His eyes lingered on her breasts and between her legs, but when he looked up again, he looked into her eyes. His mouth parted and his tongue crept out again to touch the middle of his bottom lip.

"Do you like what you do?" Her voice rasped, but Jarden didn't seem to have trouble understanding her. He nodded. His hips pushed forward just a bit more.

"I love it," he said, and she believed him.

For that moment, anyway, she allowed herself to believe him. She took a step back, toward the bed. She shrugged off her toss-away and left it on the floor without a second glance. She lay on the bed and motioned to Jared, who moved toward her with swift grace.

He covered her body with his and sought the sensitive skin of her throat again. Her legs were already opening for him, her hands reaching between them to guide his prick inside her. When Jarden pushed his cock into her, Milla groaned and lifted her hips to ease the angle. He slid in all the way to his balls in one, smooth thrust.

"Fuck me," Milla said. "Hard."

Jarden shuddered against her neck. His mouth worked. "Anything you want."

Her hands found his muscled ass and held tight. "I want it. Right now. Fuck me until I scream, Jarden."

She should have felt silly saying it, but the words tasted right. They fit. She did want to scream, she wanted to come, she wanted him to fuck her so hard she saw stars.

Jarden moved. His hips pumped. The first few thrusts were ragged, but smoothed quickly. Another thrust, and he reached beneath Milla's ass to lift and shift her so their bodies aligned in a slightly different position. Now his pelvis hit her clit with every thrust.

"Perfect," Milla gasped.

"Fuck," Jared muttered against her ear. "You're so wet."

He sounded a little surprised, but she couldn't focus on that. Milla could only concentrate on the way his cock filled her, the way his body pressed her clit with each movement. The pressure of his teeth on her shoulder. She tensed, waiting for the bite, but it didn't come, until she whispered hoarsely, "Yes. Do it."

The pain when he bit her was slight and only made the pleasure greater. Jared licked the spot he'd bitten the moment before. Then he fastened his mouth to the side of her neck and his tongue swept her skin the same way he'd used it to lick her clit.

Milla cried out. She closed her eyes, waiting for the stars, but saw only blackness. Her nails raked down Jarden's back as she hooked her heels around the backs of his upper thighs and pushed against his ass, harder. Faster.

"Harder," she demanded, and he obliged.

Milla tensed as her climax built but didn't crash over her. She strained for it, reaching for the elusive pleasure with every muscle. She moaned, arching.

"Anything," Jarden breathed, a reminder.

She didn't know what to ask for, how to articulate what her body needed. She hovered on the edge of coming, but couldn't quite get there. She let out a small, sobbing breath of frustration. Flames of desire licked her every nerve, but it wasn't enough.

It was never enough.

Even here with a man she paid to do whatever she wanted, she couldn't come.

Jarden's thrusts slowed, ragged again. He paused, finally, resting on his forearms and lifting his head to look at her. Milla looked away, refusing to give him her eyes. Jarden moved inside her, but not even the Arous-All could keep her from going cold.

"Miss?"

"Finish." She forced the sound of disdain. "I'm getting bored."

Jarden stopped moving inside her. She looked at him then. "I said, finish. I want to be done."

He gave a minute shake of his head. "You're not finished, miss."

Shame sent bile lurching to her throat. She was a failure. Again. Always. She pushed at his chest. "Get off me."

He didn't. So much for giving her anything she wanted. Jarden pushed inside her a little deeper and stayed there, but Milla unhooked her heels from behind his thighs and gave him no encouragement to move.

"You didn't come," Jarden told her. He licked his mouth again. "Tell me what you want."

"I want you to get off me," Milla said putting as much chill in her voice as she could. "Now."

Jarden withdrew. The air in the cabin had been refreshingly cool earlier, but now felt too cold. Naked, Milla shivered. She drew herself up to sit against the headboard as soon as Jarden withdrew. She curled her arms around her knees.

"You can go," she said. "I'll use my extra cred-time with someone else."

She didn't miss Jarden's blink or the way his mouth thinned, but he turned from her in a moment, so all she could see was the line of his back and shoulders.

"I'm sorry you weren't satisfied," he said, but didn't sound sorry. He sounded annoyed.

She hadn't been able to forget he was a man, a person, not a 'bot, but the tone of his voice reminded her even more why she'd wanted to fuck a thing made of plastic and metal instead of flesh and bone.

"Just get out," she told him.

Jarden nodded and stood. He bent to retrieve his toss-away briefs, but the simple fabric had already begun to disintegrate. He tossed them down the disposal chute.

He lifted a hand to open the cabin door, giving her time to realize, with some surprise, he intended to leave without even dialing for a new toss-away, when the cabin shuddered. The lights flickered and went black for a micron, then came back on. The cabin shuddered again, so hard the small plaz-glass ornamental dildo on the nightstand fell over.

Jarden put a hand on the wall. It wasn't the cabin rocking, but the entire ship. Milla cried out as the room shook again. When it stopped, even the infinitesimal shiver she felt in the pit of her belly when the cruiser was in motion had ceased.

"What was that?" she asked, hating the thin waver in her voice.

"I don't know." Jarden passed his palm over the hand panel, but the door didn't open.

"Attention, all passengers," said a pleasant female voice over the intercom system. "Attention. Pleasure Princess Cruises apologizes for the inconvenience, but we've run into some complications. For the safety of our passengers, we've docked in Newcity airspace until we can assess the situation. This is for your safety and convenience. All passengers are required to stay inside their cabins while the investigative procedures take place. Again, this is for your own safety. I repeat, all passengers are required to stay inside their cabins while the crew of the Pleasure Princess assesses the situation."

Milla got out of bed and pulled on a robe more substantial than a toss-away. "What does that mean?"

Jarden turned, his mouth set in a thin, grim line. "I'm sure it's just a minor repair job, miss. Pleasure Princess Cruises values the safety and comfort of its passengers."

The words came out as though by rote. He passed his palm over the hand panel again, but the door remained locked. Jarden punched a series of numbers on the keypad beneath the hand panel. Still nothing.

Milla watched him. "You know something you're not telling me."

Jarden didn't look at her. "Miss, I'm sure this will all be resolved shortly. Why not choose a holo-vid from the extensive complimentary library—"

"Stop," she told him. "I know you're lying to me. I'm not stupid, and you're not a very good liar."

Jarden turned, still naked, and Milla snatched up a pair of unisex sleep pants. She threw them to him and he put them on without looking at her. It was easier to face him when he was dressed.

"I can be anything you want me to be. Do you want me to be a good liar?"

Milla frowned. "No. I want you to tell me what's going on."

Jarden crossed his arms over his chest. "I don't know. There could be something wrong with the engine. These cruisers are old, and the captain of this boat would rather stretch everything on it until it breaks than spring for new. They don't tell you that in the brochure, I'm sure."

She shook her head, eyeing him. "But that's not why you're nervous."

Jarden flashed her a grin she didn't believe for a second. "I'm not nervous, miss."

"Don't call me that."

"Anything you want."

Milla frowned again and turned, pulling her robe tighter around her throat. "Damn it, I wanted a 'bot."

"Complain to the captain," Jarden said. "Maybe if he kept his fuck-crew in better repair, I wouldn't have to work constant double shifts, and you'd have been able to come."

Milla's mouth dropped and she closed it with an audible snap as she turned to him. "You're not supposed to give me attitude!"

Jarden tried the hand panel again. "Pardon me, miss, but I've got other things to worry about than being your bitch-boy."

"I told you not to call me that!" She glared. "And I knew you were nervous about something!"

Jarden made a fist and punched the wall softly. "If we docked in Newcity airspace for repairs, that means we'll be boarded for inspection. Since they rebuilt the dome, Newcity has the strictest regs in this part of the system. That's why all the passengers have to stay in their cabins. They'll try to pass it off as a quality control inspection or a satisfaction interview or something, but that's not what it is. It's not what they're looking for."

"What are they looking for?"

"Anything that doesn't conform to the Newcity Standards."

She'd heard of them, a list of requirements for citizenship in Newcity. "But the Pleasure Princess isn't required to conform to Newcity Standards. I mean, I'm not a Newcitizen. I don't have to obey their rules."

Jarden punched one fist into the other. "No, but any Newcitizen on this boat does. Any Newcitizen not conforming to the Newcity Standards can—and will—be arrested and removed from this ship. R.I.O. will be checking the Pleasurebots too. Making sure they're up to code."

Recreational Intercourse Operatives. Milla had heard of them. "But Pleasurebots aren't illegal, not even in Newcity."

"No," said Jared. "Pleasurebots aren't illegal. But I am."

Chapter 4

The woman stared at him, but Jarden couldn't care about saying too much. Even if she complained, it didn't matter. When R.I.O. rapped on the cabin door, he'd be arrested. End of story, and not happily ever after either.

"I don't understand," she said slowly. "You said the Pleasure Princess had exemptions about slaves."

Fuck, he wanted a drink. It wasn't allowed, but he helped himself to the jug of arti-wine from the table anyway. Might was well be screwed for everything as much as one thing.

"It's not because of that. There's no problem with my papers of indenture. Ninety percent of the crew on this ship are indentured anyway."

"So...why you?" Milla was her name, and she didn't want to be called "miss." She moved closer and he caught a whiff of the remnant of the Arous-All lotion.

"I'm a mecho." The words came out without inflection, though each was a barb in his throat. He waited for her to recoil, but Milla only stared at him curiously. "I'm sixty-seven percent artificial components."

She shrugged, her face apologetic. "And?"

"In Newcity I was declared a mecho. Not human."

Her lip curled, but not, he realized, with disgust about him. "They still do that?"

He nodded and finished the glass of arti-wine. It wasn't very good. It wouldn't have made him drunk even if his enhanced circulatory and filtration systems had allowed him to become intoxicated.

"That's barbaric." Milla shook her head. "And stupid."

Jarden refused to feel grateful for her "enlightened" attitude, even though he'd been expecting derision. "Yeah. But stupid and barbaric is going to land me in a work camp servicing the border patrols or something like that."

"I can imagine it wouldn't be as glamorous," she said thoughtfully. "But really, isn't that what you do now?"

"No." Jarden had to fight to keep the growl from his voice. "I'm indentured. I work for my passage. When I earn my way and save some capital, I'm off this tub for good. I'm going to get a little place somewhere, a Homestead maybe. I do what I do because I chose it, not because someone decided I'm not fit to live in polite society."

She flinched, and he realized he was shouting. She didn't back away from him, though. Instead, she poured herself a glass of arti-wine and filled his glass again.

"I'm sorry," Milla said. "I didn't mean to offend you."

He could get into a lot of trouble for talking so roughly to a passenger, but somehow Jarden doubted that would matter once R.I.O. boarded the Pleasure Princess. It didn't stop him from feeling a little bad, though. She hadn't been nasty on purpose.

"I have another year of service," he told her. "I've been on here for five."

A faint look of surprise crossed her face. When her eyes widened, he could see the bluish-green he'd noticed earlier had darkened.

"That long?"

He nodded and took another long drink. "Four years Earthside before that, just to get my passage to the cruiser."

Four years of looking over his shoulder, waiting to be arrested. Four years watching the Newcity Ruling Council write and rewrite the Newcity Standards, tightening the stranglehold on anyone who didn't meet their rigid view of who deserved to be called a Newcitizen.

"Attention, passengers," came the voice over the intercom again. "Dinner may be ordered from your servbot. Please remain in your cabins. Complimentary holo-vids are available, as well as a full array of self-stim and virtual orgy products. Headsets and visors may be found in your love cabinet. Simply log on to enjoy."

Milla made a face. "Virtual sex. No, thank you."

"Is it any different than fucking a 'bot?" Jarden asked and waited for her to flinch again.

Milla only looked thoughtful. "Oh, much different. 'Bots are real."

"They're not real," Jarden said. "They're fake. They don't care about anything but fucking and being fucked."

"They don't make judgments," Milla said, and looked away from him. "And you don't have to make them happy."

Jarden sat in the plush vibro-chair and finished his second glass of arti-wine. "What makes you happy?"

She wouldn't look at him. He watched her sip her wine in silence. He studied the tension in her shoulders and smelled the aphrodisiac lotion she'd used. He smelled her heat, unabated though he'd done everything she asked.

He'd blamed lack of sleep for his inability to give her an orgasm. His concentration had been divided. But now, watching her fingers curl tighter on the glass, Jarden thought maybe the problem wasn't that he hadn't tried hard enough.

"I wanted a Pleasurebot." Milla finished her wine and put the empty glass on the table. "Bots don't care what you look like. They get hard anyway. Pleasurebots don't need anything but a warm place to sink their dicks. It doesn't matter if you have scars."

Jarden knew about scars. His had once crisscrossed most of his body. Some from the accident that had damaged his spleen and liver. Most from the multitude of operations he'd sustained to repair the damage left behind by the unskilled surgeons who'd performed the first surgery and left infection and disease behind.

"Do you have scars?" he asked her.

She looked at him. "Not anymore."

He stood and tugged the waist of the pants she'd given him lower on his hips. He pointed to the place where an eight-foot plaz-glass spike had pierced him. "I was an engineer. I worked on the new dome. After the old one collapsed, they wanted something not prone to zips and tears. I was one of the designers who figured out how to manufacture a new one. There was an accident during the construction. I lost my liver and spleen. That was the first operation."

She looked at him, then shook her head. "I don't see anything."

"I paid for expensive surgeries after the first one. I used my entire savings to make sure they didn't leave marks. I couldn't afford to have anyone know I'd been fixed. After a while, I couldn't afford anything."

Milla blinked, then cleared her throat. "I'm sorry."

"Don't be." Jarden shrugged. "I'll design again. They need engineers on the Homestead planets. If I ever get there."

"I'm going to Selkca."

He hadn't pegged her for a Homesteader. "Yeah?"

Milla smiled, the first she'd given him. Jarden would never cease to be amazed at the power of a woman's smile. He wouldn't have minded hearing her laugh either.

"Yes. This cruise is my passage there. I figured…I've got a long time to be alone. I might as well have some fun on the way."

"But you didn't." Jarden watched her carefully. He'd been trained to find the signs of arousal. Bright eyes, flushed skin. Just like he'd been trained in a hundred ways to bring a woman to orgasm.

If there was power in a woman's smile, her frown had strength too. A Pleasurebot wouldn't want to take a woman in its arms and take away whatever was troubling her. Jarden, on the other hand, couldn't stop himself from wanting to.

When he got up and pulled her against him, Milla looked startled. "What are you doing?"

Jarden rubbed her upper arms gently. "I owe you two cred-hours."

She shook her head. "No. I told you, I don't want them."

He didn't let her go. He slipped a hand inside her robe to cup her breast. The nipple perked at once against his palm. He rolled a thumb over it and watched her mouth part.

"I think you do, Milla."

She closed her eyes, and the glimmer of tears on her lashes punched him in the gut. "I can't. Didn't you figure that out yet?"

Jarden moved his hand lower, over her belly. Tiny muscles leapt under his fingertips. Lower he moved, over the smooth mound of her pubis to the delicate pearl of her clit. He pressed it and it throbbed. She was turned on, no question of that, and not just from the Arous-All.

"I think you can."

She shook her head again, harder. "No. I can't. Maybe with a Pleasurebot—"

"You think a 'bot could do what I can't?" He really wanted to know. His fingertip pressed against her gently, and her legs parted a bit more. "Why?"

She looked at him then, her cheeks flushed and eyes bright. "Being with a 'bot wouldn't be much different from being with myself, would it? A 'bot's just like a big vibrator, only I don't have to operate it."

He slid his finger lower, along her folds. She was still slick. Hot. His cock thickened at the sensation of the wet heat on his finger. He parted her gently and found her entrance, but didn't push inside.

"A real...man..." She paused to take a breath and her eyelashes fluttered. "...expects...things."

"What sort of things?" he murmured, watching her.

Her eyes opened and she pushed out of his arms. "Things in return." Her voice shook. "Payback. A 'bot's reward is his orgasm, and he'll have one no matter what."

"Even if you have scars?" Jarden asked.

Milla turned from him. "Yes. Even then."

Someone must have hurt her, and it didn't take a genius to figure out how. "Who was he?"

Her shoulders straightened. "My union partner. His name was Derek. It was an arranged union."

The term, union partner, told him a lot about her. "You're from Nidar?"

She nodded. "Yes. Where women are only as good as the men who unite with them."

A few moments earlier Jarden had wanted to hear her laugh, but hearing it now wasn't what he'd imagined. "So you left. Lots of Nidar women do, I've heard."

She threw him a wry look. "I didn't want to leave. I loved him, even though I hadn't chosen him. He was so handsome. He was so smart. It hurt, how much I loved him, Jarden. I was foolish. I was just a girl. But Derek was all I'd ever believed I wanted."

She didn't look like much more than a girl now. "So what happened?"

She held out her wrist. "This."

Jarden took her arm and studied the faint, barely discernable line at the base of her wrist. "What is it?"

"I was shopping for union gifts for Derek's family. I needed to find something special. His family had much higher status than mine, you see. While I was at the market, there was an attack."

She pulled her wrist gently back. "I understand the ideals of the group that did it. They call themselves Imperfectionists. They cut a lot of the women in the market. Marking them. I was lucky. They only managed a slice before they were gassed. I had the wound repaired, of course, right away. The best surgeons. But that white line remained. And on my union night, Derek couldn't stop looking at it. Every time we made love, he made me hide it. He said it disgusted him. After three weeks, he said he could no longer bear to make love to me. We had a barren union."

As a Nidarian woman, she'd have been a virgin when she united, that much Jarden knew. But what she said next surprised him.

"I had an affair with Derek's business partner. His name was Stephal. He came to our house often while Derek was away. I had many affairs."

Jarden had heard stories of Nidar's unequal treatment of genders. "And what happened?"

"None of those men could make me climax," she told him bluntly. "I'd discovered I could have orgasms very well on my own. Masturbation for women is forbidden, of course, but every woman I knew did it. Pleasurebots are illegal for women too, though men can use them. I knew I could come by myself. I knew I could come with a woman too."

The image of Milla, legs spread beneath a woman's tongue, two soft and curved bodies writhing in pleasure, filled Jarden's cock a bit more. "You slept with women?"

Milla waved a derisive hand. "In Nidar, all women fuck each other. It's often the only way we have to get any pleasure. And I like women, Jarden, but they can be hard work. Women fall in love too easily. It can be…awkward."

Her eyes flashed. The folds of her robe had stayed open after he'd parted them with his hand. He glimpsed her breasts and sweet pink nipples. She'd tasted good.

"One of my lovers didn't understand the need for discretion. She fell in love with me." Milla paused, voice low. "But I didn't love her. She went to my union partner."

"What happened?" His voice was a little hoarse from the memory of her flavor.

"Derek dissolved our union. I was lucky he didn't have me put in prison for defiling our union, but when I told him about all the men—his friends and business partners—who'd also violated the union with me, he relented. The laws are more lenient for men, but the scandal would have been very bad for Derek and his family. I took the dissolution settlement and used it for a deposit on a plot on

Selkca and this trip. I wanted to fuck," Milla said with a lift of her chin. "I wanted to come with a cock inside me and hands on me that weren't my own. I wanted to just take care of my own pleasure without worrying about what my partner wanted."

"You wanted a 'bot."

She nodded. "Yes. And I got you, instead. And you see? I couldn't come, even with you."

Jarden thought of how confident she'd sounded when she'd told him to get on his knees for her. How her pussy had slicked beneath his mouth and hands, and how she'd responded. There was no problem with her being able to reach arousal.

"Because I'm not a robot?" he asked, amused despite himself. "Milla, I'm more metal and plaz than I am anything else."

"But your mind's not a hard drive," she told him with a small smile. "You're still a man."

"You don't like men?" He wouldn't have blamed her after hearing her experience.

"I love men," Milla said. "I love everything about them. I love hard, thick erections and long legs and tight bellies. I love hairy legs and arms and chests. I love the way a man feels on top of me." Her breath hitched.

"But you can't come with one." Jarden thought of how she'd arched beneath him as if by instinct. How good she'd felt. "You're beautiful, you know."

Milla frowned. "Stop. You don't have to."

Jarden made a show of looking around. "What else do we have to do?" It was the wrong thing to say, and he knew it at once. "I'm sorry, Milla. I didn't mean it that way."

She'd drawn the robe closed, tight at her neck. "No matter what you say, I know it's because you're paid to say it. So don't bother. We tried. It didn't work."

"You really think a Pleasurebot could get you off better than a man can?"

She nodded, rougher this time. "Why not?"

Good question. Pleasurebots were built to provide orgasms with no strings. She might be right about a COK or a DIK being able to bring her off, if only because she thought so.

"I'd like to watch you come." Jarden smiled.

Milla eyed him warily. "I told you—"

"No. Let me watch you. I won't do anything but watch."

She laughed, tipping her head back. This time the genuine humor in it was just how he'd thought it would be. "Why? And why would I want you to watch? I can make myself come anytime I want."

"Do you want to now?" He moved close enough to feel a flush of heat from her, but he didn't touch her. "I know you must want to. I could tell how turned on you were."

She shivered minutely, but he saw it. "It was the Arous-All. It'll wear off."

"Why let it?" he murmured. "Touch yourself. You know what you like and what you want."

She looked at him. "What's in it for you?"

He shrugged and held out his hands, open-palmed. "Nothing."

"Right."

He much preferred her smile.

"You'll just watch. You won't expect a blowjob or anything after?"

Jarden grinned. "I can't say I would turn one down, but I'm not paid to get what I want. I'm paid to give you what you want. Anything you want. And I think you really, really want to finish yourself."

He was sure he'd lost her. That she'd turn away again or yell. At the very least, ignore him. But Milla sighed, her eyes closing briefly for a moment before she looked at him.

"Oh, I do," she whispered. "I really do."

"So do it," Jarden murmured.

With one smooth, graceful motion, Milla dropped the robe from her shoulders. Naked, she went to the bed and settled herself against the pillows. Her pale hair fanned over the deep blue of the sheets. Her legs parted, giving him a glimpse of pink.

When she licked her finger and centered it directly on her clit, it was as if she'd licked him from balls to tip. His cock jerked, growing, but Jarden made no move toward her. He sat, instead, in the plush chair and watched her on the bed.

He'd seen women pleasure themselves before. Most of them did it with single-minded focus of the sort that left no doubt how necessary men really weren't. Milla, though, didn't touch herself like she was challenging him. She slipped a finger down inside herself and arched with a sigh, then drew it up to circle her clit.

With her other hand, she pulled gently on her nipples. When they were erect, she used two fingers of that hand to push inside herself as she continued rubbing her clitoris. Jarden watched, his cock getting harder by the second, as her fingers fucked in and out. They glistened now from her juices. Her pussy bloomed with color as her arousal grew. The dusky pink darkened the same way his erection was changing color as the blood rushed in.

Her moan shot straight to the base of his cock and pushed his hips forward, though his hands stayed gripped on the arms of the chair. Sweat gathered in his hairline as he watched her rock her cunt against her hands.

Any other time he'd have been on her by now, feasting on her clit and lapping up her sweetness. Sinking into her. Instead he stayed perfectly still. He could smell the musky odor of her arousal and he wanted to bury his face between her legs and drink in her essence.

There was no more powerful aphrodisiac to Jarden than a woman's flavor as she neared orgasm, and the sound of her breathing when she came. He wanted to hear Milla moan. Fuck, he wanted to hear her scream. He wanted to be the one to give her that, but he forced himself not to move. Not even to fist his prick and pump, though he was so turned on even fucking into the air was getting him close.

"Come closer," she said suddenly, her voice raw with need. "Watch me come, Jarden. I want you to see me."

He moved fast, in two steps reaching the bed where he knelt between her parted legs. Her pussy had opened, beckoning him. Her fingers slid in and out of the slick channel. She pushed upward, giving him a glimpse of the rosebud of her anus. Her clit had grown, her rubbing fingers obscuring and revealing the engorged button beneath its hood of flesh.

Jarden's cock strained, aching, his balls heavy with the need for release. Still, he did nothing but watch. The blanket bunched between his thighs teased his balls, and he fought to keep from fucking against the material.

"I see you're so close," he told her.

She moaned, her fingers slowing. She withdrew her hand from her entrance and used her slick fingers to glide over her clitoris. She paused, rubbed, paused again. She stopped touching herself and put her hands on her thighs, giving him a clear view. She rocked slightly, and Jarden could see the small clutch and release of her inner muscles.

He imagined being inside her, how it would feel to have her milk him with those muscles. How she'd pull and tighten on his prick when she came. He groaned. Her eyes opened, and she looked at him.

"You want to fuck me," she whispered.

"God-of-choice, yes, I do." Jarden didn't move.

She closed her eyes again, tilting her pelvis upward, just a little. Her bare cunt had nothing to hide it. Her clit peeked out from beneath its hood, begging for his tongue to stroke it.

"Go ahead, then," she said.

He shook his head. "No. I want to watch you come first. Make yourself come."

She let out a small, sobbing cry. "I can't!"

"You can. I'm only watching."

Her hand shifted on her thighs, but she didn't resume touching herself. "I'm so close, Jarden…"

"I know you are, sweetheart," he breathed. "I can see how close you are. Tip over the edge. You know how good it will feel."

"You want me to come for you." She moaned the words.

"No," Jared told her. He took her hand and put it on her clit. He moved it gently, in the rhythm she'd set for herself. "I want you to come for yourself."

Chapter 5

Milla shuddered on the verge of orgasm, but didn't go over. Jarden's hand covered hers, and he moved it slowly. Every shift was a pure pleasure-pain she recognized. She was so close, and yet so far.

"I want you to come for yourself," he said.

She opened her eyes and looked at him. His gaze burned into her. His fingers moved hers. Slow, slow, barely moving. Her thighs trembled.

He smiled, encouraging her. Milla arched, her eyes closing, and lost herself in the waves of desire sweeping over her. She let her body move the way it wanted to. She gave in to the familiar feeling of her hand on her clit, the way it had been so many times before. She swam closer and closer to climax and gasped with it.

The sheets bunched under her fingers as she clutched them. With both hands. Both of her hands fisted in the blankets, twisting, as the pressure on her clit continued, just the way she liked it. Just the way she needed it.

"Oh," she said, her eyes opening. She looked down her body, to Jarden's hand on her. To her body, responding to his touch. "Oh!"

At last, the stars came. One by one they exploded in her vision as her orgasm filled her. She'd teased her body so long not even fear could stop it. Jarden's touch tipped her over the edge, at last. His touch the same as hers had been. She came and came, gasping, until the stars faded from behind her eyes and she opened them.

She looked at Jarden, kneeling next to her. He cupped her cunt against his palm, holding her. She throbbed, each spasm lessening. He smiled without looking smug, and Milla laughed, suddenly euphoric.

Jarden stroked her pussy and withdrew, sitting back on his heels. His cock rose from between his thighs, thick and hard. Milla waited for him to nudge it toward her, or to look at her mouth in the way that meant he wanted her to use it, or even to take himself in his hand and spurt his pleasure all over her. Jarden did none of those things. He just smiled.

"Beautiful," he said, and she believed him.

"Jarden, make love to me."

He shook his head a little. "I told you, Milla. That was for you. It's okay."

"No, it's not." She sat, then knelt and put her hand on his shoulder, while other sought his erection. "I was wrong."

He drew in a quick, ragged breath when she gripped him. "Milla—"

She shook her head. "I was wrong. Fucking a Pleasurebot might have been good. I might have come. But you're not a 'bot. And I want you to feel good too."

He groaned as she stroked him. His hands came up to take her by the shoulders, holding her still. "I don't want you to think you have to."

"You said you'd do anything I want," she said. "I want you inside me again."

She didn't wait for him to move. Instead, she pushed and shifted until he sat on the bed and she was astride him. His prick filled her in a second. Their bodies pressed together as she wrapped her legs around his waist and his hands shifted to grab her butt. She put her arms around his neck. Face to face, she moved on him. They rocked. He was so hard inside her it almost hurt...but not quite.

She didn't expect to have another orgasm. Her body had not yet come down from the first. Her cunt and clit throbbed, still sensitive, as she moved on Jarden's cock. She looked into his eyes. She'd long known how giving another person pleasure could enhance her own. This time, however, Jarden had given her pleasure. She hoped it would increase his.

They moved together for only a few moments before his face twisted and his hands clutched her. His cock throbbed inside her. He thrust, hard, and let out a low, final groan. He gathered her close and buried his face in her neck as he pulsed with climax.

Silent, she let him hold her. Her body felt stretched. A little sore. And yet there was a promise in that feeling, a hint of possibility of further pleasure.

Jarden kissed her throat and looked up at her. He had not yet softened inside her. He moved her, just a little, to slide a hand between them. His thumb pressed her clit.

"What are you doing?" Milla asked, biting her lower lip at the pressure.

Without taking his eyes from hers, he moved inside her. Small, subtle thrusts, barely rocking. "Clench down on me."

When she did, they both groaned. She tightened her internal muscles in time to the small press-press of his thumb and the barely discernible thrust of his cock inside her. Neither of them moved even enough for anyone watching to see, but it didn't matter. It was more than enough.

She murmured his name. Her fingers dug into his shoulders. It was impossible that this should build up ecstasy inside her again, but there was no denying that's what was happening. Each tiny motion sent desire curling through her. Soon, Milla was moving faster against Jarden, who stayed still. She rode him, hoping he wouldn't move, wouldn't shift, wouldn't make her lose the tenuous thread of climax beginning to unspool inside her.

He didn't. He gave her total control, and when she came with a cry, her body shaking and shuddering, he closed his eyes and echoed the sound of her pleasure.

Breathless and boneless and utterly astounded, Milla relaxed in Jarden's arms. She blinked. She tasted sweat on her upper lip. They breathed together, in time, and she started to speak, to say something, she wasn't sure what, but the pounding on the door stopped her.

Jarden gave her a smile, but his eyes looked bleak. "You'd better answer."

Milla nodded and untangled herself from him. On weak legs, she found her robe and pulled it on and went to the door. Her mind reeled from what had happened, at last, with a stranger. Not with a Pleasurebot, but with a man.

She opened the door. Two uniformed men stood outside. She didn't step aside to let them in.

"Ma'am, pardon us, but we're conducting a routine inspection." The taller officer flashed a wrist tattoo Milla assumed was a badge, and then held up a holo-tablet with a scrolling list of numbered sentences.

She didn't have to read them to know they were the Newcity Standards. Milla let her robe gape open, just a bit, and tossed her hair over her shoulders.

"Can't you come back later?" She asked, sounding bored. "I'm in the middle of a hot fuck-and-suck. I mean, really, what sort of pleasure cruise is this?"

The officers gave each other a glance. "If you don't mind, ma'am, we need to inspect everyone here, even the fuck-crew."

These were the men who would take Jarden away, if they could, simply because he didn't conform to their standards. Milla stared them down. She'd faced scarier sights. She'd undergone a union dissolution on Nidar, after all, where women had next to no rights, except for the one to run away.

The shorter officer didn't wait for her to step aside, but pushed into the cabin. Milla turned. Jarden had already gotten out of bed and pulled on the sleep pants. He stood, resigned. His eyes met hers. She couldn't forget how it had felt to look into those dark eyes as pleasure burst through her. It was better even than seeing stars.

"Identification?" The shorter officer was asking Jarden, but Milla did her own pushing to get between them.

"Excuse me," she said, "but take your hands off my field-husband."

The officers exchanged glances again. The taller one spoke. "Field-husband?"

Milla nodded, her heart pounding. What would the punishment be for lying to a R.I. Op? Behind her, Jarden put his hand on the small of her back. She faced the officers.

"That's what I said." She lifted her chin, affecting the haughtiest attitude she could with her knees shaking and her throat dry.

"Do you have identification?"

"I do." She sniffed and took the folder of paper documents from their place in the nightstand drawer. "As you can see, I'm an official Homesteader, protected under the Homestead Council. This man is my field-husband."

She pulled out the sheaf of papers she'd honestly never expected to use. "And he's also protected under the council. So unless you have a reason to suspect—"

"No, ma'am," said the taller and presumably smarter officer. Apparently even R.I.O. respected the Homestead Council. "We're sorry for the inconvenience. It's a routine check. Sorry to bother you."

"I'll be filing a complaint," Milla said to their backs as they headed out. "You'd better believe it."

When the door closed behind them, she let out the breath she'd been holding and sank onto the bed, clutching her stomach. "Oh, God-of-choice."

Jarden sat next to her. "Thank you."

She looked at him. "You're welcome."

He smiled at her and reached to brush a strand of hair from her face. "You shouldn't have done that, Milla. They can check the records. They'll know I'm not your field-husband."

"Will it be worse for you if they find out?" The scent of their lovemaking still tantalized her nostrils. The Arous-All lotion should've worn off by now, but sitting this close to Jarden, feeling the heat of his thigh nearly touching hers, Milla couldn't stop from feeling the tingle of pleasure between her legs.

"No. I don't think it can be worse for me, no matter what you told them." Jarden stood, taking his heat and scent away from her. "But it will be worse for you."

He headed for the door, and Milla stood too. "Wait! Jarden, what are you doing?"

He stopped, but didn't turn. She watched his shoulders tense. He reached for the hand panel, though, of course, he had to know it wouldn't open. His biceps bulged. He didn't say anything.

"Are you turning yourself in?" She moved toward him. Her fingertips traced the faint, nearly invisible white line of a scar she'd never have noticed had he not pointed it out to her. "You can't do that."

"I can." Still, he didn't turn. "There's no reason for you to—"

"I have a reason," Milla told him. "Turn around."

He did, slowly. She took a deep breath. She'd ordered a 'bot and been delivered a man, instead, which was what she really had wanted all along.

"There's no telling how long they'll keep us in here," she told him. "And I have cred-time left with you."

The smallest, faintest quirk of a smile tugged at his mouth. "Yes, you do."

Milla lifted her chin and stepped back, letting her robe fall open. "Don't tell me you're going to run out on me without honoring them?"

The fact that she'd probably used up almost all but a few minutes of the complimentary time meant nothing. She knew that, and knew he knew it too. But that didn't stop her. Milla crooked a finger, but Jarden didn't move.

"Milla—"

"Shh," she told him sternly. "Does it matter if you turn yourself in now or later? Will they go easier on you for being quick?"

He shook his head. "No. I don't think so."

She crooked her finger again, feigning more confidence than she felt. "Then come here."

His smile quirked a bit higher, and Milla's stomach twisted with delight. "Anything you want."

He moved toward her and she envied his confidence. Perhaps it was purely male, that ability to put aside the past and focus on the now. Whatever it was, Milla admired Jarden's adaptability. That he'd been willing to sacrifice himself to prevent her from coming to harm had moved her too. They barely knew each other, despite having fucked together so well.

"Thank you," he said solemnly before brushing her hair from her shoulder. His fingers traced the curve of her shoulder, and Milla felt ashamed at how she'd treated him earlier.

"You're welcome." She took a backwards step toward the bed and held out her hand. He took it, following. She drew him down with her onto the softness and laughed a little. "I don't expect a bed this nice on Selkca."

He stretched out beside her, his hands already sliding beneath her robe. The bed dipped under his weight. The simple sensation thrilled her.

Jarden slid a hand to her knee, then higher, to her thigh. "That's a hard planet."

Milla arched, her robe parting for him, and in moments she lay naked. Jarden eased out of the sleep pants just as fast, but didn't move on top of her. He sat, his hands idly tracing patterns on her skin.

"Yes," she said, "I know. But the compensation package is three times larger than for one of the other Homestead planets."

He looked at her, his fingers easing closer and closer to her center. "Is that why you need a field-husband?"

Milla parted her legs for him. "It will make it easier, but…ah."

She sighed as he found her warm and willing flesh and stroked it. Jarden smiled and moved closer to use his tongue on her thigh. His fingers and mouth moved in tandem as he eased his lips over her skin, moving toward the place she wanted him to lick and kiss.

Jarden asked no more questions, just bent to her waiting cunt and kissed her there. The pleasure wasn't intense, or sudden, or shocking. It was exquisite. She sighed at the warmth of his tongue and lips on her heated folds. As his mouth moved on her skin, Milla reached to run her fingers through the silk of Jarden's hair.

"How could I have thought I wanted a 'bot?" she murmured, looking down to watch him nuzzle and lick between her legs.

He paused to look up at her with a grin. "I told you I could do anything you wanted."

What might have felt awkward became comfortable with their shared laughter. Milla'd had many lovers, but few who'd laughed in bed with her. Derek never had. Derek hadn't laughed much at all…ever. She reached again to smooth her fingers through Jarden's hair.

"Come here," she said, and he did.

He moved up her body with fluid grace and settled himself between her legs. His cock was a thick heat against her thigh, and Milla shifted just a little to move him closer to her. Jarden looked down into her face with a faint smile toying on his lips.

"Thank God-of-Choice Pete broke," he murmured before dipping his head to kiss her throat.

Milla tipped her head to give him more room to get at her skin. "Hmm?"

Jarden laughed. "Never mind."

He had to be thinking about what was going to happen if the R.I. Ops checked her story, but Jarden didn't falter as he used his mouth and hands to urge Milla's body toward pleasure again. He'd been good the first time, when she hadn't been able to allow herself to climax, but now there wasn't any barrier. She moved beneath him, reacting. Giving in.

And Jarden took what she offered. He had to be paying careful attention to what was working for her, and to Milla, it seemed as though he never faltered, not once. She didn't even consider blaming the Arous-All this time. This was all the man before her. His hands, his mouth, his tongue, his body.

She fisted her hand in his hair and brought his mouth to hers, hard. Bruising. Jarden opened to her and their tongues dueled. He was inside her a moment after that and Milla gasped into his open mouth. She wrapped her legs around his thighs and twisted them both. There was no way she could have turned him if he hadn't allowed it. He was too big. But Jarden rolled with her, still connected. He knew what he was doing, too, because Milla ended up straddling him.

She sat up straight, already moving. Her head tipped back, her eyes closed, as she rode him. Jarden's hand slipped between them, his thumb stroking directly on her clit. Milla shuddered, no holding back this time, no hesitation.

She climaxed with a cry, her body shaking. "Jarden, come with me!"

He did, with a final thrust and a groan that sent more shocks of pleasure through her until, exhausted, Milla sank down onto his chest. She sighed. The pounding of his heart echoed in her chest where their bodies aligned. The puff of his breath caressed her hair. He put his arms around her and held her, tight.

"Don't go," she whispered. "If they come back…we'll deal with it then. But don't invite them to take you away."

Jarden said nothing, but beneath her, his muscles tensed. He was going to turn himself in anyway. She knew it. And why? To save her? Because if he were discovered, her lie would hang her as neatly as his truth?

Milla pushed herself up to look into his eyes. "It doesn't have to be untrue, you know."

He frowned. They parted, their bodies slick with sweat. She reached for her robe and drew it around her, but Jarden seemed as comfortable in his nudity as he did in clothes. He sat up against the headboard.

"I don't know what you mean," he said.

She glanced toward the folder of documents on the desk. "Those papers are my future. I've been granted a field-husband. I didn't think I'd actually find one. I wasn't sure I wanted one…not really."

Milla shrugged and got up, padding across on bare feet to take up the folder. Jarden's gaze weighed her as she did, but he still said nothing. That was fine. He didn't have to speak. Made it easier, in fact, if he didn't.

"I wasn't sure I wanted to be tied to someone else again." She held up the folder. "But I knew that Selkca isn't an easy planet to homestead. I knew having a partner would make it easier. Someone strong."

She looked at the firm, strong lines of his body.

"Someone smart." She smiled, and he smiled too. "An engineer would know how to fix equipment and build new tools."

"Are you asking me to be your field-husband?" Jarden's smile didn't falter, but it hadn't quite reached his eyes either. "Why? Because I made you come?"

Milla shook her head. "No. Because I realized I need someone strong, and smart...and noble, Jarden."

Now he laughed and got to his feet. "I heard Nidar was old-fashioned, but I didn't know you'd be looking for some sort of champion."

"Not a champion. Not a savior." She lifted her chin. "I left my family, the only life I'd ever known, the only world I'd ever known, to make my way. I expect it to be hard. I don't want or need anyone to save me from it. But it would be easier with someone to share it with."

Jarden paced. "You barely know me."

"You barely know me," she pointed out. "But then, most field-husbands don't know their partners before agreeing to the union. Most don't know if they'll really be compatible. We have that advantage."

He looked at her, that faint smile still tugging the corners of his lips. "I meant to be a Homesteader. Not a field-husband."

"You'd still have rights," she told him. "It's a contract. Like any other. And you wouldn't have to wait another year."

They stared at each other. Jarden crossed his arms over his chest. "If I wait another year, I'll be my own man. Owing nothing to anyone."

She could understand that, and she nodded. "It's an offer, Jarden. That's all. I like you."

He nodded then, like her words had made sense, but he'd expected them. "Are you sure?"

Before she could say more, the lights flickered again.

"Attention, all passengers. Attention." The modulated female voice was the same as it had been before, but the sound of it sent a bolt of anxiety through Milla. Jarden looked up toward the ceiling speakers. "Attention. Pleasure Princess Cruises apologizes for the delay, but we'll be departing Newcity airspace in approximately two ship-hours. Please be prepared for any final inspections. Thank you."

Milla looked at Jarden. "Final inspections?"

He looked grim and bent to pull on his thin sleep pants. "It means they've found something they want to check. Again."

Him? Milla swallowed, hard. "Sign the forms, Jarden. Become my field-husband. I can transfer the credits directly into your account. It'll be a legal transaction. Don't tell me you'd rather be put in prison than work and live on Selkca. Even if it's with me."

"That's not—" The pounding on the door stopped him. Despite his bravado, Jarden's face paled.

Milla handed him the documents. "Mark your name there."

She was already pulling out her cred-account card and sliding it through the wall-reader. She punched in her passcode. "What's your account number for the transfer?"

"You can't do this."

"Miss, we're sorry to disturb you, but you need to open the door or we'll open it for you."

"They're not sorry," Milla told Jarden fiercely. "The number!"

He rattled it off and she punched it in. She forced herself not to think of what that money could've provided for her on Selkca. Jarden's hands flew over the document folder, adding his name to the contract. They both finished as the door rattled again, and she opened it.

"I told you, I'm in the middle of a hot fuck-and-suck!" she complained with a pout.

"We're here for him." The tall R.I. Op gestured at Jarden.

"I told you before," Milla said. "He's my field-husband."

"Yeah, let's let the scanner figure that out," said the shorter one.

But in another minute they were backing out the door, apologizing. The transfer of funds and documentation had gone through, and Milla waved them away without a hint of her relief as she sent up prayers to God-of-Choice that they hadn't waited even a moment longer.

"Thank you." Jarden said the words stiffly. "Should I get my things?"

Milla shook her head. Her heart still pumped faster than normal, from the delicious orgasms he'd given her and the close call with the Newcity officers. "No."

"No?" Jarden frowned.

Milla turned from him. He didn't want to be tied to her. She understood that, and knew it had nothing to do with her scar. Nothing to do with her. She paused, her fingers working the robe's stick-seam closed. She smiled. Jarden's rejection of her had nothing to do with her, and she was still smiling when she turned to face him again.

"No. You go." She eased the field-husband contract from its place in her folder and pressed it into his hand. "You don't want this. When we're far away from Newcity, you can annul this contract. It will revert to me. You won't even lose the money. All the details are in there."

He stared at her. "But..."

Milla shook her head again, her smile faltering. She turned away. "No, Jarden. I mean it. I couldn't have let you sacrifice yourself to protect me, and I can't bind you to me either. I know what it's like to be bound to someone who doesn't love me. I don't want to do that ever again."

The soft sound of his breathing was all she heard. Then the soft pad of his footsteps as he went to the door. The room shuddered. The lights flickered. The automated announcement told them the Pleasure Princess was once more engaged in interstellar travel.

And when she looked up, Jarden had done just what she wanted.

He was gone.

Chapter 6

"Hot pussy," Pete moaned. "Hot, wet, slick pussy."

"Yeah, man. Whatever." Jarden rolled over in his bunk to face the wall, while Pete watched the jack-off channel. "Take my shift and get all the hot pussy you want."

"You mean it?" Pete sounded happy.

Fuck. Pete always sounded happy. "Yeah, man. I mean it."

"You don't have to work?"

Not with the credits in his account, he didn't. Jarden pulled the covers up higher around his neck. In two more days they'd reach the end of the cruise and he'd be able to get off this ship too. Pick a destination, any one he wanted.

Or he could give her back the money, annul the contract, stay on the Pleasure Princess as she turned to make her way back across the universe, and wait another year while he earned his freedom with his cock.

Jarden groaned.

"You all right?" Pete placed a hand on Jarden's shoulder. "Do you need the medbot?"

"No. Just tired."

Pete didn't really understand tired, but he left Jarden alone. Which is what he wanted. Wasn't it? With another groan, Jarden punched the pillow.

He'd been with hundreds of women, and Milla Sulay wasn't the first who'd tasted good, or smelled good, or who'd writhed on his cock like a goddess. She didn't have to be the last either…but she could be.

Muttering, Jarden rolled onto his back to stare up at the top of the bunk above him. Field-husband. A fancy word for indentured fuck-slave, wasn't it? Sure, field-husbands weren't contractually bound to have sex with their partners. They got a share of the land, the profits. Field-husbands had rights.

But they were still bought and paid for, and that was something Jarden had vowed not to be once he got off this ship.

"Can I really have your shift?" Pete asked when the service light started blinking.

"COKs never quit, right?" Jarden didn't look at him.

"Never quit!"

"Go for it, buddy."

Jarden didn't turn to watch him leave the small room they'd shared for five years. Pete didn't bother saying goodbye or anything like that. COKs weren't known for their manners.

Jarden rolled onto his stomach to bury himself in the darkness beneath his blankets, but sleep eluded him. Instead, a fall of sleek, pale hair and bright, twinkling blue eyes formed a vision in his head. Milla.

He'd seen her a few times before voluntarily imprisoning himself in his room. In the dining room and once on the vast star deck. She'd smiled at him and nodded, but made no move to talk to him, and he felt like more of an ass than ever for leaving the way he had.

His stomach growled now, but the thought of ordering another meal in this room defused his hunger. The thought of watching another porn-vid, or reading another holo-bloid turned his stomach too. In fact, Jarden thought, as he tossed off the blankets with a growl, being in this frigging room much longer was going to drive him crazy.

If he couldn't even stand to stay in a cruiser cabin for a few days, how could he ever have imagined he'd be able to make it in prison? And he'd been saved from that certain fate by whom?

Milla. The woman who'd offered him the chance to have everything he'd been working for. And what was keeping him from taking her up on her offer?

"Nothing but my damned pride," Jarden said aloud.

Too bad he didn't have anything else.

Chapter 7

Milla had waited until the sun dove behind the mountains before dipping herself a drink from the jug of water on her counter. Real, fresh water, a luxury she needed to carefully parcel out to herself, but one she deserved.

She'd worked hard, supervising the fields that day and making sure her workers had all been paid before they took off for the three-day Selkcan holiday. She planned to use those three days to sleep, eat and read the carton of magazines that had finally arrived in the last shipment of supplies. Real paper magazines, something she hadn't seen in years on Nidar, but which were common enough in Selkca's single city. Out here on the homestead, a good magazine could be read over and over, then recycled into many uses.

Milla was looking forward to the next three days, when she'd be without duties to perform. The Selkcan 'steaders had formed a close-knit community. She had friends. She'd even been courted, sort of, by a few of the single men and by one or two of those with wives too. Her life on Selkca was fulfilling and good…and incredibly hard. Could anyone blame her if she chose to stay at home, relaxing, instead of mingling with the rest of the holiday celebrants?

So, when the knock came at her door, Milla was less than pleased. Assuming it was Heldaig, the Selkcan native she'd hired to assist her, Milla flung open her door with a sigh.

And promptly lost her breath.

"Jarden?"

He nodded. "Milla. Hi."

She stepped aside at once to let him in, her mind already whirling with the thoughts about how he didn't have to wait for her to open the door. He could just push inside. Technically, he owned part of this house. This land. Part of everything she'd worked for, so hard, because though he hadn't come there with her, he'd never had the contract annulled.

"Thanks." Jarden smiled at her, and her heart leaped at the memory of his touch.

She served him sweet Selkcan tea and cookies from a tin that had traveled far and were a welcome treat despite being stale. They sat across from each other in her tiny kitchen. Their knees bumped beneath her table.

"So," she said when she couldn't stop herself from it any more, "why are you here?"

Jarden pulled a small cloth bag from the pocket of his jumpsuit and pushed it across the table to her. "I owe you this."

Milla didn't take it. "You don't."

He smiled. "Yes, I do. And I worked my ass off for a year to get it, so don't turn me down."

She didn't have to open the bag to know it contained Selkcan crystals. Currency. She looked up at him. "You never annulled the contract."

Jarden shook his head. "No."

"Why?"

He sighed and scrubbed at his face. "I didn't want to. But I didn't want to show up with a debt on my hands either."

He got up, paced the floor, looked out her small window to the night beyond. When he finally turned to her, Milla realized she was holding her breath. He moved fast, too fast for her to get away, and took her hands to pull her to her feet.

"You still don't know me," he said.

She shook her head, but didn't pull her hands from his. "No. But you don't know me either."

He stroked her hair away from her face. "It's crazy to make a life with a stranger, isn't it?"

"No more than many others have done," Milla replied. Her mouth parted, waiting for him to kiss her, but Jarden didn't.

"You'll take the money?"

"If you want me to." She smiled, inching closer. "It's not like I couldn't use it."

"You've made a success of this place," Jarden said as the distance between them became nothing.

"I have. Thanks. But there's still more work to do. Always more. And I could really use someone to share it with, Jarden." Milla stretched onto her toes to give him her mouth.

This time, he took it. His hands tightened around her. He tasted of sweet tea and crumbled cookies, and his body was hard, tight and welcome against hers.

"And you're willing for that person to be me?" he asked into her ear. "You're sure?"

Milla laughed gently and pulled away to look into his face. "There are worse things to base a relationship on than sexual compatibility."

Jarden laughed, too, after a minute, then hugged her tight to his chest. "Don't you want to ask me why I came here?"

"No." She sighed, holding him. "But if you want to tell me, please do."

"I couldn't forget you," he told her. "Milla, I don't know if this is going to work, but if it doesn't—"

"It's a contract," she reminded him. "And you'll owe me nothing."

"And if it does work?" he asked.

Milla smiled, already leading him toward the bedroom. "Then you won't ever have to try to forget me again."

He followed her willingly enough. "Just like that? We're going to try this?"

"Jarden," Milla told him as she undid the stick-seam on his jumpsuit, "you're the only man I've ever had an orgasm with. Aside from that, you were willing to sacrifice yourself to keep me from harm, and you barely knew me. I think that, no matter what else might happen, I'm willing to give this a try. Yes."

She bared him and ran her hands down his smooth skin, then looked up to his handsome face. A face she was willing to accept as her field-husband, her partner. A face she was willing to try to love.

"Jarden?"

"Yes, Milla?"

"I haven't made love in over a year. I'd really like it if we could celebrate our new partnership the old-fashioned way."

His grin took her breath away, as did the way he dipped her down to kiss her thoroughly. "Anything you want, Milla. Anything you want."

EVERYTHING COUNTS

*For anyone who's looked up at the stars and wondered
how many there were.*

Chapter 1

Change was coming. Elspeth Valerin knew it. She'd seen it this morning in her daily calculations. The date, her name and birthday, the color of the sky and what she'd eaten for breakfast—all had been given a numerical value and figured in an equation along with a dozen other factors.

Everything counts, she thought as she followed Gabriana through the carved wooden door to The Slaughtered Lamb. For most people, Arithmancy was no more than a jumble of numbers. For Elspeth, it was her life.

"I'm so pleased you decided to come out with us tonight, Elspeth," Gabriana said over her shoulder. "We've been asking you for ages. I thought you'd never say yes."

"The stars must finally have aligned," teased Dayla Mornit. Dayla taught Runes at Somnus Keep.

"No," interjected Callis Dardin. She taught Astronomy. "The numbers finally added up. Am I right, Elspeth?"

Elspeth smiled a bit as she followed her colleagues to a table toward the back of the pub. "Something like that."

The scent of sawdust, alcohol and food greeted her, and she paused to look around. Seventeen tables, each with three or four chairs. Six windows. A long, polished wood bar stretched along the left side of the room. Twenty-two stools lined up along it. Toward the back, a swinging door leading to the kitchen, and a hallway. A dartboard with eight darts stuck into the cork. Six musicians in the corner struck up a tune to cheers from the substantial crowd.

She was counting again and took a deep breath to force herself to focus on the quality of the pub rather than the quantity of the items within it.

"I admire anyone who can make sense of Arithmancy, much less teach it," said Dayla. "I can't add the contents of my pocket, much less turn everything I do into an equation."

Elspeth gave a tentative smile. "It's useful to know how to do it. But it's just as useful to know someone who can make the calculations for you."

Dayla stared at her for a moment. "Is it possible our quiet Elspeth has just put me in my place?"

"Oh, no, I—"

"Hush," said Gabriana. "She's teasing you."

Callis laughed, looking at the serving lass headed their way. "Ignore her, Elspeth. She's a sour old biddy because nobody likes Runes either. And good eve to you, Gretel Deloras!"

Elspeth couldn't help staring at Gretel, whose smile was almost blinding in its brightness. Her lush curves threatened to burst the seams of her simple peasant shirt, worn so low off her shoulders the dusky hint of aureoles peeked out from the lace around the edge. A man's hands would easily span her waist, while her hips swelled out below with the promise of sensual delights any man would be unable to resist.

"Who's your friend?" Gretel's voice oozed such blatant sensuality it turned the heads of the men at the next table. She leaned forward to smile directly at Elspeth. "Hello, honey. I'm Gretel."

"Elspeth," she stammered, overwhelmed by Gretel's presence.

Gretel laughed, tossing back her mane of blond curls so they fell down her back. "Welcome to The Slaughtered Lamb, sweet thing. What can I get you? We have everything you could want and probably some things you don't."

Elspeth hated the heatroses that bloomed in her cheeks and hoped the pub's dim lighting hid them. At the school she managed to maintain the near-constant cool and collected demeanor necessary to keep her students in line. Here she was out of her element, unused to the attention and uncertain how to react.

Gretel took their orders and glanced again at Elspeth, her bright blue gaze lingering. "Sure I can't bring you something strong, sweetheart? You're a mite pale. Maybe an ale would do your blood some good."

"All right," she answered, surprising herself. "Ale would be lovely, thank you."

Gretel raised one perfect golden eyebrow, as though Elspeth's politely phrased response had surprised her, but she smiled. "Grand, lass. I'll bring your drinks right over, ladies."

"Sweet Astria, if I looked like her, I'd never get out of bed." Callis shifted in her chair, watching Gretel sashay away.

"You wouldn't?" Elspeth turned to look at the Callis. "Why not? She's beautiful."

Callis looked perplexed for a moment before laughing. "Oh, Elspeth, you're such a dear."

Damn. She'd said the wrong thing. Again. 'Twas a talent, she supposed, to consistently come out with the wrong words.

Gabriana came to her rescue again. "Callis didn't mean she'd stay abed out of grief, Elspeth. She meant that if she looked like Gretel, she'd have so many lovers, she'd never get out of bed."

Again, Elspeth blushed. "Ah. Of course."

In a world where lovemaking was as practiced a pastime as playing a sport or taking up a hobby, the subject of sex was not one that ought to have brought such heat to her cheeks. Yet of course it did, because though lovemaking was considered not only an enjoyable part of life but a necessary one, Elspeth did not partake.

Her colleagues wouldn't have known that, of course. It wasn't good manners to ask, and she doubted they'd assume she was celibate. She was a magicreator after all. An instructor at Somnus Keep. Arithmancy, the study of numerical values used to make predictions, meant she rarely had to harness the power of the thrall. Nobody had to know her control of it was flawed, that although she could sometimes form an orb of power, she could never sustain it or make it do anything more than look pretty sitting on her palm. She was a magicreator who could not control the high magic and therefore could not use it. She was a failure, and worse than that.

Elspeth Valerin was a fraud.

"Here we go, ladies." Gretel returned bearing a tray of glasses she set down in front of all of them with the unerring memory of a good server. "Ale for you, my lovely."

"Thank you."

Gretel smiled and put her hand on her ample hip. "Anything else I can get for you, loves?"

"This will do for now." Dayla sipped from her glass, the foam from the ale coating her upper lip.

Gretel moved away, and Elspeth watched her work the tables. She flirted with the men, and if her obvious pleasure at their attention was false, she did a fine job of making it believable. Envy, fierce and shocking, made Elspeth gulp her ale. A woman with control like that over her body could do anything.

"Two sevendays of freedom!" Gabriana crowed. "What will you do with it?"

"Sleep late!" Callis wriggled with a gleeful sound.

"Stay up late," Dayla countered.

"What about you, Elspeth? Have you any grand plans for the holiday?"

Elspeth intended to do the same thing on her holiday she did all the rest of the time—study, read, knit. Perhaps continue to work toward advanced certification in her field.

She opened her mouth to answer, but before she could, Callis pointed discreetly and gave a whispered giggle. "There he is!"

"Who?" Elspeth asked, even as she followed Callis's pointing finger with her gaze.

"The owner. Conn." Dayla giggled too. "I forgot you've never come with us before. Isn't he beautiful?"

Conn. The name was not uncommon. Hundreds of mothers must have named their sons the same. The man who owned this pub, the beautiful man who had all the ladies giggling and pointing, did not have to be the same Connell from her past.

But he was.

Chapter 2

"Your admiration club is here," said Gretel as Connell came from the storeroom, hefting a fresh keg to tap.

He settled the keg behind the bar and gave her a grin. "Yeah? Which ones?"

"You're too convinced of your own charm." Gretel rolled her eyes, but nodded toward the back of the room. "The ones from up the hill, from the Keep."

Connell chuckled, bending to drive the spigot into the new keg and sliding an empty glass with practiced ease beneath to catch the spurt of ale. No sense in wasting it, so he swallowed the mouthful and set the empty glass in the bin to be taken back for washing. "The ones who're so free with their coin? Sure and they're always welcome."

Gretel poured some shots and set them on her tray. "They brought a new little mouse along with them tonight."

"Yeah?" He stood, wiping his brow on his sleeve, scarcely interested in whatever giggly miss they'd dragged along with them beyond what coin she might spend.

"Pretty thing with a mouth like sugar."

He laughed. "Yeah?"

Gretel nodded. "Shy, though. I thought she was going to burst into flame when I asked her name."

He rolled his head on his shoulders, cracking his neck and shaking out the tension. "Not everyone can flirt with you, love."

Gretel smiled. "That's what you think, Conn-me-love."

He laughed again as she swished her hips and headed back to serving. Gretel liked to give him a bit of a wink and a nudge, but she saved her real charms for men who didn't pay her wages. He looked out over the room, eyes taking in everything. Connell Byrne prided himself on running the finest pub in town. The Slaughtered Lamb was a clean joint, with the best food and beverage he could provide, the fastest service, the liveliest entertainment. He didn't allow dirty dealings in the Lamb either, and if that meant cracking a few skulls to keep out the riff raff…well, he wasn't above it. Bar fights were part of the business, but as he examined the crowd, he saw no sign of belligerence waiting to erupt into violence.

The trill of feminine laughter from the back of the room caught his ear, and grinning, he turned to look. Gretel was right in saying he knew too well his own charm. The ladies came in to eat, drink and be merry, and if a little harmless flirting made them merry, Connell wasn't above that either.

He recognized the group just as Gretel had said he would. They were all magicreators from up the hill. Instructors at the Keep, which meant they always had plenty of coin to spread around. That suited him fine. Magicreators didn't cause trouble either, because even a group of unattended women wouldn't be bothered by the most boisterous of his customers. No man would mess with a magicreator who could take off his nuts with little more than a flick of her fingers.

Connell walked around the edge of the bar and headed toward their table, intending to give them a smile and a laugh, and a round of free drinks in appreciation of their business. Maybe let them think they might have the chance to take him to bed. It never hurt to lead them on. Made them spendy, it did, even if it never led to anything but stories they took back with them.

"Good evening, ladies," he said, hands on his hips, looking round at each of them. "A pleasure to see—"

The words caught in his throat at the sight of her. The same dark hair, worn tied up instead of loose, but still as smooth as silk. Time had sharpened her features and turned her from a girl into a woman, but the better-defined cheekbones and jaw only made her that much more beautiful. The lush lips he'd once kissed with such passion parted as he spoke, and the remembered taste of her set his mind reeling.

"Hello, Conn." This came from the red-haired woman to his left. She eyed him without a speck of coyness. "Nice to see you again."

"And you," he answered, eyes locked on Ella's familiar blue-gray gaze. The eyes he'd never thought to see again.

The other women didn't seem to notice his lack of attention, for they giggled and flirted while his mouth made replies his mind did not bother to track.

She was terrified. He could see it in the way her eyes grew dark and her fingers tightened on her glass. Her entire body vibrated like she meant to run away, but was unable to move.

He scared her, 'twas no great feat to see it, and even after all this time, the fact she would fear him tightened his jaw with anger. He'd never done aught to harm her. All he'd ever done was love her. And even now, ten years after he'd told her he would never love another woman the way he loved her, she wanted to run away from him again.

"...on the house," he heard himself say, and waved away the ladies' half-hearted protests. "I insist. On me."

"Ooh," purred the woman with black hair. "Really? Drinks on you? That would be interesting."

Where he'd have given her a grin and a wink before, now Connell only managed a faint smile. "Be careful, madam or I'll think you fancy me."

This made the women at the table erupt into giddy laughter. All but one. He stared hard into her eyes for one more moment before turning away.

Chapter 3

Three ales. She'd kept careful count, as she did of everything, even now when the alcohol fuzzed her brain and made her unsteady.

The others had become raucous as the night wore on, setting up challenges with the table of men beside them. Drinking games. Wagers. Callis had settled herself upon the lap of a brawny man with a ginger beard and a booming laugh. Dayla and Gabriana had agreed to a game of darts with two men, though their opponents had declared the match unfair because the women could use magic to their advantage.

Everything in pairs, Elspeth thought as she stared at the bottom of another empty glass. *Two by two. Neat and tidy. No room for three.* She was drunk, which surprised her into laughter. She put her hand over her mouth to stifle it, though nobody would have noticed with all the noise.

"What's with your friend?" she heard the brawny man ask Callis. "She don't like comp'ny?"

Callis murmured something Elspeth couldn't hear and she stared at the table. Men had been speaking to her all night, but she'd put them all off. The only man for whom she had eyes had not looked at her again, a fact for which she was intensely grateful as his studied lack of attention allowed her to watch him, unnoticed.

Connell. Ten years had been kind to him. They'd broadened his shoulders, lengthened his hair and touched the corners of his eyes with lines that showed he, at least, had spent his time smiling. He wasn't a lad any longer, but a man. Then again, she supposed she could no longer consider herself a girl.

She was no fool. She was an Arithmanticist. Elspeth knew better than anyone how small choices influence greater ones, and how one seemingly unimportant decision can affect an entire outcome. *Everything counts.*

If she was here and Connell too, it meant that somehow along the way both of them had done something, made some choice, taken some branching path that led them both to this spot. It would not have happened otherwise. She would have refused the invitation to join her colleagues, or they'd have taken her to another pub. Or going further back, he'd not have opened his place in this town where she'd chosen to live.

She was here, and he was here, and there was a purpose to it. A fate she could not comprehend. An equation she did not know how to calculate.

All at once the drinks, the smoke and the laughter made her blink against an onslaught of dizziness. She stood, touching one hand to the table to steady herself.

"I'm going to get some fresh air," she told Callis.

"Are you well?" Callis looked concerned, as though she meant to get up from her companion's lap.

"I'm fine," Elspeth answered quickly, adding a smile to be more convincing. "Just need a bit of a breeze. That's all."

Callis nodded, but sank back onto her seat. "If you're sure…"

"Yes. I'm sure." Elspeth smiled again and moved around the table, avoiding the leer and lewd greeting of one of the men sitting there.

Darkness shrouded the hallway leading to the washrooms, but Elspeth had never feared darkness. She went past two doors marked with symbols—one for male and one for female. Again, a pair. The door at the hall's end bore no marking, but she knew it led outside, and so she pushed through it and ventured into the chill winter air.

The fenced courtyard behind the Lamb contained no pretty garden or bubbling fountain, only a path of fitted slates leading to a leaning, decrepit shed and scrubby grass interspersed with patches of bare earth. Large refuse bins lined one side. Some benches lined another, and 'twas there she sought to rest her legs and catch the breath which had left her with such sudden ferocity inside.

Above her, the stars gleamed pure white against a black, clear sky. The moon hung like a coin amongst them. She smelled snow despite the lack of clouds. She tipped her head to stare up, and her eyes followed the lines and curves of the constellations as she began to count the points of light.

She'd never counted them all. She never could. It brought her peace, though, to try. Stars were just about the only limitless thing in the world, the only things she could not reach the end of, and the numbers rose higher and higher in her mind, wiping out everything else for the moment.

When she lifted her palm, fingers slightly curled, not even the numbers in her head could push aside the sight of the glimmering silver orb that formed there. She could count forever and still remain unable to wipe from her mind how the orb shimmered and shattered before she could push it into anything else. She closed her fingers tight on the remaining shards of what should've been great power and were instead nothing but broken pieces of what she could never have.

A star has fallen to earth.

Not a star, and not a piece of her broken orb either. An ember. A cheroot, the tip flaring as its owner drew in the smoke, then arcing through the air as he tossed it to the ground and left it without bothering to crush it with his boot. A smaller piece of blackness separated from the larger shadows, and she stood, stepping back against the fence.

"How many are there?"

She'd known it was him the moment she stood. "You know I can't know that."

"Not even you? Not the Countess?"

"Don't call me that." The retort came out sharper than she'd intended. The fence pressed against her back. A splinter gouged her arm. She'd come out without a cloak.

Connell stepped closer. "You used to like it when I called you that."

"That was a long time ago." Elspeth couldn't back away any further, so she straightened her spine. *And you used to say it with love in your voice.*

Connell's eyes flashed in the starlight, and a moment later, his teeth as he grinned. "Aye, and so it was. A long time ago and a place far away. But you haven't changed, have you? You're still counting."

He'd moved so close to her she could smell him, and it made her weak. He'd used to smell of the sea. Salt. Sun. Sand. The tang of sweat.

Now he smelled of ale and smoke, but underlying it still a hint of sun and wind and sand. He was different and yet the same; the remembered taste of him flooded her mouth and made her heart thump in her chest.

"I'm still counting." Her voice scratched and cracked, embarrassed her.

His hand came out to twirl a strand of hair that had fallen over her shoulder. A handspan separated them, no more. He tucked the hair behind her ear. His fingers cupped her cheek, then trailed along her jaw, down the line of her neck and came to rest upon her shoulder.

She shivered, not from cold but heat, which had sprung up along the path of his fingers. Shadows veiled his face again, but she heard his breath, felt it on her face, and she could almost taste his lips on hers.

Connell didn't kiss her. "I didn't believe my eyes when I saw you sitting in my pub. After all this time and there you were, looking like an angel. I thought for sure I was dreaming."

She wanted to tell him she was sorry. She hadn't meant to run away. She hadn't meant to hurt him. She hadn't meant any of it, that long ago night when she'd told him she could never love him... But unlike numbers, words never came to her rescue when she needed them.

Closer still he moved, his body against hers, pinning her against the fence, and Elspeth shuddered with a sudden force of desire so strong it forced a low cry from her throat. Ten years, and he still affected her this way. The only man who ever could.

She was already opening her mouth to his kiss when he pulled away, leaving her cold instead of hot. Connell backed away with a muttered curse. She blinked, trying to see his expression, but could make out nothing more than the flash of his eyes again in starlight.

"Why?" he asked her, one word that meant so much and had so many answers.

She didn't know which to give him. "Connell..."

He backed away from her reaching hand, putting both his own up as though to make sure there was no way they could possibly touch her.

"Why, Ella?" The agony in his voice broke her heart all over again. "Why now, after all this time, when I finally thought—"

But he'd say no more, just backed away another step. This time, she was the one pursuing, moving across the slate path toward him. "Connell, wait."

"You're still afraid of me!" he cried. "I saw it inside, and I felt you shaking just now! You're afraid of me, even now, when I'd never do aught to hurt you!"

"I know that. I know it. Connell, love, please..."

He'd backed into a patch of moonlight, and to her horror, she saw tears glimmering in his eyes. She'd made him cry before, and it seemed unfair now that she'd made him weep again when tears would never come for her no matter how much she might wish for the relief they brought.

He ran a hand through his hair, messing it, and let his hand rest on the back of his neck, his eyes turned away from her. "Why?"

"Because I was a fool," she answered. "I didn't deserve you."

She reached for him again, a hesitant hand that did not quite touch him. "I was a fool who did not know the gift she held, Connell. And I plead your mercy."

He shook his head. "You left without a word. I never knew where you'd gone, or if you were all right. I never knew if you were alive or dead, sick or well. I never knew if you were happy."

"I'm sorry." It was all she had to say, and it was not enough.

"All I ever did was love you," he said in a low voice. "And you treated me like I wasn't even worth it."

Then she was in his arms and his mouth was on hers, bruising. She didn't resist, didn't protest, just let him walk her backward and put her up against the fence, his hands on her waist and his mouth crushing, crushing.

She opened beneath him and his tongue swept inside. She tasted ale and smoke. She tasted Connell, a flavor she'd never forgotten, and it made her gasp as she put her arms around his neck and clung to him.

He pushed hard against her, the way he used to when they were in her garden and desperate to steal one more kiss before she had to go inside. He bunched the fabric of her skirt in his hands and slid beneath it to the bare skin of her thighs atop her stockings. His hands cupped her rear and he lifted her, holding her so tight she had no fear of falling. The heat and hardness of him pressed against her, and she gasped and tightened her thighs around his hips.

She tasted blood from the force of his kiss, from a spot where her teeth had caught the inside of her lip. The metallic, salty taste of it made her think of the way they'd been, and how she'd once taken him in her mouth while the ocean crashed so close to them the spray had wet their clothes.

Desire, unaccustomed and overwhelming, flooded her, but she didn't fight it. Her arms tightened on his neck and she kissed him as fiercely as he did her, their mouths meeting again and again, reminding her of the way eagles mated in the sky, soaring and plummeting as they screeched their pleasure.

He held her against the splintered wood with one hand while the other slid between them to fumble with the laces at his waistband. His hand rubbed her through the thin material of her undergarment, and she shuddered with want.

He'd be inside her in another moment, and oh, by the Astria, she wanted him there. Inside her. Filling her. Making this feeling grow until she exploded the way she used to when they were young, before it had all gone so wrong.

He shifted her weight and she tensed, waiting for him to enter her. Then, in the next moment, she stood on her own, her skirt falling down around her ankles and the fence the only thing holding her up. She blinked, bereft and abandoned, her body not yet adjusted to the loss of his hands on her. She licked her lips and tasted more blood, and she lifted a shaking hand to wipe them clean.

"You might not have changed," he said in a shaking voice. "But I have. I'll not be used like that again, no matter what treasure you hold between your legs."

His words hurt, that he thought she'd ever used him. He twisted away from her when she tried to touch his cheek, and she let her hand fall. He ran his hand again through his hair, then crossed his arms over his chest. The white moonlight made stark lines on his face, cast his eyes into shadow and highlighted his scowl.

"All these years," he told her. "You've no right to come here, to my place, looking as though naught's changed. No right."

His words were unfair, but she accepted them with a nod. "I'll go then, shall I?"

"Aye, go." He bit out the words like they tasted bad. "Get out of my place, and don't come back here."

She didn't move. They stared at each other until at last she nodded again. "I plead your mercy, Connell. I never meant to hurt you."

"No." His reply was colder than the winter air. "And I can see by your tears how grieved you are."

His short, sharp burst of laughter pierced her heart.

"Ah, but then, you've never wept, have you? Why should I expect you'd bother to cry for me?"

"If I could have, believe me, I would."

He didn't answer. She backed away from him, turned and left the courtyard, wishing desperately she could have given him tears but as always, finding none to give.

Chapter 4

She came to him in dreams, as she always did. The girl he'd loved so much it had been like dying when she left him. Tonight she was the woman she'd become, the one he did not know.

The taste of her had changed, as had the curve of her hips, the fullness of her breasts, the timbre of her voice. He took her in his arms and she yielded, offering her mouth to his kiss and her body to his hands.

He took her without a word, as once they'd not needed to speak. She opened beneath him. His tongue stroked hers. His hands roamed her body. She linked her arms behind his neck, and he lifted her, laying her down upon a bed of flowers that filled the air with their scent as the weight of their bodies crushed the petals.

His mouth traced the line of her chin and the slope of her throat. Her pulse beat under his lips and he licked the spot. Ella arched beneath him, murmuring the name only she had ever called him. To everyone else he was Conn. To her, he'd always been Connell, and she always made it sound noble.

"The name of a prince."

Her smile made his heart thump inside his chest and he kissed her again, covering her with his body, the body of the man he was now and not the lad he'd been.

"I'm no prince."

"You have ever been my prince." Her eyes shone. "Ever and always."

And the thing of it was, with her he had always felt a prince, rather than the beggar he really was. A nobleman, not the son of a butler and a cook. Ella made him feel as though he could be and do anything, that he needn't contort himself into the place his parents had expected him to take.

"Everything I've become is because of you," he told her.

Her hands linked around the back of his neck, pulling him down to her mouth again, and he kissed her like it was the last thing he'd ever do on this earth.

His hand slid up to cup her breast through the thin flaxene of her gown, and he passed a thumb over her nipple. In another moment, he slid down to take it in his mouth through the cloth, and in the next, the dream shifted and they were both naked on the bed of flowers which he knew from real life to be somewhat scratchy but here, in the dream realm, were as soft as feather bed.

She tasted of sunshine, his Ella did. His mouth moved along her body, along the soft curve of her belly, the slope of her hip, the warm skin of her thighs. He found her center. The sound of her low cry when he kissed her there made his cock twitch in response. He licked her, and she arched upward. Her fingers tightened in his hair. He found the small button of her pleasure and stroked it with his tongue until she gasped his name over and over again.

He had always loved making her shudder beneath him. He loved the taste of her desire, and the way her smooth folds swelled as she grew hot with passion. He loved the way her clit grew stiff between his lips, and the way it throbbed when she came.

"I love you," he said into her ear as once again he stretched his body along hers. "I'll never love any woman the way I love you."

And because this was a dream, thank the Astria, she did not turn him away but looked into his eyes and put her arms around him, and she took him inside her body.

"I love you too, Connell," his dream-Ella told him as urged him to move with an upward shift of her hips. She said the words she'd said to him once before, long ago and far away, before it had all disintegrated around them. "Make love to me."

Long ago and far away, he had not been able to do as she'd asked. He'd made love to dozens of women since that night. Fair-haired and dark, with eyes of blue and green and brown and gray, with bodies of every shape and voices in every tone. Every one of them became Ella at the moment of his climax.

But now, in this moment, as he moved within her, it really was Ella and he didn't have to pretend. He kissed her, the taste of her spurring him on. Her nails raked down his back and he moaned, though the pain only enhanced his pleasure. He moved faster.

"I love you," she said, her blue-gray eyes never leaving his. "I always have. And I always will."

Ecstasy boiled inside him, making him shake, and he wanted to bury his face in her hair, but couldn't pull himself from the sight of her eyes. He moved inside her heat, watching desire make her tilt her head on its pillow of lilies. Her gaze never left his, and he drowned in those eyes, the color of the sea on a cloudy day, her eyes that never wept, and he saw himself reflected there as he climaxed.

And woke, sweating, the sheets a tangled mess around his ankles and his cock throbbing with a need for release so great it made his stomach hurt. Connell sat up and scrubbed his face with his palms, breathing hard. A dream was all it had been, but he mourned the loss of it anyway, because dreams were all he had of her.

He swung his legs over the side of the bed and went into his washroom, seeking the solace of a cold shower, the only relief he'd have that night. As he closed his eyes against the needling spray, he saw her face, and he whispered her name, letting his mouth fill with water that couldn't wash away the memory of her flavor.

Chapter 5

"Mistress Valerin, sit." Riordan de Cimmerian, Instructor Primus of Magical Theory and Practice, indicated the chair in front of his desk.

Elspeth sat. She slid a sheaf of parchment across his desk. "I've completed the requirements for the Consummo degree, sir. I would request you review the work and approve it before I send it to the Arithmancy Accreditation Committee."

He nodded and pushed the papers to one side. "Quite a lot of work for you to be doing during the winter break. You're entitled to some time away from your job, Mistress Valerin."

She gave a small smile. "As are you, sir, and yet here I find you at your desk."

The Instructor Primus had a reputation for being a man quick to anger and swift to disdain, and though Elspeth had seen him behave that way with many others, with her he seemed more often to maintain an air of quiet bemusement or consideration. What, exactly, he was considering about her she never dared ponder. She didn't wish to know. It was enough for her that he had hired her knowing her control of the thrall was flawed, and that he never asked her of her past. He'd earned her loyalty for that alone, and Elspeth's loyalty, once earned, was fierce and unrelenting.

"Mistress Valerin," de Cimmerian now said, "I must speak with you on a matter of some import."

"Sir?" Her stomach twisted. His dark eyes traveled over her face, and he had that look again. As though she were a puzzle he meant to decipher.

"You have been a teacher here for seven years."

"Yes, sir."

"And in all that time, it has never come to my attention that you've taken a lover."

For a moment she didn't know quite what to say. Her mouth parted in surprise before she closed it. Those words were the last she'd ever have expected from him. Of course the Instructor Primus would certainly be aware of any and all who formed bonds in the Keep...and of those who did not. It was his place to know such things. Still, his statement shocked her not because she was startled that he knew, but because she had never expected him to be concerned.

"Sir, I fail to see—"

His raised hand stopped her. "When I hired you, I understood your control of the thrall was...limited. But as your position didn't require its use, I felt your inability to harness it properly was less of a deficiency than your extreme skills in your chosen field were an asset."

She drew in a breath, ready to explain though she had no idea of what she could possibly say to make any of this better. Again, the Instructor Primus raised a hand. He needed no orb of power, no use of the thrall to silence her. The power in his gaze was enough.

"Mistress Valerin, I assumed your control of the thrall would grow in time and with practice. That you would acclimate yourself here at Somnus Keep, become a true member of our staff. You've held yourself back from us." He paused. "Yet in all this time, I have watched you teach your craft to class after class. You are one of my finest instructors. You have an easy way about you that makes Arithmancy appeal to even those who find numbers appallingly difficult. You care for your students. I know you have open office hours longer than any of your colleagues, and I know as well the number of students you counsel."

"They come to me because I listen to them," she said.

"Because once you needed someone to listen to you and had nobody."

His assessment of her made her body stiffen so suddenly she pushed the chair back from the desk. "Sir—"

Again, he raised his hand and she fell silent. "I've watched you teach, Mistress Valerin, and I've seen you are capable of passion. So tell me, please, why you can express it with equations and calculations, but not with a lover?"

She wanted to run, but could not. His dark eyes pinned her in place. She shook her head slightly and had to wet her lips, but still could not speak.

"Who hurt you so badly you can't open yourself?"

She had seen him be cold to others and had seen his sneer. This was worse, this penetrating insistence upon truth. Nobody else seemed to notice or care about what was inside her, but this man did. She couldn't hide from him. He was the most powerful magicreator in the Keep, the strongest she'd ever known. Perhaps the strongest anyone had ever known.

"I have never asked you why your control of the thrall is incomplete," he told her, his voice gentler than she'd have expected from him. "But I don't have to ask to know. I've seen it before. Rarely, thank the Astria, for it rarely happens. But I do know."

Her throat closed. Another woman would have cried, but again the release of tears was denied her. She ducked her head, eyes fixed upon her hands fisted in her lap. "I have worked hard, sir, to gain better control of it. I am much improved."

"You shouldn't have had to work so hard."

The anger in his voice made her look up, but he was not angry with her. He was angry *for* her, and Elspeth understood something about him few probably did, for he hid his heart beneath an exterior of disdain as she did behind a mask of dispassion. Riordan de Cimmerian cared deeply about his students and his staff.

He cared about *her*.

"Who was he?" he asked. "The one who took from you instead of giving. Tell me, and I'll see he's punished for it, no matter where he is."

"He is dead. Beyond punishment. He slit his wrists and bled to death in our mother's rose garden. I was ten-and-eight." The implications of what she'd revealed hung between them. She met his gaze and didn't look away.

"Then you've never had an *ahavatara,*" he said quietly. "No first true lover whose duty it is to open your body to love and your soul to the glory of the thrall. You were forced."

She nodded. She had never spoken to anyone of the things Des had done to her. Never admitted her shame. Not since the day in her mother's garden when she'd lied and told Connell she did not and would never love him.

"Elspeth, you are not to blame."

She nodded again. "I know."

"But you don't believe."

She gave a small shake of her head, a shrug. "It was a long time ago."

The Instructor Primus stared at her for a long, silent moment. He sighed, and again she caught a glimpse of the man he hid from everyone else. "'Tis not my place to tell you that you must take a lover who will open you to the thrall in the proper way, how it is meant to be done. I do well understand your reluctance to do so. But you do understand that the damage he did you need not be permanent, do you not? You need not forever mishandle your magic because of one man's disservice? There are ways to remove his tithe upon you and replace it with one more proper."

"I didn't know. I thought—" She'd thought she was destined to be this way forever. Ruined.

"Come here." He stood, and she obeyed, her heart hammering.

He waited until she stood in front of him. He was a tall man, and he put a finger beneath her chin to lift it. He bent to kiss her, his lips pausing before they touched hers. "You trust me, don't you?"

"I do, sir."

"And yet you are shaking, and not from desire."

She looked into his eyes. "I plead your mercy."

He ran a hand along her neck, down her shoulder, brushing the hair off it. Then he stepped back. "You need plead nothing from me, Elspeth. I would not force attentions upon you. Tithed to me you would achieve great power, but it must be your choice. Without true desire, no matter how brief, binding us, what I can give you would be worthless. I understand why you shield yourself."

Looking into his eyes, she thought he did. Riordan de Cimmerian had his own demons, his own reasons for keeping his heart as closed as hers. That he had been willing to help her meant all the more.

She thought of Connell. The courtyard. His bruising kiss and the inside of her lip still wounded from it.

She looked at de Cimmerian. "I made a mistake ten years ago, and threw away the love of a man who would have given me everything."

"A magicreator?"

She shook her head. "He was the son of my parents' butler and cook. We had known each other since infancy. We played together as children. And when we got older..." She smiled a little. "We were foolish. We thought nobody would know."

"But you could not take him as your *ahavatara* because he did not have magic."

Again, she nodded. "Yes."

"Did he know what happened to you?"

She hesitated, remembering. "Yes. He knew. He blamed himself for not protecting me. But when he tried to love me, I couldn't let him. I ran away."

"And now?"

"Now," she said slowly, "I have found him again."

"Then might I suggest, Mistress Valerin, you don't let your opportunity slide away again?"

Once again he was the Instructor Primus, distant, though now his consideration of her had disappeared. *Because he knew,* she thought. She was no longer a mystery to him. He understood her now, and he did not despise her for her past.

She'd experienced moments of revelation in her work when the columns of figures had formed a picture so clear and precise it was impossible to ignore. Now, even without the equations, she understood something so clear and shining she felt the worst sort of fool for being blind to it before.

Riordan de Cimmerian, a man neither kind nor generous by any description, knew her truth, and he did not hate her for it. He did not turn from her in disgust, and he did not even love her.

If a man who did not love her did not turn from her in disgust, neither would a man who did.

"I understand, sir. And, sir, if I might be so bold…" She paused. "You might take your own advice."

His eyes narrowed, and again she caught the glimpse of the man who so many feared. "You *are* bold."

She nodded. "I plead your mercy."

He stared at her a moment longer, the weight of his gaze unreadable. "You're dismissed, Mistress Valerin."

"Thank you, sir."

He nodded, not looking at her any more. Elspeth left his office with much to think about.

Arithmancy was a far more precise practice than Divination. Divination used signs and portents to predict the future, while Arithmancy used numbers and calculations to determine how choices would affect outcomes. The difference of something as simple as one number could result in an end completely different than if one used another number or calculation to figure it.

She spent several hours at her desk, running numbers. She factored every possible equation, ran every scenario she could think of, added and subtracted every element. It was, perhaps, the mathematical equivalent of "he loves me, he loves me not," but it was what she knew best how to do. In the end, it came down to two results, the difference of one small equation, one factor, a single number that when used or eliminated in the overall formula created two results. One, positive. The other, negative.

When it came down to the line, there was nothing she could do to determine which of the sums was going to be accurate. No choice she could make to sway the results. Two outcomes seemed equally likely.

She couldn't put a numerical value on love; couldn't use addition and subtraction on the human heart. It didn't work. She could fact and figure her way into an assumption of the future, and use the numbers to lead her choices toward positive or negative, but in the end, it all came down to something she could not control.

Either Connell loved her, or he did not. And no matter how many times she looked at the numbers, she wasn't able to decide which of the two most likely results were going to happen.

Chapter 6

"Connell."

His eyes opened wide to darkness and he sat up. The curtains blew in the open window. The chill, salt-scented breeze made him shiver.

"Ella?"

A portion of the darkness peeled away from the doorframe. In the next moment she slid under the covers and into his arms. His nose filled with her scent, while the dark silk of her hair tickled his bare chest. She wore a thin flaxene gown, and his hands told him she was bare beneath it. The points of her nipples rose hard against the cloth, and at the feeling of them, he was hard too.

"Make love to me, Connell."

Oh, how badly he wanted to. Her mouth was already on his, her tongue darting between his lips with the delicate aggressiveness that never failed to stiffen his cock and make his heart pound. His hands tangled in her the glory of her hair, and she moaned when he tugged it. She moaned louder when his teeth found the soft flesh of her throat.

He had no fear they'd be overheard. His secluded rooms over the garden shed meant only someone standing down there in the night, listening on purpose, could possibly hear her. Yet something made him hush her. He put her from him a little more roughly than he'd intended, and the whimper as his fingers gripped her arms made his heart lurch with grief.

"Ella," he said. "I want to make love to you. But we can't."

She sat up. Moonlight filtered through the window and flashed in her eyes. She was crying. "We have to."

Connell shook his head, pushing her hair away from her beautiful face. He was dreaming this as he'd dreamed so many other times. He already knew her reasons for seeking the safety of his bed when they both had always known he could not be her first lover. Her *ahavatara*.

Connell didn't have magic. Giving him her virginity meant she'd tithe herself to him forever, her use of the thrall would be compromised and she would never reach her full potential as a magicreator. They'd always known it. They'd always known their desire needed limits. One day she would no longer be his Ella but belong to someone else.

"I don't care," she whispered. "I love you, Connell. You. And I want to be with you. I don't care if I never harness the thrall, I don't care—"

She did care. He knew that. She had to. She had no choice. Elspeth had magic, and it couldn't be denied. He had nothing but a strong back and hands that could build. Nothing but sweat and effort. She had the chance to have it all, but not if she wasted it on him.

"Ella, I can't let you."

"Please, Connell!" Tears choked her voice, and she shook in his arms. "Please, before it's too late! Once it's done, he'll be able to do naught about it."

"Who, Ella? Who?"

Silver tears slipped down her cheeks like trails of star fire. "He said he'd make sure Mother and Father put you out...and your parents too. And that he'd kill you himself, if he knew you'd laid a hand on me again. He said I'm bringing shame to our family, that I'd better not disgrace him by tithing myself to someone with no magic!"

"Your brother doesn't scare me," Connell said angrily, but the sight of her face made him fall silent.

For the first time, he saw why his Ella had gone so pale and thin the past few months. Why she'd stopped smiling. His fingers tightened further, and her small cry made him relax. His heart lodged in his throat. "I'll tear him apart."

"I'll give it all up. I don't care." She sounded hoarse, her voice like glass, brittle. Ready to shatter. "Make love to me, Connell, and all I'll lose is the thrall. I can live with the rest of my life doing only low magic. I can. But I can't live the rest of my life tithed to him. I can't! Not that way!"

He hushed her, gathering her into his arms, burying his face in her hair. He didn't want to ask her what Des had done or what he was trying to do. He didn't want to believe it. His stomach twisted, but the words she'd said no longer mattered. She was with him now. His Ella, the only woman he would ever love.

And then, another figure appeared in the doorway. The shouting began. Desmond Valerin, his parents' pride and joy, and supposed defender of his sister's virtue. He'd cried of scandal and threatened to kill Connell, and because Desmond was a magicreator and Connell not, the fight had been brief and unfair. By the time the binding spell wore off and Connell could leave his room, much had happened. The rose garden had been painted with Des's blood.

And Ella had been lost.

"Connell."

His eyes opened wide to darkness, and he sat up. He was no longer dreaming. A shadow in his doorway had him on his feet in moments, fists raised.

She murmured a word and the fire flared. She pushed her hair off her shoulders and looked at him, her eyes glimmering in the light. "I didn't mean to scare you."

"You didn't." He ran a hand through his hair, then looked down, self-conscious at his bare chest and the loosely tied sleeping trousers he wore. "What are you doing here?"

Ella—Elspeth, he corrected himself, looked hesitant. "I came to plead your mercy. For everything. All of it. I have no excuses. I was cruel then. You deserved better."

This wasn't what he'd expected, and though her words softened him inside, he did his best not to show it. "You have my mercy. Now you can go."

She did something he had not expected. She crossed the room and went to her knees in front of him, head bowed. "Connell, please, please forgive me."

And he could no longer hold onto his anger. It had burned through him like a hot coal in a napkin, leaving behind a hole, but no more heat. He got down in front of her, unable to bear seeing her abase herself like that. "I forgive you, Ella. I told you that."

She looked up at him. "Do you still hate me?"

"I could never hate you."

Her smile was small. "You told me you hated me."

"You told me you'd never love me."

"I didn't want to hurt you." She looked at him. "Des was dead by his own hand. My mother—"

"I remember."

Her mother had given her favored child a funeral full of pomp and circumstance, of glitter and glory. Amarata Valerin had slapped her daughter's face in front of the mourners, called her a whore and blamed her for Desmond's death.

"When you found me in the garden afterward and took my hand, all I could do was think how my mother was right." She took a deep breath and reached for his hand. She linked their fingers together. "How it was my fault Des had died. And how I couldn't let her know how much I loved you, Connell, or else she'd send you away or find a way to hurt you out of spite for me. So I told you I didn't love you, and I pushed you away because I didn't know what else to do, and I went away because I couldn't bear to live with how much I'd hurt you."

He pulled her into his arms. "You weren't crying. I thought you meant it. I shouldn't have believed it, Ella. I should've known different."

Against his cheek, she shook her head. "You couldn't have."

He held her tight against him, stroking her hair and losing himself in her scent the way he'd done so many years ago, when they were no longer children and not quite adults. Tears wet his face, and he wasn't sure if they belonged to her or to him, only that she was laughing and crying at the same time, and then she was kissing him.

"Make love to me," his Ella said to him once again, after all this time. "Please, Connell."

And this time there was no hesitation, no reason to say no. This time, he took her in his arms and carried her to his bed where they fell, both of them laughing until the laughter became sighs.

Chapter 7

He laid her down and covered her with his body. His hands came up to cup the sides of her face and brush the hair away. He looked into her eyes. Then he kissed her with such gentleness it made her want to weep again.

She gave him the tears she'd been unable to shed for years, and he kissed them away. He kissed her eyes, her cheek, the line of her jaw. Connell nuzzled her ear, then the curve of her shoulder, and she tipped her head back to give him access to her throat, and he kissed her there too.

His mouth, wet heat with a hint of teeth, made her gasp. He took her skin in his teeth and she arched into his bite. His hands moved down along her sides, then up to cup her breasts through her gown. She moaned his name.

"Ella," he whispered, "I never stopped loving you. Not ever."

"I never stopped loving you either."

He paused in kissing her to prop himself on his elbows and look into her eyes. "I should've protected you."

"Shhh." She shook her head. "That's all gone. He's gone. It's in the past. Let's make the present, here. Now."

She reached up to pull him down to her. Their mouths met, opened, tongues darting, and it was as though no time had ever passed between them. He set her on fire as he always had. As no other man ever had. She took his hand and brought it again to her breast.

He shivered and bent back to her neck, kissing and nibbling. She arched into his touch, encouraging him with small moans. He knew already how to touch her, how to urge her passion from her, only now each touch, each lick, each stroke and nibble, was magnified because it had been so long for her without pleasure, without passion, so long without the ability to feel.

He moved down, undoing the small pearl buttons that lined her dress from throat to hem. Connell laid open the throat of her gown, baring her skin to his kiss. He found the curve of her collarbone and nipped it, earning a gasp, then smoothed his tongue along the place his teeth had already found. He kissed further down, his hands undoing the buttons without hesitation.

He undid the buttons to her waist. Under her gown she wore a thin flaxene shift tied at the throat with ribbons. Connell unlaced her slowly while he kissed her mouth. The heat of his hands on her bare skin made her gasp.

"Your skin is like silk," he whispered.

His fingers circled her nipples, already hard, and he rolled them in the way he used to. The way that made tingling sparks of pleasure flood her veins, move along her body with each beat of her heart. Something had happened to her that made her gasp at the realization.

"I've stopped," she said.

He looked at her. "Stopped what, love?"

"Counting," she said, and kissed him again.

He left her mouth and moved downward again, lips sliding over her skin until he replaced his fingers with his tongue upon her nipples. He suckled first one, then the other, and she shivered under his touch. His hands slid down along the curve of her hips. His mouth kissed her ribs, then the hollow of her naval and the slight curve of her belly. He licked and kissed and nuzzled her skin.

He paused to take her hand and pull her up so she could slip her arms out of her clothes. Sitting, she bared herself to him, nervous for the first time. She was no longer the girl he'd loved. Time had been kind to her, but her body had changed. She pushed the material down over her hips and watched him watch her, his dark eyes gone darker with passion.

"By the Astria, you are beautiful."

Other men had told her so. Ones she'd ignored or avoided. Being told of her beauty had always made her stomach twist, made her turn away. Made her go cold inside.

Not with Connell. His words made her smile. Heat bloomed inside her, sending a flush along her chest and up her throat to paint her cheeks. She wriggled the rest of the way out of her gown and lay back against the headboard, holding out her arms to him.

He stretched out along her once more. They kissed. Long ago they'd spent hours kissing, tongues stroking, lips nibbling. Hands touching first over clothes and then, when it became too much to bear, fingers sliding beneath to pet and rub. And finally, clothes removed, mouths and hands arousing each other, doing everything but the one thing they couldn't do because it would change their lives forever.

His erection rubbed against her through his sleeping trousers, and Elspeth reached down to stroke him. Connell, face buried in her neck, shuddered when she touched him. His teeth closed on her skin, giving her the pleasure-pain she'd always loved.

She let her hand move up and down, then reached for the ties at his waistband. "I would see you."

He nodded and helped her undress him as he'd helped her. In moments he was bare, and she put her hand upon his shoulder to push him back against the pillows. She wanted to see all of him. She wanted to drink the sight of him like she'd drink fine wine, wanted to consume him with her eyes.

His body had changed too. He'd always been strongly built, with muscled arms, broad shoulders, lean hips and strong legs. As a lad of ten-and-eight, dark curling hair had thatched the base of his penis and run in a line up his belly. Now, as a man of eight-and-twenty, the line had thickened. More curling hair scattered over his smooth skin and surrounded the dark circles of his nipples.

She bent to lick one, then the other. He tasted spicy. She sucked his skin gently, hair tickling her cheek, then let her mouth linger on his skin. Warm. Smooth. The same, but different. His body had grown more defined with age. A rippled scar curved along one shoulder.

She moved to kiss his mouth again, her hands running down his arms to circle his wrists, and she pulled away to turn over his hands. The palms were rough. Scars dotted his skin there too. Marks of hard work. She traced them with her fingertips first, then her kisses, and held them up.

"Each of these must tell a story."

He nodded, drawing her closer to kiss her. "For another time."

She laughed as he put his arms around her to hold her close. Their bodies, length to length, skin warm, fit together like puzzle pieces. She took his kiss and gave it back.

"Another time, oh and aye," she agreed.

Her hand found his cock again, and she stroked him gently, fingers barely grasping him. She let her palm roll over the head, then twist around and down the shaft. Up again, the rhythm familiar even after so long.

He sighed into her mouth. She took his breath. He entered her lungs. Became part of her. His hand found the back of her head and held her mouth against him as his hips lifted into her touch.

She broke the kiss to catch her breath. She shifted her legs, and the sensation made her shiver. Heat filled the pit of her belly and lower. She felt swollen, slick with arousal, empty and yearning to be filled.

The first time she'd taken him in her mouth, he'd cried out her name so loud it had startled a colony of gulls. She'd been clumsy then, her love for him making up for her lack of skill, and it had taken only moments for him to spill inside her mouth. Time had granted both of them greater control. The memory of it, the musky, ocean taste of him, made her clit pulse.

Elspeth slid down his body, her mouth leaving a trail of slickness along his skin. She let her breath caress his length, her lips hovering but not touching him. She heard him take in a breath, but did not hear him let it out, and she smiled. She licked the head of his cock. Connell moaned.

She could not torture him longer, or herself. She wanted to taste him. Elspeth took him into her mouth, the entire length as far as she could. The brush of his pubic hair tickled her lips. He cried her name, and though there were no gulls to scatter above them, the sound of it well-pleased her.

She slid her mouth upward, following behind it with her hand so he was not left bereft. She suckled the head of his cock in time to her hand's stroking. Then down again, slowly, deliberately, until again her mouth brushed his dark hair and her hand slipped down to cup the weight of his balls.

She had always loved doing this for him, giving him pure pleasure. Letting him fill her mouth gave her almost as much pleasure as him filling her, because she loved him.

"Ella." His voice hoarse, Connell moved his hips in time to the pace she'd set. His fingers tangled in her hair, not forcing her to stay there, but moving with her as she moved.

He grew harder under her tongue. His breathing got faster. Between his legs his heartbeat quickened when she pressed the seam of his skin below his testicles. He moaned louder when she ran her finger along that soft skin and pressed in time to her sucking.

A drop of salty fluid coated her tongue and she swallowed it. The taste made her clit swell further, begging for attention. She slid a hand between her legs to stroke herself. Her fingers had made no more than one full circle when she felt his hand upon hers.

In the next moment, Connell shifted to the side, pushing at her hip in the same motion. He rolled her so skillfully she did not lose him from her mouth. He settled himself full on his back, hands on her hips and her heat poised over his mouth.

She paused in her sucking when she felt his breath upon her. Then the next minute her own cry burst from her throat at the sensation of his tongue licking her. Heat on heat, wet on wet, he circled her clit then kissed her. Soft, firm kisses. The tip of his tongue stroked her clit.

She lost her concentration at first from the sheer ecstasy of it. It had been so long. So long even since she'd made love to herself. She couldn't breathe or move, could only let the glory of Connell's mouth upon her wash over her.

His hands stroked her hips, urging her to rock them in time to his kisses. This made it easier. She took him in her mouth again and let him move her body. Back and forth. He licked her while she sucked him.

She couldn't think. Could do nothing but ride the waves of pleasure. Her rhythm stuttered. She lost her place. Her hips moved against him until at last his hands held her still and he licked and licked and her entire body shook with climax. Her fingers clutched the bed clothes. She put her forehead to his thigh, her hair falling down over them, tangling round his cock, slick from her mouth.

His tongue fluttered on her. She broke. She shook. She came so hard she couldn't even think.

He rolled them again. She became aware of the softness of his bed beneath her back and the weight of his head upon her belly. He was stroking a hand along her hip and side, over and over. She blinked and looked down to see him looking up.

Grinning.

"Come here," she said, and he did at once.

She tasted her joy on his lips, and it made her shiver again. She held him close to her. He settled between her legs, his belly against her still-pulsing center. He pushed her hair off her face. He kissed her mouth, her cheeks, her eyes, her forehead, then rested his forehead against hers and looked into her eyes.

"I love you, Ella."

"I love you, too, Connell."

He smiled and kissed her once more, like he couldn't get enough of her, and she understood because she felt the same. She thought he would enter her, but he did not. Connell seemed content to lie upon her, kissing her, and Elspeth was content to let him.

She did not think her body could respond again to him. Her climax had left her shaken. But as Connell kissed her, soft, hard, gentle and fierce, once again heat pooled between her legs. Her body became pinpoints of sensation. Her lips. Her nipples crushed against his chest. Her clit rubbed the firmness of his stomach.

Connell shifted, still kissing her, never stopping. The tip of his cock nudged her. She sighed and tilted her hips to aid his entrance. He did not push inside her.

Instead, he kissed her more. His hips made slow, gentle thrusts. His pelvic bone rubbed her clitoris with maddening continuity. His hand slipped round beneath her neck to hold her head as he kissed and kissed and kissed her.

Tongues stroked. Lips nibbled. Mouths opened, breath passing from one to the other. She no longer knew where she ended and he began. She no longer cared. She didn't know the moment he began to fill her, only that he slid the tip of his cock along her folds. She arched to take him further. He withdrew.

Their bodies had joined, melded by sweat and the slickness of her arousal. Nothing scraped, nothing pinched, nothing caught or tugged. Everything had become smoothness, like silk, like oil. Liquid and languid and flowing.

He slid inside her without pause. His cock nudged the entrance to her womb. His belly teased her clit. He began to move.

She heard herself murmuring his name, words of love, and heard him answer, but they came with no conscious effort on her part. They slipped from her lips as easily as breath. She could not think of words, could think of nothing but him moving inside her and his mouth on hers. Nothing else mattered.

"Ella—"

His surprised tone made her open her eyes. The air glimmered around them. The thrall filled her, making sight replace sound, sound become taste, taste transform itself to sight. Connell tasted like singing and smelled like sunshine. She had covered them both with the high magic without knowing it.

He moved faster with long, smooth strokes. The thrall glimmered and shimmered around them both. Her hands ran down his back to cup his rounded buttocks as he pushed upward on his hands to keep his weight from crushing her. Elspeth angled her hips and hooked her ankles around the back of his calves, urging him forward.

"Look at what you've done." Connell shivered. Sweat dripped from him. She slid her hands up his chest to tweak his nipples. "Look at you, Ella. Look what you can do."

The thrall danced within her and around her. Connell did not have magic. She wanted to share it with him.

"Kiss me," she said.

He did. It should not have happened. It wasn't supposed to happen. Everyone said it could not happen.

Yet when he kissed her, it did. He opened to her out of love, and she gave him what she was feeling, seeing, tasting, smelling. He had no magic, but she gave him some of hers.

His eyes opened, glazed with passion, and she lost herself in his love. They moved together. He bent to kiss her again. He tasted like love. Together, they made love while the thrall covered them and urged them on, taking them higher.

I love you.

He answered her thought with his voice. "I love you too. My Ella."

His pace became ragged. His breath shortened, and hers did too. Starlight filled her, tension coiling, every part of her focused between her legs where the pressure built and built until it let go and she surged with climax again.

Connell thrust inside her once, twice, the last time falling forward to bury his face in her neck. He cried her name and gathered her into his arms.

His cock pulsed inside her. The thrall let her feel his seed filling her. Connell's climax sounded like moonlight and tasted like thunder, and it left her gasping and quaking with a third and final orgasm of her own.

The thrall had never filled her the way it just had. Connell rolled off to lie beside her, his head next to hers, his lips pressed against her shoulder. Elspeth lifted her hand and formed an orb. It was perfect, without flaw, a deep and gleaming gold tinged with blue the color of summer sky.

She closed her fingers and it absorbed into her skin. She made another, as perfect as the first. This one she released. It hovered above them, waiting for her to command.

It was almost too much. She closed her fingers again and withdrew the orb. Her body hummed. Every sensation remained colored by a new awareness. By the thrall. By the magic Connell's love had let her access at last.

Elspeth began to weep.

"Ella, love, what's wrong?"

How could she explain how it felt to hold the thrall in her hands rather than have it slip away from her grasp? To know she could do anything now, make anything happen, create and destroy. How could she tell him, who had no magic, how the years of working so hard to harness what she'd been born to do had left her convinced she would never be able to do it?

How could she explain to one who did not have magic how empty she had been, and how full she was now?

"Ella?"

She looked down at him and brought him to her again for a kiss. "Thank you, Connell. Oh, thank you."

His brow furrowed at her tears, but he held her in his arms and kissed them away. "Shh, love. Please don't cry."

How could she explain that she wept from joy, not grief? That she had found her way at last along the path she'd thought never to walk. How could she tell him she had believed she would always be alone.

She could not. Numbers, not words, were her strength. She could not find the means to tell Connell everything in her heart.

She could only tell him what she'd already said. "I love you."

And it was enough, because he demanded no more from her. Her words were not inadequate to him. They were enough. At last, for her, everything was enough.

A DREAM UPON WAKING

In the eight seasons since she'd been at Somnus Keep, this was the first time Noa had been to this part of the manse. She'd followed the winding stone corridors and descended the curved stone stairways, and now she stood in front of a massive wooden door carved with all manner of designs. She'd stood before this door many times in her dreams, but the reality of it now made her heart thump fiercely in her chest.

Behind the door were the private chambers of Riordan de Cimmerian, Instructor Primus of Magical Theory and Practice. He was the most powerful magicreator in the realm. And her *ahavatara*. Her first lover.

She hesitated before knocking, though she'd planned this night for weeks. The time of her first flow had come and gone, and seven days had passed since the white cloth she pressed between her legs came back unstained. She'd had to wait much longer than other young women, most of whom earned the right to practice their magic by the age of ten and six. Noa was five seasons beyond that. The time had come to lose her virginity. After tonight, she'd not only be a woman, she'd be a full magicreator.

Still, though this moment had haunted her dreams for nearly five seasons, she almost turned around without knocking. She could make another choice…find another man. She'd had many offers, for she was already an accomplished user of the low magic. The loss of her maidenhead would allow her to access the high magic, and the man who broke that barrier, her *ahavatara*, would gain some of the power for himself.

Before she could leave, the door swung open on silent hinges. Noa took a deep breath and stepped over the threshold. The door swung shut behind her. She heard the click of a lock, engaged by invisible hands. Despite herself, she jumped.

"Are you afraid of me?"

The voice, like smoke, curled out of the dimness toward her. Noa shut her eyes against its touch on her cheek, her throat, and the twin mounds of her breasts rising beneath the cloak. When she opened them, she saw him in his chair across the room.

"No, sir."

His next words were spoken in a voice so cold it made an instant liar out of her. "Perhaps you should be."

Noa took a step toward him and passed through the haze in the air. She murmured a clearing spell under her breath, and the dust motes hanging in the candle's flickering glow moved aside to clear her view of him. He sat in his high backed chair, a sardonic smile on the mouth she'd tasted so many times in her dreams.

"Sir." Noa bowed her head. "If you would have me fear you, I will."

A low, rumbling chuckle curled through the air toward her. "Are those the games you'd like to play, then?"

Without her even knowing he'd moved, he was next to her. Riordan lifted her chin until she looked up into the depths of his black eyes. His finger stroked the line of her jaw. Noa's knees shook, but she forced herself to stand firm.

With the quickness of a snake, Riordan's hands tangled in the lengths of her upswept hair. The fullness of it tumbled from its pins to cascade down her back and over her shoulders. Vanity swelled in her for a moment at how the sight of it made him run his tongue across his lips.

Then she gasped in pain, because he'd tightened his grip in the handful of hair at the base of her neck. He pulled her head back until she stared up at him. Noa felt her knees give way, and he pushed her to the stone floor in front of him without letting go of her hair.

"Should I make you kneel before me?" he asked as calmly as though he offered her a cup of wine. "Take out my cock and have you suck it? Push you down on the floor, spread wide your legs and ram my length inside you until you scream as I burst the precious veil of your maidenhood?"

Tears sprang to her eyes, but she forced herself to say, "If it would please you to do so, sir."

He let go of her so abruptly she fell to the stones. Her hands slid over their smooth contours. She waited for his next command. This, too, she had dreamed.

Riordan sighed. "By the teeth of Adon'ai, girl. Get to your feet. I prefer a little more expertise in those who seek my bed. Go back to your classroom to your giggling girl friends. Make eyes at some young swain who will woo you with flowers and parlor magic."

Silently, her tears of pain turning to humiliation, she shook her head. She had chosen this man. She would have him.

"No? You defy me?"

Riordan stalked a few steps from her then turned to look back. Noa risked lifting her head to meet his leveled gaze.

"You've heard the tales, haven't you?" he asked her.

She nodded and got to her feet. She stood before him, hands clasped in front of her as she'd been taught. She did not flinch when his gaze swept over her. "I don't believe everything I hear."

He ran a hand through the dark thickness of his shoulder-length hair. The strands glimmered purple, green and blue in the candlelight, a sign of his power. Sparks jumped from the tips of his fingers and lit the planes of his face.

"I don't want to bed you, girl."

Now Noa set her jaw stubbornly. "I am not a girl any longer. And I've come to claim what's mine by right."

He stared at her for so long she thought he might explode in anger. When he spoke, his voice was soft, but deadly. She'd heard it before, when a student failed at some simple task. It was the calm before the storm.

"You know the consequences, don't you?"

She nodded. "But I will attain the high magic."

"You could do that with lesser men than I." Riordan slanted a sly smile across his full mouth. "Kinder men than I."

She stepped toward him. "I want you."

Her declaration seemed to stun him. "For the love of Adon'ai, why?"

Because I love you, she wanted to whisper, but did not. The words fluttered on her lips and passed silently from her mouth to dance among the golden motes of dust. She could not tell him the truth—that she'd watched him the past five seasons. That she'd sat in his classes and tried to concentrate on the spells he taught and not the way his hands would feel on her skin. She could not tell him that his face haunted her dreams, and the scent of him lingered in her nostrils even after he'd passed her in the hallways.

"Because you are a good teacher," she said at last.

He slid his fingers across his mouth then peered at her again. "And because I am the most powerful man in Somnus Keep? Because when I fuck you, you'll attain power most chits can only dream of?"

She shook her head. "I don't care about that."

"And you don't care that you'll link your soul with mine forever either?" Riordan's mouth twisted into a sneer.

I long for it, she wanted to say, but again kept silent. Noa's tongue swept along her lips in a nervous gesture, and she was rewarded when Riordan's hungry gaze fastened on her mouth. Her breath grew lighter, faster. Her breasts rose and fell beneath the weight of her cloak. She clenched her hands to keep them from trembling.

"I should turn you away," he said. "I have other occupations to fill my time this eve. I don't have time to waste on an untried girl with her heart full of stars…"

"You can't send me away. By Shalhevet's Mercy, you must take me because I am a virgin of common origin, and a magicreator. I can't afford the luxury of hiring a doxy to train me in the art of love."

"Shalhevet's Mercy?" Riordan shook his head. "Girl, that edict has not been enforced in nearly a hundred seasons. You know as well as I that you may choose your first partner from anyone you like. Indeed, 'tis better if the first bond is one based on friendship or love, rather than simple attraction, because you will tithe your soul to the one who takes your virginity and gives you access to your full strength."

Noa lifted her chin. "Shalhevet's Mercy, sir. I choose you."

Riordan went to his chair, a massive piece of furniture covered in studded velvet. The swish of his robes on the stones caressed her ears as it had so often when she sat in his classroom. Noa's nipples peaked, and warmth grew between her legs.

He expertly flicked the flowing cloth of his black cassock to prevent it from tangling as he sat. Riordan steepled his fingers under his chin and stared at her without speaking. Noa forced her back to remain stiff, though the way his eyes crawled over her cloaked form made doing so difficult. She wanted desperately to go to her knees before him to take him in her mouth as he'd so crudely offered already. The thought of it made the juncture of her thighs tingle. She bit back a sigh.

"Come here."

Could he read her mind? Noa did as she was bidden, her heart thumping like the sound of a thousand feet running on wooden floors. She kept her hands clasped in front of her, deferent, as she'd been taught.

"Get on your knees."

Oh, how many times she had longed to hear him say those words! So many times she'd dreamed of it as she touched herself in the loneliness of her narrow bed and tried to reach an ecstasy denied her. Noa slid gracefully to her knees in front of him. Her fingers pressed against the chilly stones. She could not bring herself to look at him, for fear her face would give away the intensity of her passion.

As if he could read her mind, Riordan tapped her head to make her look up. Noa felt the heat of a blush steal across her cheeks, and she couldn't stop her tongue from stealing across her lips again. Riordan made a low noise in his throat.

"Touch yourself."

Whatever command Noa had expected to hear, it was not that. Hesitantly, she lifted her hands to the swell of her breasts beneath her cloak. She rested her fingers there, conscious of the way her nipples nudged at the heavy fabric.

She dared not take her eyes away from his. He gazed at her with the familiar, sarcastic look she knew so well. She felt the heat on her face and between her thighs deepen. Noa bit her lip.

"Touch yourself as you do when you are alone. When you think about me."

Noa shuddered, not from fear or from cold, but from the fierce bolt of desire that shot through her. For a moment, she had to close her eyes against the way the room swam in front of her. Drops of sweat collected on her brow and at the nape of her neck, though the room was cool.

"I gave you an order."

"Sir, I—"

"Question me and I'll put you from my sight. Do it."

With trembling hands, Noa spread her knees gently. The folds of her cloak fell into the space between her legs, protecting her from exposure. She touched herself through the fabric, twice.

"More."

She undid the few hooks holding the cloak closed above her knees. The fabric parted with a whisper. Noa looked down at her hands, startled to see them against the whiteness of her skin instead of the cloak's dark gray. She slid a hand inside and found the softness of her pubic curls. She stroked softly and could not stop the sigh that escaped her lips.

Her other hand kneaded the fullness of her breast then undid several of the tiny hook-and-eye closures down her chest. She slipped a hand inside there, too, and found the peak of her nipple with her thumb and forefinger. Noa stopped, uncertain of how to continue. She could feel what her body wanted. She'd spent enough nights doing these very same actions, but never with an audience.

"I did not give you leave to cease."

She gave another brief shudder that pushed the mound of her womanhood more firmly to her fingers. She moved them in a circular motion, just above what her Sexual Arts teacher called "the monk in the pulpit." Around, around, then a quick dip down to find the rising slickness coating her folds. All the while, her hand rolled her nipple in her fingers.

Noa's breath came short in her lungs. She bit her lip again, harder. The sensations flooding her were not new. Tonight, however, she'd achieve satisfaction instead of frustration.

Noa's magic surged inside her as it always did when she touched herself this way. The power slid through her pores and along the strands of her hair, until they stood gently on end. She heard the crackle of the magic as it flowed from her scalp and burst from the ends of her hair in sparks of violet and red.

"What do you think about when you do this?" he asked her.

"You." The words felt thick on her tongue. She expected them to slur.

"Me?" Riordan sounded quizzical. "Doing what?"

Noa's head bent lower. Her eyes fluttered, so she could glimpse her hand where it disappeared into the opening in her cloak one second, then nothing but the blackness of her lids the next. His voice stroked her as she stroked herself. "Touching me."

"Where?"

"My breasts. My thighs. Between my legs."

Faster now. Her fingers were slick with her own juices and sliding without effort over her clit. She thought she might feel shame at performing this intimacy in front of him, but the movements of her hands quickly swept anything but the frenzy of pleasure from her mind.

"What else?"

She took in a deep, shuddering breath. "Kissing me. Making love to me. Telling me…" She faltered at having to reveal to him her secrets. "Telling me to get on my knees before you and to take you in my mouth."

She heard him shift in his chair and risked a glance. He wasn't looking at her. His attention seemed focused on something far away.

His voice had grown rougher. "How long have you thought these things?"

"A long time." She stuttered as her fingers swept again over her clitoris. The muscles on the insides of her thighs jumped. The stones bit into her knees and her heels gouged the softness of her buttocks. She longed to change position, but the ecstasy that seemed only seconds away kept her in one place, afraid to disturb the rhythm.

"How long?"

She thought back, with difficulty, to the first time she'd sat in his classroom. Though his reputation was legion in Somnus Keep, she'd had no more than a passing acquaintance with him until she was a third season student.

"Since I was ten and six, sir. Since I first sat in your classroom. I am one and twenty now."

"Five years?"

Noa paused in her movements. Beneath her fingertips her clit pulsed in time to the beat of her heart. Exquisite pleasure-pain radiated from that spot, tempting her to press lightly, then slip her fingers down to probe her opening.

"Yes."

"Sweet stars." Riordan put both hands to his face for a moment.

The haze of Noa's arousal hung in the air between them. It was a pale gold color, tinged with pink edging to red. She could have whispered another clearing spell, but chose instead to watch the aura undulate with her growing sexual excitement.

"When do you think these things?"

She thought of long afternoons watching his hands demonstrate how to work the low and the high magic, the hands she longed to feel against her flesh. She thought of evenings in the older students' lounge, watching him play at Quoites or arguing magical theory with students bold enough to risk his acerbity. Meals in which she'd scarce eaten a bite because she'd had the fortune to sit in view of the teacher's table, where she could watch him eat and talk with the rest of the Somnus Keep faculty. And of course, the nights when her dreams had filled with his face, his voice, his scent.

"All the time."

"Tell me again what you imagined."

She looked to see if he mocked her, but saw no sign of anything but curiosity. "I imagined you licking me. Touching me."

"Fucking you?"

"Yes!"

"Tell me something, sweetling. Are you going to come yet?"

Noa's drowsy lidded gaze snapped wide open. "I want to. But not alone."

She wanted to weep with the unfairness of it. Normal people—those who lacked the nature forces that made her a magicreator worthy of Somnus Keep—could achieve sexual satisfaction at their leisure. She needed a lover to reach her full potential.

Tears pricked, hot at the back of her eyes. What a picture she must make. Her hair had tangled over her shoulders. Her cloak gaped open, barely concealing her nakedness. She pulled her hands from their actions and clutched them in her lap.

"Shalhevet's Mercy," he murmured. "I am not so pitiless that I can ignore that. Not when it is so clear to me how badly you need release."

He pitied her, which was something altogether different than mercy. Noa pressed her lips together, then rehooked her cloak. She got to her feet.

"I don't want your pity, no matter how much I might deserve it." She turned, humiliation burning in her chest. The tears clouding her vision made her stumble, and she caught herself with one hand on the edge of a table. She paused to blink her vision clear. Her body ached from unfulfilled desire, but it was no different a sensation than had haunted her many nights before this.

"I did not say you could leave!"

The thunder of his voice, so familiar, stopped her. Noa didn't turn. She straightened her back and clenched her fists at her side, then twisted her head until she gave him her profile.

"You take my truth and you throw it in my face to shame me?" she asked. "They say you are arrogant, and I've seen they are right. They say you are powerful, and I know that account to be true as well. But no matter what stories they whisper about you after you pass, no matter what tales the older students use to frighten the younger, I have never believed it when it is said that you are cruel. Until now."

"Take not one step further," he said in warning.

She whirled to face him. "Or what? What shall you do? Bid me get on my knees again? Bid me to lay down on the floor so you can strip my innocence from me while you mock my desire?"

"I am not in the habit of deflowering maidens with such lack of finesse," Riordan replied.

Her anger, spurred by her humiliation, had not abated. "No? From what I heard, you're not in the habit of anything at all!"

His eyes narrowed. "Now what tales do they tell of me?"

She allowed the twitch of smile touch her lips, though she'd never felt less like laughing. "They say you haven't brought a woman to your bed in nearly six seasons. Nor a man. That you spend each night alone, no matter how many willing partners you might have. Some say 'tis because you wish not to dilute your magic with excess sexual congress. Others claim your preferences run to the perverse—that the mere flesh of another human can not satisfy your urges."

He lifted an eyebrow at her. "Really? And pray tell me, pretty one. What do you think?"

Noa replied calmly, "I think you are afraid of intimacy."

His laugh was short and cut off abruptly. He sneered and flicked his hand at her dismissively. "Then you are wrong."

"I asked you to give me Shalhevet's Mercy. I take back my request."

Again, she turned to leave, and again his command forced her to halt. She knew he could have used the force of his will to glue her feet to the floor, but it took only his words to keep her from moving.

"And if I won't let you? If I insist you stay?'

Noa bent her head for a moment, worrying the soft flesh of her lower lip with her teeth. Everything had gone so horribly awry. She'd been a fool to think he'd want her when even the loveliest women at Somnus Keep hadn't been able to lure him into their beds. She'd asked him for Shalhevet's Mercy because she thought it was the only certain way to get him to agree to be her *ahavatara*, and she'd even failed at that.

"You don't even know my name," she whispered, broken, her heart cracking beneath the weight of the love she did not wish to have for him.

She was at the door, her hand on the great brass latch, before he spoke.

"You do me great disservice," said Riordan. "Noa."

Her fingers clenched on the smooth, cold brass.

"Turn around."

She did, hope setting her heart to a frenzied beat. He hadn't moved from his chair. His hair looked rumpled, as though he'd been running his hands through it. He lifted his hand and crooked a finger at her.

"I cry your mercy, Noa. I was unkind because…because I have no excuse. I was cruel to mock you, and I cry your mercy."

"You shall have it."

"As you shall have mine, not Shalhevet's," Riordan said. "Come here."

She went to him as though upon a cloud of air. Again, he whispered the words she'd dreamed so often, though now they were less a command and more a request. "Get on your knees."

She did.

"Slide up my robe. To my thighs."

Bright sparkles of color flickered in Noa's vision the first time she touched the heavy linen of his black cassock. She heard the soft chuff of his laughter and humiliation stabbed at her. He could see the sparkles, too, and could sense the arousal triggering them to dance around her head. Still, he said nothing, so she continued.

The cassock was lined with crimson satin. She'd glimpsed the color often as she watched him pace the classroom. When he turned corners, the red beneath the black winked at her. Now she let her fingers slide across the luxuriant fabric and imagined it as his skin.

She gripped the robe's hem and lifted it to his ankles. His feet were bare despite the cold floor; his toes long and his ankles strong. She lifted the robe over his calves, scrunching the cloth between her fingers. Her thighs shifted as she knelt, and she fought a shudder as the first coarse hairs on his legs brushed her knuckles. She lifted the hem to his knees, then to his thighs.

Noa stopped, still gripping the handfuls of his cassock. The red satin shimmered in front of her. Riordan hadn't moved.

She waited, aching to move further, but not daring. Her fingers opened and closed slightly on the bunched cloth. She wanted to feel his flesh beneath her fingers, not the damn robe!

"Farther."

She pushed it farther, to the spot where the hair grew sparser and his skin paler. He shifted to allow her to push it higher. Fear struck her suddenly, and she stopped.

"I didn't give you leave to stop."

"Forgive me." Noa had to force the words from a throat gone dry. "I've never... I never have..."

"Of course you haven't, Noa. That's why you came to me, isn't it? To give up your maidenhead in return for the power I can give you?"

Noa nodded, thinking he could never know her real reasons. "I've waited a long time."

"Push it farther."

She took a deep breath and did as he commanded. He was as bare as she beneath the robe, and she wondered for the first time if he'd been expecting her. Then he lay exposed to her, the part of him she'd dreamed of when she squirmed on the hard desk during spells lessons. She blinked and forced herself not to look away.

"You are...magnificent," she breathed.

Her words seemed to startle him, because he let out another low noise. "Take me in your mouth."

Oh, gladly! But Noa had no idea of how to practically do so from her position. She lifted herself higher by putting her hands on his thighs. Now her face was close enough. She closed her eyes, opened her mouth and slid the first inch of him into her mouth.

She could not hold back the moan. Instinctively, she rested her belly on his knees and gripped the length of his shaft with her hands. Oh, she had dreamed of this, but even in her dreams she'd not imagined the sensations would shoot through her like comets in the night sky.

Riordan lifted himself slightly and nudged himself further into her mouth. For one panicky instant Noa tensed, certain the feeling would make her gag. She thought a conforming spell, a calming spell, then could concentrate solely on the pleasure pouring through her.

Though she'd never done this act, she'd spent enough time preparing for it in Sexual Arts class. She let him slide out, then in again, then suckled gently on the contoured head of his erection. Her hands found the weight of his testicles and she stroked them in time to her mouth's movements.

Eager to taste and touch every part of him, Noa slid her mouth down the shaft to the swell of his balls. She pressed her mouth to them, then slid out her tongue to run it along the puckered line leading from the root of his cock. His hands gripped her hair harder, and she thought he muttered a curse.

She slid a hand beneath her robe. She needed no more than a series of light strokes to return her to the quivering brink of climax. Noa slid a finger inside herself, imagining it as Riordan's cock. She eased it in, then out, letting only the tip enter her slick hole. Her thumb rubbed her clit, and her hips bucked.

Noa licked Riordan's balls, losing herself in the sensual onslaught overcoming her. He closed his hand around the base of his cock and slid it up and down as she tongued his testicles. Beneath her cheek, his thigh tensed and relaxed as he stroked and she licked.

Noa no longer had to touch herself to continue her arousal. Just shifting her thighs, slippery from her juices, against one another kept her clit throbbing. She pushed her pelvis against Riordan's chair, aware her body was setting its own pace and following its own urges.

His hands entwined in her hair and she welcomed his instruction. He pulled gently, and she left the sweetness of his balls and returned to his length. When he tugged her hair, she pulled away, and when he pressed gently, she took him back in. She never left him completely. His cock grew slick with her spittle, and she tasted a musky, slippery fluid on her tongue.

Startled, Noa pulled away. It was over so soon? "Sir?"

He'd thrown his head back against the back of the chair. His eyes had closed. Now they opened, and she was surprised and flattered to see his gaze was glazed.

He looked down at his erection, the slickness of her saliva giving it a shimmer in the candlelight. " The deed isn't done. Only a taste of what's to follow."

She nodded and pressed her mouth lightly to his cock again, grateful he hadn't mocked her. He could be cruel in the classroom, and vicious to students who hadn't done their lessons. Though his arrogance was part of what drew her to him, she was glad he wasn't showing it now.

She took the head of him in her mouth again, but this time, he stopped her. "It's not too late to leave."

"No." Noa pushed herself off his lap in dismay. "If I'm not pleasing you, I'll do better."

He made a noise that was nearly a growl. "Not please me?" He grasped the thickness of his erection and slid his hands along its length. "Think you this an indication that you do not please me?"

"I want to please you." Noa moved to go to her knees again, hungry for his cock, but he stopped her.

"There's more to lovemaking than this. And I would serve you the way you seem determined to serve me."

"Sir?"

"On a bed," Riordan said patiently. "You've chosen me, despite the warnings and the stories. I would have you enjoy the experience at least."

Did he think she wouldn't? "Merely being with you is joy enough."

He gave her a sharp glance. "Now it's your turn to mock me?"

Noa refused to look away from his steely glare. "I cry your mercy. I don't mock."

He stood, the folds of his cassock falling back down to his feet. Noa made a small, involuntary noise of protest when the material hid his beauty from her. Then she let out another unintentional noise of surprise when he swept her into his arms.

Noa's breath caught in her throat with a sting like the prick of thorns. For an instant, she fancied she even tasted blood. Riordan's powerful arms cradled her against his muscled chest. He strode without hesitation toward the arched doorway to his bedchamber.

Noa put her arms around Riordan's neck, lost in his embrace. She put her face to his chest and breathed in the scent of him. Smoke and musk...and, incongruously, the scent of flowers. All Soul's Bucket.

He shifted his arm so she slid down to stand before him. Their bodies pressed together. Noa was taller than most of her female classmates, but in Riordan's arms she felt petite. She had to tilt her head back to look at his face.

He gazed down at her, his black eyes smoldering with flashes of gold and red. He gave a sharp twist of his head toward the fireplace in the corner, and it burst into heat and light. He gave another glance at the lamp next to the bed, and its light was extinguished. The scent of flowers grew stronger, briefly. The length of her hair crackled with the spark of Riordan's power.

Now the room was bathed in black, red and gold. Purple and green still gleamed in his dark hair.

He was going to kiss her. Noa let her head fall back further to allow him access to her mouth. Ah, he was going to kiss her, like she'd dreamed, like she'd prayed about…

He didn't kiss her. She opened her eyes, embarrassed to be acting like the mooning schoolgirl she hadn't been before. Riordan tilted his head, his mouth parted. But he didn't kiss her.

Disappointment flooded her, but Noa made no protest when he told her to get on the bed. This was it then. The time had come.

She closed her eyes again, waiting for his weight upon her, waiting for the stab of pain that meant her time with him was over. Tears burned against the backs of her lids.

She felt gentle hands on her, opening her cloak's catch at her throat, then the line of hooks and eyes down the front. She felt the whisper of the fabric against the sheets as it slid from her shoulders. She heard Riordan's sharp intake of breath when he saw she was naked beneath it.

Noa tensed, waiting. At last she opened her eyes. Riordan knelt between her parted legs, his gaze solemn. He looked at her breasts and the nipples she knew must be pink and rigid. His gaze took in the soft curve of her belly, and the circular tattoo that marked her as common born. He looked at the mound of her cunt with its crinkly hair a shade darker than her ash blond head. She parted her legs wider to allow his gaze to caress her everywhere; especially there, where she'd yearned so long for his touch.

Riordan rested his hands lightly on her ankles. His fingers closed on the fragility of her bones. She felt the strength in those fingers she'd seen painting thousands of designs in the air. He could break her bones with little more than his will, but Noa didn't fear his strength.

He slid his hands up her calves, then to her thighs, mimicking her earlier journey. Riordan stretched himself down on the bed's softness. His breath puffed against her center. Noa squirmed.

At last, he kissed her. His lips pressed lightly on the her clit. Noa sighed and shifted beneath him. Her legs parted further, without effort. His hands touched the inside of her thighs and opened her even more. She was exposed to him completely.

Riordan flicked his tongue against her folds, then on her swelling bud. Noa gasped. Riordan swiped his tongue more firmly against her, then took her clitoris gently between his lips and suckled.

Noa's hips rolled upward as the sensation rocked through her. Sweet Stars, but nothing had prepared her for this! She arched her back, helpless against the feeling of the exquisite softness of his mouth on her, the feather-light probing of his tongue along her folds. She'd thought she'd gain pleasure from this night if for no other reason than she loved him. She hadn't dreamed he would see so thoroughly to her pleasure as well.

"Stars above, but you are sweeter than honey."

He continued to stroke her with the fullness of his tongue, pausing now and then to probe with only the tip. Noa rocked her hips, aching for release.

Riordan slid his finger inside her gently. She felt him probe the barrier that had held her back from reaching her full strength. A pain, brief but sharp, stabbed her, and she winced.

What would it be like when he filled her?

Riordan gave her no time to ponder. He slid another finger inside her, stretching. All the while he continued the relentless pressure of his mouth and lips and tongue. He moved the two fingers in and out in rhythm to his strokes, much as Noa had done earlier with her mouth on his cock.

She heard noises coming from her own throat and was helpless to stop them. Words, pleas, his name over and over.

"Riordan!"

She had never called him that before, always referring to him deferentially as Sir or Instructor. Now the syllables of his name rolled from her lips with the ease of water flowing to the sea.

His pace quickened and she rode with it, meeting the thrusts of his fingers and tongue with her own. The bed enfolded her, embraced her. Noa felt as though they lay on a ship's deck, moving with the wind and the waves to some distant shore that was rapidly approaching.

He paused. She protested. Her head tossed side to side on the pillow. It was the place he laid his own head at night to sleep and dream, and that thought had her suddenly cresting toward her climax more than anything else.

For this one night, she shared Riordan's bed.

Just when she thought she might cry with frustration, he kissed her again. This time, the gentle pressure of his lips on her aroused clit sent her over the edge. Something cracked within her, exploded, shattered, and she soared on the sensation and rode it toward the stars. Her back arched and her arms came up to cradle her chest and her throbbing breasts.

He pressed against her again, and she surged again, more briefly this time, and less intensely. When she opened her eyes, Noa felt certain she would be in her own bed, waking from the frequent dream.

But no, Riordan stared at her from his place beside her on the bed. She hadn't noticed him moving from between her legs. Now he rested on his elbow on the bulk of her cloak still tangled in the sheets.

Riordan's dark hair fell across his shoulders. A band of red peeped out from above the high, banded collar of his cassock. Against the ivory of his flesh, the color spoke of lust and power, like the man himself.

"You have the most intriguing eyes."

Noa's hand went to cover her face. Her eyes, one green and one brown, had been a source of shame her entire life. Some said the mismatched set was the reason she'd taken so long in reaching her womanhood. Others said it must be the result of her common birth. Nobody had ever called them intriguing.

"Take your hand away." Riordan's voice brooked no rebelliousness. "I would see your face."

She looked at him.

"You were not too self-conscious to meet my eyes before. Why is that?"

"I wasn't thinking about my eyes before."

He passed a finger along the edge of her hairline, then down her cheek. "I liked it better when you spoke my name."

Her cheeks flamed even as her heart leapt. "I shouldn't have taken the liberty."

"You came to my private rooms, naked beneath your cloak, and demanded I make love to you in accordance with an ancient law no one bothers to uphold any longer. You took my cock in your mouth and came with my name on your lips. I think you earned the right to address me by it now."

She had never felt so naked as she did then, with him still fully clothed beside her. Though her nipples still peaked with arousal, the rest of Noa's body felt warm and languid. Her vagina felt stretched and slightly sore.

She sat and tried to gather the folds of her cloak back around her.

"Don't do that. I want to look at you some more."

She let the garment fall back to the bed beneath her, but gave in to her sudden desire for modesty by pulling her knees to her chest and clasping her hands around her shins.

"Perhaps I should leave," she said in a soft voice.

Riordan tilted his head to look at her. "Do you wish to leave with the task unfinished?"

"No." The boldness of her answer surprised her, but once the word shot from her mouth Noa didn't regret it. "I want to stay with you."

Forever, she thought, but didn't say. Some faint echo of her thoughts must have reverberated between them, however, because his mouth thinned and his dark eyes sparked. Riordan left the bed and paced in front of the fire for a moment before turning to face her.

"I give you one more chance to go," he told her. "And you will owe me nothing."

"No." She shook her head until the pale strands covered her shoulders.

"Stay and be bound to me forever, is that what you want? For me to hold a piece of your soul until you die?"

More than anything.

"You make no protest. I might think you do."

Noa could only stare at him. The fire outlined his silhouette in gold. With every movement, his cassock swirled around his bare feet. The pulse of his magic crackled along the garment's lines and added bursts of color to the dark cloth.

His voice was cold when he spoke next. "And if I refuse you? If I send you away? What will you do then?"

Noa lifted her chin, her heart turning cold. "Would you have me leave? Did I not please you?"

He turned from her to face the fire, and though his words were pitched low, she had no trouble hearing them. "You please me too much."

"Then why won't you look at me?"

"I thought you were a quiet little mouse." Riordan turned back and pierced her with his eyes. "Seems I was mistaken."

Noa, emboldened by his admission, smiled. "We are not in the classroom, my… Riordan."

Ah, she liked the way that sounded. My Riordan, as though he belonged to her. A giggle burbled in her chest and she bit it back. It would not do to laugh right now.

"Nay, but you have chosen me as your teacher, have you not?"

"And I am your willing student."

Noa let her arms fall away from her knees and found the bulk of the pillow behind her back. She allowed it to support her as she let her legs fall open just slightly.

She watched his face, reveling in the opportunity to do so. So often she'd been too shy to look at him when she thought he might be able to see her watch him. She knew intimately the curve of his ears, the line of his jaw, the strands of his hair and shape of his body…but she'd never been able to indulge herself in complete and utter contemplation of his face.

His skin was pale in sharp contrast to the ebony of his hair, eyes and brows. His nose was thin, but his mouth full and red. His teeth, when they flashed in a rare smile, were perfectly shaped and white as pearls.

He wasn't smiling now. His mouth thinned as his eyes raked over her. He focused on the space exposed between her legs. She felt the weight of his gaze there, and she shifted again to flaunt herself.

He put a hand to his throat. His fingers worked the buttons. His cassock opened like a crimson-lined mouth. He slid it from his shoulders and tossed it to the floor.

Noa's breath caught in her throat at the sight of him. He was magnificent from his broad shoulders and finely muscled arms down past his trim waist and long, lean legs. The hair tufting under his arms and between his legs was as purely dark as that on his head, while the line of hair on his belly and covering his legs was of a slightly lighter shade.

His cock stood only half-erect, but under her perusal it rose to nearly meet his belly. Noa took in the sight hungrily as his balls tightened and relaxed. His erection pulsed a little as it lengthened, and she felt an answering throb in the place he'd earlier stretched her.

"You've always been one of my brightest students."

"I never believed you noticed me before." Noa leaned back further on the pillows. She touched her breasts lightly then ran her hands down to the slight curve of her belly. She ventured no further. The touch of her hand would be a sad substitute for Riordan's.

He crawled up the bed toward her. He kissed the inside of her calf, paused to press his lips on her inner thigh, passed over the juncture of her womanhood and slid his tongue across her belly. He moved his mouth first to one breast, then the other, suckling briefly at each nipple while she writhed beneath him.

"That is so sweet," she murmured as warmth burst inside her.

Then his face was before hers, and his weight rested along the length of her. Noa froze, shy again. Riordan's gaze didn't waver as his nose brushed hers lightly.

Then, at last, he kissed her. His mouth was warm and full as he slanted it along hers. She'd never been kissed before, preferring not even to participate in that level of sanctioned experimentation among the other students at Somnus Keep. She'd been saving herself for him.

She sighed and her lips parted. Riordan slid his tongue inside her mouth. He stroked her with its velvety softness, slowly in, then out, in a rhythm she ached for him to repeat with other parts.

"Let me hear you say my name," he whispered.

"Riordan."

"Noa," he whispered back against her lips.

His mouth left hers and she gave a whimper of protest that quickly turned to a gasp of pleasure when he found the sensitive spot beneath her ear. He gathered a handful of hair and pulled it up to further expose her neck to his questing mouth. Riordan nipped at her. "Stay still."

She could not obey. Every touch had her squirming against him. His hardness pressed her belly, hot like a brand.

Riordan slid his mouth along her shoulder and again to her breasts. This time he paid them more attention. He took one firm globe in his hand and sucked the nipple until it stood up in his mouth. He painted moistness on her breast with his tongue then blew on the heated flesh left behind. The combination of heat and chill made her wriggle all the more.

Riordan bent to Noa's other breast and lavished the same attention on it as he had the first. His hands still caught in her waist-length hair, and he held her so tightly in place she could no longer arch beneath him.

"Stay still, I said." His command was firm but not cruel.

"If it pleases you," Noa managed to say. Her voice sounded husky and low, not like her normal voice at all.

She wondered if he might move lower again and the thought of it made her feel faint. He came to her mouth again and captured it. His chest crushed hers, and for a moment, she felt truly light-headed, until he released her hair and rested his weight on his palms, one on either side of her.

His scent filled Noa's nostrils, her lungs. She breathed his breath and felt him become part of her, and she exalted in it.

"Are you ready?" he asked.

She nodded her assent, though, just as suddenly, nervousness assailed her.

"Don't worry, Noa," Riordan said. "It will only hurt for a moment."

She couldn't imagine a pain worse than she expected to feel when she had to leave him when this night ended. "I'm ready, Riordan."

Her slickness aided his entrance. He did not have a gentle nature; she'd known that and loved him despite that. So it didn't shock her when he took no time to ease his way inside her, but instead plunged in directly to the root of his cock.

Noa bit her lip to prevent the cry that rose in her throat. Riordan hushed her with kisses, soft and tender, and he didn't move.

In a moment the pain faded and was replaced with a pleasant sense of fullness.

"It is done," Riordan said. "The barrier to the high magic is broken for you."

Noa searched inside herself for a sign they were joined. She felt no different in his presence than she ever had. If being joined meant she sensed him with every breath, then she'd joined with him long ago.

He moved. Pleasure ebbed and flowed along her breasts, between her legs. Noa slipped her arms around his back and held him closer. His skin was smooth and warm beneath her fingers.

Riordan gave a small twist of his hips that ground his pubis into hers with a delicious burst of pleasure. His cock slid in and out of her slickness. Noa curved her heels over the back of his calves while her hands found the lightly furred mounds of his buttocks.

Faster, she urged him with her mouth, hands and hips. Her body forced her to action—her mind would have had the moment last without cease so she could remain in Riordan's arms.

He buried his face in the crook of her neck and ceased his thrusting. With a slow, steady movement he slipped his arms beneath Noa's back and rolled her over. So smooth and skilled was the motion she ended atop him, still impaled on his length.

The new position rocked her forward. Her sensitized clit brushed against the flat plane of his belly as she leaned forward at his urging. Their mouths met again. The curtain of her hair fell around them, shielding them. Hiding them from everything else.

If only they could stay hidden away forever.

The light from the fire shone through the veil of her hair and cast it in shades of orange and red. Shadows fell on the angles of Riordan's face, highlighting the spots she bent to kiss.

They rocked together. His hands found her hips and clasped her, but Riordan no longer guided Noa's pace. An urge inside her set the rise and fall, the twist of her pubis against his, the brush of her breasts against his chest.

She splintered and broke inside again, this time with a cry so loud it seemed to make the very walls ring. Noa threw back her head, helpless to stop riding him. Not wanting to stop.

Her climax burst through her. She gripped his sides, and his hiss of pain only made her squeeze harder.

Riordan met her thrust for thrust. A line of sweat had broken out on his brow. His hands bruised the flesh at her hips, but Noa didn't wince, didn't care. She felt nothing but the splendor of his cock thrusting inside her, and her own bursting orgasm.

After a moment, she realized he was muttering softly to himself.

"Thebasile rath manlel," he whispered. "Ganme raht."

"A containment spell?" She questioned. She ran her fingertips along the line of his jaw, then down to tangle briefly in the silk of his hair. "Riordan, are you all right?"

"My sweet, some of the stories you've heard about me are true." He pulsed inside her, briefly, and began to awake her again. "I've not made love in nigh on six seasons. If I would serve you properly, I must...contain myself."

Noa arched a little and felt him throb again inside her. She twisted her hips, amazed she should feel the beginnings of arousal again so shortly after being so completely fulfilled. She put her hands on his chest and caressed his nipples.

"Riordan, don't hurt yourself on my account."

He laughed, and she laughed with him. Her love for him burst through her in that moment, so bright she thought for certain it must shine out of her every pore, impossible not to see. She loved him so much, now more than ever that they could laugh together during such intimacy.

"Ah, love, the pleasure will be that much more intense because of the little bit of pain I must endure to reach it."

He'd called her love. A casual endearment...or more? Noa put the thought from her mind. She had one night with him. Let tomorrow come and bring with it what it might—tonight she would not ponder overmuch.

She waved a hand over his face and released a tendril of her magic to caress him. Already she felt the change within her. Spells for which she'd had to work hard now rose to her fingertips with the briefest of thoughts. She lifted her palm and formed an orb of power within it, pulsing the same golden pink as her aura had been earlier.

Riordan raised his own palm revealing his own orb, larger than hers and of a dark, steely gray edged with crimson. With his eyes on hers, Riordan took Noa's hand and pressed them together. Their orbs co-mingled and became one. Their fingers linked. The single orb broke beneath the pressure of their palms and its energy crackled along their arms.

Riordan did not let go of her hand and kept his fingers locked with hers. With his other hand, he lifted hers to his mouth and kissed the palm, then pressed her hand down to the skin over his heart. It thumped beneath her fingers, the throb of its rhythm echoed with that of his penis still inside her.

"I've waited a very long time," Riordan whispered.

"Surely you could have had your pick—" she began, but the shake of his head stopped her.

Riordan's voice was serious. "No, Noa. I've been waiting for you."

He thrust inside her as he spoke, and Noa moaned. "Riordan?"

"The first time I saw you, you stood in a patch of sunlight shining through the window of the library on what was otherwise a gray and dreary winter day. The sun lit up your hair like spun gold and shone in your amazing eyes. You were still a maid at ten and six, though most of your classmates had already chosen their *ahavataram*. You moved out of the sunlight and back to your books, and I felt my heart crack a little at the loss of such a lovely sight."

He thrust again, smoothly, and the hand that had moved hers to his chest now crept between them. His thumb pressed a counterpoint to the movement of his hips. As he slid deeper inside her, he slid against her swollen bud, and when he pulled out, he pressed again, so the pressure on her clit was constant.

"The second time I saw you, you passed me in the hallway as I was on my way to teach a class. You were laughing, your teeth like shining pearls against the blushing rose of your lips, and I envied the boy who had made you smile. Me! Riordan de Cimmerian, master of the high magic, Instructor Primus of Magical Theory and Practice, jealous of a pimply faced schoolboy?"

His hand squeezed hers. His heart thumped in his chest. His cock stretched her, his thumb stroked her, his gaze held her.

"It." Another thrust. "Was." A roll of his hips. "Intolerable." A final tweak of her clit had her gasping his name.

"When it came time to have you as a student in my classroom, I had to force myself to ignore you, Noa."

Riordan's breath had become as ragged as her own. His pace quickened. Noa rocked with him, her climax building more slowly this time but no less exquisitely.

"I feared you would take one look into my eyes and see the truth I could not bear to lay before you. You were right when you said I was afraid of intimacy. Afraid to bare my soul to someone who could see my sins and the cruelties I've committed from arrogance and ignorance, and judge me for them. It never mattered before, you see."

"I knew none of this," Noa whispered.

Their linked fingers glowed with the force of their mingling magic.

"When you came to me tonight," Riordan said, "I wanted to send you away, not because I held you in contempt, but because I have loved you from afar for so long, Noa, I was afraid I would lose that. I would lose you. You would take what you needed from me, and leave. Not even the tithe would be enough to keep you close to me."

"You won't lose me, Riordan." Noa threw back her head as the first wave of another orgasm rippled through her. It was calmer, this time, gentle. Small, perfect spasms of bliss. "I know who you are. I've watched you, too, and heard the tales. I believe what I see for myself, and not what others tell me."

"Tell me again why you chose me," he asked.

Noa bent her head to meet his gaze. "Because I love you."

At her words, his hips jerked. A stifled cry burst from his lips. His cock throbbed inside her.

"I love you," she repeated. "I've loved you for so long, Riordan, I can't tell you when it started. I only know it will not end."

His back arched. "Noa!"

His cock erupted inside her, and she along with it. They surged together, and the bright, shining light of their magic surrounded them in its glow. Bands of color—gold and gray, pink and red—hummed around them.

The full force of the high magic burst through Noa along with her orgasm. The firelight sounded like music, the rustle of the sheets smelled like the ocean, and her name coming from Riordan's lips looked like the dawn.

Their words of love joined in front of her, twisted and became shimmering motes that disappeared into the orb formed above their clasped hands. Noa felt them go, felt them enter her palm and knew Riordan felt the same. He cried her name again, hoarsely, and thrust one last time.

Slowly, as though drifting through water, Noa slid down to rest her head on his chest. Riordan rolled over gently until they faced each other, side by side. She tucked her head beneath his chin. He put his arms around her and held her close. The pattern of their breathing meshed until the rise and fall of his chest matched hers.

"I'm honored you chose me," Riordan said quietly.

"As if I could chose any other?" Noa ran her hand over his hip then rested it on his thigh.

"I love you, Noa."

She wanted him to laugh with joy, but instead he only looked at her seriously. "You've a whole world ahead of you now, Noa. Your power is yours to fully command. Every door is open to you."

"And I shall open all of them," Noa said. "As long as you are there beside me with the key."

"Everything begins now," Riordan told her, and kissed her again.

Noa returned his embrace. "With you. Forever."

And this time, Noa thought as she drifted to sleep in the arms of the man she loved, she needn't regret waking.

The dream would still be with her…along with a whole new world at her fingertips.

TRIAL BY FIRE

Chapter 1

Noa woke and stretched without opening her eyes. Her entire body still sang with contentment, and she smiled as she turned in the bed to reach for Riordan. Her hands touched the smoothness of empty sheets and her eyes flew open. The smile turned to a frown of confusion.

She was in her own bed. Alone.

She sat up and looked around. She didn't recall coming back here, which meant he'd magicked her while she slept. Noa looked down at her bare flesh, still marked in places by the lovemaking they'd shared the night before. She had gone to Riordan and demanded he take her maidenhead in return for a small portion of the power she'd gain with its loss. He had obliged her well and thoroughly, albeit reluctantly at first. And now...now what had he done?

Noa left her bed. She needed no looking glass to know she had changed. The lengths of her hair crackled with sparks of blue and gold as she paced the narrow strip of stone floor between her bed and the wall. She lifted her hands and with a thought formed an orb of magic that pulsed on her fingertips. Then she let it fall away.

She'd been a good student at Somnus Keep. She'd studied hard and done well in all her classes. She'd graduated with honors--no small feat since she hadn't had the advantage of the full magic strength so many of her classmates had already gained. When her flow finally came, she'd chosen Riordan de Cimmerian as her *ahavatara*, her first lover. With the breach of her virginity, she had reached her full potential and, because of her earlier training, she already knew how to wield it.

"Show me," she commanded as another orb flourished on her fingertips.

The ball of light glimmered and grew to reveal the face of the man she loved. She recognized the background. He was in his chamber. His brows were drawn in an expression she well recognized. He scowled.

So soon after their night of love he had returned to his former ways? And he had transported her from him to wake alone? This was intolerable.

The Noa of last night had needed to find the strength to confront a man she loved. The Noa of this morning was already strong. With a word and a gesture, she clothed herself. With another, she flung open the door to her spinster's room. The hall outside was deserted. The summer term had just begun and all students not enrolled had already gone home.

"Good morn, Noa." The young man who greeted her stepped out of her way as she passed.

"Caylen." She nodded, but didn't pause.

Caylen kept step with her. "You did it, didn't you? You chose your *ahavatara*?"

She swiveled her head to glance at him. "Aye, Cay. Last night."

He gave her a grin that stopped her furious pace. "I can tell. You look...lovely."

His eyes had gone starry as he stared at her. She gave him a smile and touched his shoulder "Cay, it's me, Noa. Stop looking at me like that."

He blinked and grinned. "It's the thrall. I can see it all around you like a rainbow. Tell me what it's like?"

Noa thought. "I don't know if I can, Cay. It's like nothing I've ever known."

"Can you truly hear the birds on the other side of the Keep? Can you see my thoughts, hear my dreams, and smell the colors of my clothes?"

"I smell breakfast," Noa replied. "And I hear your stomach rumbling. Go eat. I've got something I need to do."

"Who was it?"

At first she couldn't answer, but Cay had been a friend for a long time. "You know who I asked."

His eyes widened a bit. "You asked *him*?"

"Who else?"

"And he said yes." Caylen shook his head and let out a slow whistle. "I'm happy for you, Noa."

"Don't be." She frowned. "I woke up this morn alone."

Caylen winced. "You knew he might not feel for you what you felt for him."

"That's the problem," Noa said. "He says he did."

His eyes widened again. "So then why?"

"I'm going to ask him that very question."

Caylen stepped back and gave her a lingering stare. "You've changed. I can see it in you. It's more than the thrall. This is more."

She laughed, though she didn't feel much humor this morning. "Go on. I'll see you later."

He left her, and she turned back to her mission. Anger, tempered by anxiety, churned her gut. Why had Riordan sent her away? The night before he had told her he loved her, as she did him. What could have changed?

She'd hesitated before opening the door to his chambers last night but didn't pause this time. The door refused to open at her touch and, without thinking twice, she raised her hands and blew it nearly off the hinges. She strode through it and into the now-familiar chambers beyond.

If she'd startled him, he gave no sign. He didn't even turn from the row of bubbling beakers in front of him. Noa stopped and waited for him to speak.

"Next time, try not to break my door."

The calmness of his response, spoken in the familiar, sarcastic tone, deflated her a little. Set her back. Made her doubt.

"I woke up alone, Riordan."

Did she imagine his shoulders tensing, just a little? "I know."

"Why?"

His glance over his shoulder made a shiver run down her spine. "Because I desired it should be so."

"And what of *my* desires?" She took two steps toward him. Her entire body hummed with tension. Strands of her hair began to lift around her, but she made no effort to smooth them.

He turned back to his beakers. "You got what you wanted from me, Mistress Kahane. Take it and be glad of it, and leave me alone."

His words infuriated her. "I thought I had gained your heart, which was what I truly wanted."

"You gained the thrall. As for the other..."

"Yes? The other? 'I have loved you from afar for so long.'" She threw his words back to him. "Did you lie to me last night?"

"Mayhap I merely told you what you wished to hear."

She gasped as though he'd slapped her. "Look me in the face and tell me you lied to me, Riordan. Meet my eyes and tell me last night was fulfillment of your duty and naught more. Convince me, and I'll leave you alone and not bother you again."

He sighed, and the sound encouraged her for it meant he was unable to immediately spout anger at her. He turned, his shoulders slightly bent, then straightening as he faced her. His eyes met hers without blinking.

"I did not lie to you, Noa. But I spoke wrongly."

She lifted her chin and faced him squarely. "You don't love me?"

The mouth that had given such pleasure thinned. Again he wore the long, high-necked robe of his office as Instructor Primus. Crimson peeked at the hem and just above the collar. A length of black cord tied his dark hair back from his face. Her heart broke from looking at him.

"Riordan?"

He gave an infinitesimal shudder that nonetheless gave her hope. "It's impossible, Noa. It can't work."

"Why not?"

He held out his hands, palms up. "You have your entire life ahead of you. You have the chance to be one of the greatest magicreators this land has ever seen. I can sense it in you. You need to reach that potential."

"And loving you can play no part in that? If I have that power, it's because part of my soul is tithed to yours. Riordan, no matter where I go in this world, part of you will always be within me. You can't send me away as though I'm of no consequence to you. You have some of me within you, too."

"I have some of lots of people inside me," came his cruel reply. "I have been the *ahavatara* for many young magicreators."

"I am not they," she said quietly. "You love me."

"Don't make a fool of yourself. Go away and leave me alone."

"Why do you seek to push me away?" she cried and advanced on him. "Why fight me like this? What are you afraid of?"

His retort thundered in the chamber. "I fear nothing!"

"You are a liar!"

He raised a hand and she stumbled back. Her powers had grown, but his were stronger. She could not fight him with magic and expect to win.

Instead, she went to her knees in front of him. Her hands lifted the hem of his cassock and exposed the dark leather of his boots. He stepped back, but his thighs hit the table behind him and he could go no further.

"I offered this to you last night, and you took it."

"Any woman who gets on her knees before a man to try and woo him to her wishes is an idiot."

She shoved him harder and the table crashed against the wall. "I'm not wooing you."

She pushed the cassock the rest of the way up his thighs. He wasn't bare beneath the cloth as he'd been last night. His linen drawers bulged with his erection, and she nuzzled him through the thin material. Her mouth pressed his cock through the linen and left a spot of wetness.

Without finesse, she reached up and yanked the loose drawers down to the floor. She tucked the cassock around his hips, pinned by his buttocks to the table. Noa put her hands on Riordan's thighs and, without preamble, took the length of him completely in her mouth.

His groan rasped on her ears. She slid her tongue along his cock, down to the base, then up to swirl around the head. Her hands reached up to cup his testicles, and she stroked her thumb along the smooth seam of skin between his balls and his anus. She drew him into her mouth again, then out. The taste and scent of him filled her. Her clit swelled beneath her gown, and she rubbed her thighs together to stimulate herself as she sucked him.

With a subtle shift of concentration, she allowed the thrall to overtake her. All at once, she could hear the blood surging in his veins, smell his heart beating, and hear his arousal growing with every minute. The magic grew and crackled around them. Her hair stood out from her head in floating, shimmering waves, alive with the colors of their passion.

He made as though to move away from her, and she pinned him with a gesture of her hand. That he could have easily broken her hold meant nothing, for she knew he would not. He leaned back against the table. His thighs had begun to tremble with an erotic tension that tasted like lemons and berries, sharp and sweet at the same time.

Her nipples ached for his touch, and her center pulsed in desire for his caress, but this act was not about mutuality. It was about love and truth. She drew him in again, loosening the muscles of her throat to take him in as deeply as she could.

His hands tangled in her hair. He groaned her name, and she saw his voice as bright bands of throbbing color--blue, green and fiery gold.

He was going to climax. She eased off for a moment, left his cock for the softness of his testicles and licked him there while his hips surged and thrust on empty air.

The slickness of her arousal coated her erect clit. Noa rocked her hips, seeking release, but unable to find it. She needed more, and in the moment she thought it, the thrall gave it to her.

She gasped as a thick, solid phallus entered her slick tunnel. She shuddered as a tongue began to dance upon her clitoris. Was this her magic or Riordan's? It didn't matter. She took him into her mouth again and made love to him with her lips, teeth and tongue until he began to thrust against her and shout her name in hoarse gasps.

Her cunt clenched on the phantom phallus penetrating her. Her clit spasmed. She burst into orgasm as Riordan's cock throbbed in her mouth.

His hands pulled her hair hard enough to bring tears to her eyes. He pulled her to his mouth and kissed her so fiercely it left her breathless. With a smooth, powerful motion, he lifted her and plunged his cock inside her all the way. Her legs went around his waist, his hands beneath her buttocks.

Another burst of orgasm wracked her body. Her teeth sank into his neck just above the crimson-edged collar. She tasted blood and smoothed the wound with her tongue to heal it. She arched in climax as he lifted her up and down, then shuddered into his own final ecstasy.

For a moment afterward, he held her. At last, Noa unwrapped her legs and disengaged herself, less awkwardly than she might have imagined. Riordan's cassock fell down to his ankles again. Noa stepped back, her own gown falling to the floor.

"What of my desires?" she asked again.

His chest still heaved from the exertion, and a faint, brick-red blush painted his cheeks. He ran a tongue across his lips, then a hand through his hair. His fingers made a fist when he dropped his hand to his side.

"I plead your mercy." He turned. "But this...this means nothing."

"It means everything." Noa forced herself to remain calm, even as she felt like screaming. "Last night, you told me you loved me. I believed you. What has changed since then?"

"Nothing." His sigh lifted his shoulders, but she still could not see his face. "Nothing but the morning."

"And what has morning to do with it?" she cried, but he gave no answer.

She gathered her pride about her like a tattered cloak and left his chambers. Her eyes stung with furious tears. A wind gathered in her wake as she swept through the halls of Somnus Keep. She sought privacy and solace, and though all who knew her would surely have said Noa Kahane was as mild and even-tempered as any woman they knew, not one person dared stand in her way today.

She climbed the stairs to the Keep's tall main tower. She refused to weep. The wind followed after her, sobbing and crying because she would not.

Chapter 2

"Sex is nothing like they teach you in sex arts class," Bragnon Hucka said smugly as he leaned back and crossed his arms. "Believe me, it's one thing to read about it in a book, and another to actually have a woman's warm and willing tits in your hands."

Caylen rolled his eyes, making certain Bragnon didn't see him. Though only older than Cay by two seasons, Bragnon had been chosen by his *ahavatara* when he was only ten-and-six. Six seasons ago. He hadn't ceased wooing and bragging since.

"I'm more interested in the thrall," Caylen spoke up finally, unable to listen to Bragnon's descriptions any longer.

Bragnon paused and looked at Cay, and so did the rest of them sitting around the table. "You would be."

Cay bit his tongue before he could say something he'd regret. Of the five lads at the table, he was the only one who remained a virgin. He ducked his head and concentrated on not clenching his fists.

"Hairy Mary and her five daughters is no substitute for a real woman." Bragnon's crude joke made the others erupt into laughter. "Just like the low magic isn't substitute for the thrall."

"I know that." Caylen got up from the table. "I'll see you all later."

He tried to ignore the laughter following him, but it rang in his ears until he left the room. He paused in the hall to calm himself. There was no sense in fighting with Bragnon and his toadies. It wasn't their fault Caylen hadn't yet been chosen by his *ahavatara*.

He watched a group of giggling sorceresses pass by. The scent of them filled his nostrils and made his cock a hard, throbbing spike between his legs. They were all at least two seasons younger than he, but the way they swung their hips and made casual orbs of magic as they gestured proved they'd all gained the high magic already.

It's easier for girls, he thought a little angrily. They got to choose their first lover. Their only requirement was that they'd reached their first flow. Allowing them to choose meant they were never forced by someone stronger than they. Though Caylen had never known of a young woman to be raped at Somnus Keep, he knew it happened in other places. Men who didn't respect a woman's right to say no might be punished in other places, but in Somnus Keep, they were killed.

Men had it harder. They had to wait until an eligible female chose them for their first sexual intercourse. There were plenty of older, experienced sorceresses who enjoyed being *ahavateram*. A young man could count himself lucky if he caught the attention of one of them. Bragnon, with his handsome face, tall build and swaggering manner, had attracted the attention of several who had actually competed for the chance to become his first lover. Some of them still warmed Bragnon's bed, a fact he never ceased to brag about.

Caylen suspected that was the real reason Bragnon hadn't left Somnus Keep to seek further employment, though his studies had ended two seasons before. Out in the real world, he'd be another magicreator in service to a monarch or working for his supper. Here in Somnus Keep, Bragnon was practically a king himself.

Caylen was no king. He knew he wasn't hideously ugly or stupid. He simply...was. Thick brown hair, pale blue eyes, average height, average strength, and nothing special to set him off from the others. He didn't have the gift of speech Bragnon had, or the skill of gaming or sports. Girls liked him well enough when it came time to study for exams in classes like Introductory Arithmancy or Runes. For tests in the Sexual Arts classes, Caylen had needed to use one of the Keep doxies.

One of them had kindly offered to be his *ahavatara*, but Caylen declined as politely as he'd been able. The woman was kind enough, but to be tithed to her for the rest of his life...even now the thought made him shiver. The person who gave you access to the high magic needed to not only have adequate control of the thrall herself, she needed to be someone you wouldn't mind being a part of.

Someone like Gabriana. Even now, the thought of her made his groin tighten. She'd been the assistant teacher in his Scrying class last semester. She'd helped him pass the class he otherwise would have failed. She smelled like flowers all the time. They'd spoken often of what controlling the thrall would be like when it came to be his time.

He'd taught her to play Quoites. She'd introduced him to the pleasures of honey on apples. When he had finally passed Scrying, he'd made thin excuses to be around her, and she'd allowed him to. Sometimes, he saw her watching him with an expression he couldn't identify on her lovely face, and he wondered if she remained his friend because she pitied him. He didn't want that to be true. He'd waited for her to offer to be his *ahavatara*, but she never had.

Caylen had left the Keep and reached the lawn outside while he thought. The sun overhead beat on his head with a fierceness that seemed too strong for Fivemonth. He shielded his eyes against the glare and caught sight of a familiar form in the distance. His breath caught in his throat at the sight of her long, golden hair, unbound and gleaming in the bright sunshine.

Gabriana.

She disappeared beneath one of the drooping loveapple trees. Caylen paused for only a moment before deciding to follow her. A shiver tickled his spine as he ducked beneath the trees' hanging branches and entered the shadows. It was a lot cooler there than it had been outside, and the glare had been cut considerably. He blinked to let his eyes adjust, and then he saw her.

"Gabriana?"

She turned, her eyes glittering with tears and her pretty mouth turned down in a frown so fierce it hurt Caylen's own face just to see it. "Cay."

"Are you all right?"

She nodded, then shook her head, then shrugged. "No."

He moved closer and sat the stump at her side. "Want to talk about it?"

"I don't think so."

He nodded and said naught more. The faint whistle of a bird caught his attention and he tilted his head to listen better. The forest seemed hushed unless you really, really listened. Someday, when he had the thrall to command, he would be able to see the bird songs, hear the trees growing, smell the sun shafting through the leaves. For now, he had to content himself with what his own ears and eyes could provide.

Gabriana sat beside him and gave a sigh so deep her shoulders lifted. "I don't want to leave Somnus Keep, Cay."

"Why would you have to?" The thought alarmed him.

She bent her head to stare at her hands folded in her lap. "How long can I expect to continue as an assistant instructor? I have the thrall, I'm qualified to teach, but how long, really, can I stay where I am?"

"Won't they let you teach a class on your own? You're a good teacher, Gabri. You're very patient, even with the younger students. Won't they let you teach them?"

"They have enough teachers, or so Hedavarius told me when I asked. There are too many magicreators who want to stay at Somnus Keep instead of heading out into the world. There aren't enough jobs for all of us. I have until the end of the summer term, and then I must leave."

"They can do that?"

"Of course they can." She made a face. "While fools like Bragnon Hucka stay on, leeching off the Keep, magicreators like me have to leave! It's not fair."

"I'd like to leave. I look forward to the day when I can make my own way in the world." Cay's words startled him, for he'd never thought of that before.

Gabriana looked at him carefully. "Do you?"

He nodded. "Neither of my parents have any magic. They're merchants. They work hard for what they have. I'd like to help them out a bit."

"That's nice."

What she meant as a compliment sounded sour to his ears. "I'm tired of being nice while men like Bragnon get everything they want."

"Men like Bragnon have little going for them other than a handsome face and an attitude. You have more than that, Caylen." Gabriana touched his sleeve.

He fancied he could feel the warmth of her fingers through the lightweight fabric.

His laugh sounded bitter and he knew it. "Sure I do. I have one more term to finish for my advanced studies."

"And then you'll go out into the world and help people." She smiled.

He looked at her. Could she not know? "Gabri, there's no point in my leaving Somnus Keep until I can summon the thrall."

Her lips parted. In that moment, he wanted to kiss her so badly he could nearly taste her lips.

"Cay?"

It was bad enough to face Bragnon's mockery. It was a thousand times worse to have to share his shame with Gabriana. Caylen got up from the stump and turned his back.

"I told you, I don't have the same appeal as Bragnon."

"I think you do. You're bright, you're kind, and you're compassionate. You use your strengths wisely and never to the detriment of others. You have every quality a woman would like to tithe. I'm surprised no sorceress has asked to become your *ahavatara.*"

He thought of Bragnon. "I'm not handsome enough, I guess."

She put her hand to his cheek. "You're no pretty swain like Bragnon, it's true. But your face is fair pleasing, Cay. To me, it is."

He turned to face her. "Gabriana, you were my teacher first, and we've been friends for quite a while. You know the rules. Women choose their first lovers. Men don't."

"I'm sorry, Caylen. I didn't realize. You've always impressed me with your skill...I just assumed..." Her voice trailed away and she stood. She came closer to him.

His heart thudded so hard in his chest he thought he could hear it, even without benefit of the thrall. Gabri put her hand on the spot. His nipple tightened beneath her touch and breath hissed from his lips.

"Caylen, I would be honored if you would allow me to be your *ahavatara.*"

It was everything he'd ever dreamed. And yet he couldn't, in good conscious, take it. "I'm honored you'd choose me. But I don't want you to do this because you pity me."

"I don't pity you," she whispered. "Cay, you're my friend. How can you think I pity you? If it's enough for you that you accept my gift, I'd be happy to give it."

His cock swelled from the sound of her voice, the scent of her skin, the whispered touch of her lips upon his.

"Cay, it's all right. Really." She tilted her head. "Unless you don't want me."

"By the Knight!" he cried. "Gabri, I want you!"

She kissed him, and it was better than anything he'd ever imagined. Her tongue nudged his closed lips, and he opened to her. Her hands clutched his shoulders and drew him closer to her.

Caylen knew what to do to bring a woman pleasure, but pictures in a textbook couldn't compare to the real thing. He tried to still the trembling of his fingers as he slid his hand up to cup the fullness of her breast. Her nipple peaked through the material, and he ran a thumb across the tight bud.

He couldn't really believe this was happening. He half-feared he'd wake in his bed, rigid with arousal and aching from being unable to release. His cock thrummed with heat and pushed at the front of his trousers.

Her fingers found the bulge and stroked him through the cloth. She unfastened the ties at his waist and slipped her hand inside to cup his testicles and stroke his shaft. She closed her hand around the head of his cock and squeezed lightly. Caylen surged against her hand and let out a low, strangled moan.

Before he knew how she'd done it, Gabri had gone to her knees in front of him and loosed him completely from the trousers. Her hot, wet mouth enveloped him, took him deep, to the root. He pushed into her mouth in an instinctive rhythm she matched with her tongue, teeth and hands.

"How does the magic know?" he managed to gasp.

She paused long enough to ask, "What?"

"How does it know the difference between my own hand and your mouth?"

"I don't know." She licked him slowly, in small circles, while his hips rocked. "It's the thrall."

He began to sense something different in the magic he'd carried with him for as long as he could remember. He could use it well, but now it swelled and surged within him along with his growing need for release. He could begin to smell the passion between them, hear the beat of Gabri's blood in her veins. He looked up and heard the sunlight cascading through the trees.

"It's wondrous!"

She chuckled. The sound vibrated his shaft and made his balls tighten with desire. He lifted his hips to the sensation, and Gabri took him deep within.

The barrier had begun to crack, but it didn't break. Gabri left him and lifted her gown off over her head, then laid it on the ground. She lay down on it and parted her knees, and Caylen responded eagerly to her silent invitation.

He knelt between her legs and parted the soft, golden curls with one finger to see the upright nub of her clitoris. He slipped his finger between her folds to find her slickness, then brought it up to circle gently on her button. Her legs fell open wider. The small nub pulsed beneath his touch.

Caylen bent and used his tongue to echo the movements of his finger. She sighed and lifted her pelvis toward him. He took her clitoris between his lips and suckled gently. He gave up trying to remember what the classes had taught him and relied on instinct and Gabri's response to tell him he was doing well.

Her slick channel begged for him to insert his finger, and he did while he continued to lick her. His cock throbbed as he slid in and out of her warmth. He ached to be deep inside her.

Her bud twitched beneath his tongue and she gave a small cry, then tugged so sharply on his hair he thought he might have hurt her. Instead, she pulled him up until his mouth could take hers again.

Gabri urged him to remove his shirt, which he tossed aside. Her hands smoothed his back and sides, the curve of his pectoral muscles. She tweaked both his nipples and his cock spasmed. A drop of liquid oozed out, and his vision swam at the extreme sensation.

He didn't need to ask her if she was ready. He moved over her, and she helped him position his cock at her entrance, then eased him inside her passage. He held himself back from thrusting too deeply, afraid of hurting her, but Gabri lifted her hips to draw him in further.

Caylen paused before beginning to move. His body shuddered as he blinked at the colors and patterns moving in the air around him. Sounds had become scent, scent became noise, sight became scent. The thrall overtook him like a lightning bolt and shook his body with a pleasure-pain so fierce he ground his teeth together to keep from screaming.

Gabri waited patiently for him to gather control of himself. "You're feeling it, aren't you?"

"The thrall." Caylen bent his head to the curve of her shoulder. "Yes."

She smoothed his hair. He began to move against her. In moments, his buttocks tensed with each thrust. His balls became heavy with seed, burning with desire to get out. His shaft was lost in

Gabri's slick heat, with every thrust coming that much closer to the final climax.

"Let go," she whispered in his ear. Her hands found his rear and cupped him, pulled him closer, urged him to push into her harder.

With a shout, he did. His cock tensed, long and hard, and he shuddered like a man caught in the chills of fever. He spurted, each gush another burst of ecstasy.

When he finally caught his breath, he opened his eyes to look down into her lovely face. "I'm sorry."

She raised her eyebrows. "Why, by the Lady? Why would you be sorry?"

"Because I didn't make it good for you."

She shifted him so he moved off her, then sat up and took his hand. "Caylen, you were wonderful."

"But you didn't climax. I could tell." With the thrall humming in his veins, he knew many things he wouldn't have guessed before.

"And you worry about men like Bragnon being better than you." Gabri gave a rueful shake of her head. "Men like Bragnon wouldn't even bother to ask their partner if she climaxed."

"But you didn't."

"Cay, this wasn't for me."

The thrall had backed off a bit, but still sparked on his fingertips when he reached down to touch her belly. "Let me make it better."

"You know you don't have to. It's not a requirement. You have the thrall--"

He stopped her with a quick kiss. "But I want to."

She searched his eyes with hers. A faint expression he wasn't sure he could or wanted to identify crossed her face. She bit her lip, then nodded. "All right."

Without his own lust urging him to frenzy, Cay found it far easier to concentrate on giving Gabri the same pleasure she'd given him. He stretched out beside her to kiss her while his hand slipped down to the tangle of curls between her legs. He easily found her still-erect bud, and began to circle it gently with the tip of his forefinger. In moments, her hips lifted under his touch. Her clitoris grew larger, hotter, harder. He felt the beat of heart in the small nerve center.

Her body shuddered. Her back arched. He slipped a finger inside her and felt the wondrous contractions bearing down on him. She cried out against his mouth and grabbed his hair.

She relaxed and sighed. He withdrew and simply cupped her heat with his palm. Gabriana gave him a sleepy smile.

"Thank you."

"I should thank you." Cay nuzzled her cheek with his lips. "You've given me something much greater."

"Use it well," Gabri said. "But I don't need to tell you that, Caylen. I know you will."

Chapter 3

"Instructor!"

Riordan, his hands overflowing with texts and parchments, paused in the doorway to his office. A dark-haired girl with brilliant blue eyes hurried toward him. He caught the scent of heartflower, an aphrodisiac, in her hair.

"I'm very busy. What can I do for you?"

She actually fluttered her eyelashes at him. "I was wondering if I could talk to you...in private."

Riordan waited a moment before answering. The thrall curled around his ankles and twisted up his body to tickle the back of his neck. This girl was up to something.

"I'm afraid I don't have time right now." He shifted the papers in his hand to get a better grip and moved off down the hall.

His brow furrowed. He was done with classes for the day, and he wanted to get back to the privacy of his chambers. He needed some time to think about Noa...

"Instructor, wait!"

Incredulous, for most students at the Keep regarded Riordan with awe, and sometimes fear, he turned again to face her. "If you'd like to speak to me about class work, you can schedule an appointment with my secretary."

She reached for his elbow to stay him. "I'm not in any of your classes. I want to talk with you about something else."

He raised an eyebrow at her and frowned. "Mistress?"

"De Yourk. Solveig de Yourk."

"Mistress de Yourk. You do realize who I am?"

She simpered. "Of course I do. Everyone knows who you are."

"Then you must realize I am extremely busy. And extremely bad-tempered. Good day." Again, he moved away from her, but the chit had the gall to catch the sleeve of his cassock.

"I said I wanted to speak to you in private." Her voice had grown hard beneath its veneer of flirtation. "Unless you'd like the entire Keep to know about our conversation."

"I don't respond to blackmail, Mistress de Yourk."

She let go of his sleeve and gave him another flirtatious smile. "Please?"

He ground his teeth, but gestured toward the door to his office. "Come inside."

She closed the door behind her and passed her hands over the lock in a simple charm to keep it closed. The thrall tickled him again and he raised his hand to undo the charm.

"There's no need for that."

She shrugged. "It's your office."

He sat in his chair behind the desk and gestured for her to sit in the chair in front. "State your business quickly. I grow impatient."

The flirting and the simpering fell away. Her pretty face became shrewd. "I want you to be my *ahavatara*. A man of great power such as yourself is the perfect choice. Any who tithe themselves to you can count on achieving great things."

"Or terrible things." Riordan watched the girl as she leaned back in her chair. There's something feral about her. Feline. Her eyes gleamed with an intelligence he would have admired, had the expression in them not been so predatory. "You are a very bold young woman to approach the Instructor Primus."

Solveig ran a hand over her breasts and belly as she spoke. "I want you. I want the power you can provide me. I demand the very best when it comes to my clothing, my accommodations, my steeds. Why should I not demand the best when it comes to my *ahavatara*?"

"I'm not a stud service, Mistress de Yourk. And you demand nothing from me."

"Why deny me?" She twisted in her seat. Her gown rode up to expose an expanse of creamy thigh. "I'm young, I'm beautiful. I excelled in my Sexual Arts classes and I can assure you I'll give you pleasure."

"I can see all that. And still, it's my right to deny you."

Her eyes flashed. "My father pays your salary, Instructor."

"Your father is Hedavarius de Livanone?"

"So my mother tells me." She smirked. "He's never denied it. He brought me here. He pays for my schooling and anything else I desire."

"Unfortunately, mistress, he can not pay for me. I long ago stopped serving as *ahavatara* to students. I found it unseemly."

She narrowed her gaze at him. "You did it for that common-born wench with the mismatched eyes. Noa."

"How do you know this?"

"Sir," Solveig said sarcastically. "The entire Keep knows it. We all know she's finally reached her command of the thrall. That's hard to miss since she's so old. We all knew who she yearned for. It was apparent every time she looked at you. Frankly, I'm surprised you accepted her request when you're so reluctant to fulfill mine, but Shalhevet's Mercy is a powerful tool--"

"Close your mouth, girl." Riordan sat up straight in his chair. "Don't sully Noa's name with your lewdness. It's none of your concern, or anyone else's, why I agreed to become Noa's *ahavatara*."

For the first time since stopping him in the hallway, Solveig seemed taken aback and a little nervous. "What other reason could it be? You can't possibly...love her?"

He did love Noa, no matter how he might try to deny it. To hear this spoiled bitch in front of him--a wench who'd never had to work for anything in her life--speak of his beloved in so mocking a fashion made his stomach churn. It made him ashamed of the way he'd spoken to Noa earlier.

"You do love her. By the Lady." Solveig sounded stunned. She sat back in her chair, all attempts at seduction disappeared. "You actually love her!"

She began to laugh, a mocking, cruel sound that had Riordan across the desk with the neck of her gown in his fists before she could speak. "'Ware who you mock, lady. Your father might be the head of this university, but you are still a student here."

"Get your hands off me!"

He let go and brushed his hands to rid them of the filthy feeling touching her had given him. "Get out of my office."

Solveig sneered. "I'm going to give you one last chance. I don't like the idea of sharing my *ahavatara* with someone like that common-born slut, but you are the best. And I take nothing but the best."

"You'll take nothing." Riordan watched her pretty face darken as he rejected her again.

Incredibly, the chit ran her tongue over her lips and lifted her gown to reveal her bare thighs. The dark curls between her legs showed she was bare everywhere else, as well. She parted her legs and used her hand to show him the pinkness of her intimate region. He was unmoved.

She slid a finger inside herself and gave a soft moan. "I'm tight and hot, and I'm wet for you, Riordan. You can't tell me you don't long to fuck me."

"I wouldn't fuck you with an enemy's prick," Riordan replied calmly. "Now get out."

Her legs clamped together so quickly the hem of her gown bunched between them. "How dare you! I'll have my father--"

"Yes, tell your father your story. How you approached me with lewdness and arrogance instead of the proper behavior of a maiden. Tell him how you threatened me. See what he says."

Hedavarius might have spoiled his bastard daughter, but the old man wouldn't approve of her behaving like a common whore. Solveig hissed and stood. Her blue eyes burned with fury. "You'll be sorry!"

"I have only one action for which I am sorry." Riordan thought of how he'd turned Noa away this morn. "And it has nothing to do with you."

At last, she left with a swirl of her gown and slamming of the door. Riordan rubbed his temples. He'd handled that badly. The past two days had turned him upside down, a feeling he wasn't used to and definitely did not like.

He needed to find Noa.

Chapter 4

Noa had always enjoyed the view from the tower. From its small, arched window, she could see for many miles, over the top of the forest, even to the base of the mountains beyond. She'd grown up in farm country, the child of a shepherd and shepherdess. The land of her childhood had been gently rolling hills of grass. Seeing the majestic woods and mountains surrounding Somnus Keep always took her breath away.

Her throat hurt from the effort of holding back her grief, but she still refused to let the tears fall. She should have known Riordan's love would be nothing but the dream she'd thought she might keep upon waking. If only she could still be asleep.

She rested her elbows on the windowsill. This high up, the breeze whipped strongly around the stone tower. It tugged the edges of her hair and lifted it toward the air outside. She closed her eyes to feel it touch her cheeks as softly as lover's caress.

She sensed him before she heard him whisper her name. She kept her face toward the window, but a smile parted her lips. At last, the tears fell.

"Noa, I plead your mercy." Riordan put his arms around her, tentatively, as though he were afraid she would reject him. She'd never expected him to fear.

She leaned into his embrace. "Riordan, I love you. I don't care about the magic. I care about you."

"I know. I'm an old fool."

"You're not old," she said as she realized she wasn't even certain if that was the truth. The thrall gave those who could summon it extra life, if they used it wisely. "Are you?"

He chuckled, his breath hot on her ear and cheek. "I'm old enough. I've lived so long alone, I don't think I know how to live differently."

"I have every confidence you can learn."

His hands tightened on her waist. He nuzzled her neck. Her nipples tightened at his touch, and her heart lifted. She didn't even care about the tears slipping down her cheeks. She turned and kissed him. Their tongues darted and danced. His hands moved down to cup her buttocks through her gown.

"Noa, can you ever forgive my foolishness?"

She looked at him seriously. "Do you plan on doing this every morning?"

"No."

She linked her hands around the back of his neck. "Then you don't even need to ask."

He moved one hand to support her upper back and lifted her into his arms. He kissed her long and thoroughly, then brought her close to his chest and held her there. "Hold on."

The room whirled around her and she closed her eyes against the sudden dizziness. When she opened them, she lay on Riordan's bed with him stretched out beside her. A chill went down her spine at the feeling of the thrall surrounding them, then quickly passed.

"We could've walked, Riordan."

"Ah, but then I'd have wasted precious minutes when I could have been making love to you." His hand slid from her belly to cup her breast, and pleasure tingled through her entire body.

"I like you this way much better," she said.

"Way?"

"Teasing and smiling. You are so much handsomer when you smile than when you scowl." She touched his cheek and ran her fingertips over the curve of his lips. "I think your smile is all the more precious because it's so rare."

"I've not had much to smile about. Until you."

His answer surprised her. "I would think you have much to be happy about. You have wealth, power, and security. You hold a position of prestige in the most respected university of magic anywhere in the world."

"And all of it empty...until now. Without love and someone to share it with, none of the rest of that matters." He touched the tip of her nose.

She had to ask the question. "Then why turn me away this morn? Why push me away from you?"

He sighed so heavily his breath gusted her hair. Riordan turned and lay on his back, arm flung behind his head. "Noa, I learned long ago I don't care for rejection. It's always been my choice to keep those who could hurt me at a distance."

"I don't intend to hurt you." She turned on her side and put her head on his shoulder. She ran an idle hand over his chest, down to his belly. The material of his cassock was smooth and heavy, yet she could feel the heat of his body beneath it.

"I know you don't intend to. But you could do it."

It moved her to hear his honesty. Noa shifted onto her elbow so she could stare into his face. "I can't predict the future, for it's not my talent. But I can promise you I will never choose to bring you harm."

He didn't answer with words, but with a kiss that reached into her very soul. The thrall sparkled between them. They'd become joined in spirit when he took her maidenhead, and now that connection burst open in her mind and heart like sunrise after the longest night. Noa opened herself to it and to him. He filled her.

His tongue stroked hers. His hand came up to cradle the back of her head and he rolled her onto her back. His weight pinned her, but didn't crush her. He nudged open her legs with his own and settled between them, the bulge of his erection a delightful pressure on her center.

"Too many clothes," he murmured and made a pass down her body. Her gown disappeared.

Noa laughed and did the same to him. Naked, his flesh was hot as fire on hers. His cock brushed her belly, then settled lower against her hardening clit and her soft folds. He didn't enter her, though she ached for him. Instead, Riordan rubbed his erection against her and coated himself with her slickness.

He kissed her shoulders and neck, then moved downward to slide his tongue along the first swell of her breasts. A moment later, his lips found her nipple, still erect with arousal, and he suckled it. Sensation burst through her and she arched her back to push herself against him.

His mouth left her and the air caressed the heat he'd left behind. She shivered. He kissed her belly, ran his tongue along the circular tattoo there, then went lower to press his lips to the soft curls between her legs. He parted her thighs and licked her from the base of her tunnel to the upright nub of her clitoris with one smooth motion that made her purr.

Noa sighed as Riordan centered his attention on her bead. He didn't bother teasing her. He set immediately to a pattern of smooth circles that covered her completely. The thrall filled her, covered her, wound around her and Riordan and drew them together tighter than any rope.

Riordan slid his hands beneath her buttocks and lifted her closer to his mouth. His tongue delved deeply into her folds and stroked inside her. His breath warmed her. He slid up again to lick at her button, around, up and down, then back again to her center.

The first spasms of climax shook her, and he withdrew to blow brief, pointed breaths on her pulsing clit. The teasing caress drove her closer to the edge, but not quite over.

She needed him inside her, and as she thought it, he gave her what she needed. First one finger, then another, and he stretched her passage slightly as he continued to puff repeatedly on her trembling clitoris. Her bud swelled, grew impossibly hard, while her passage clenched on his twisting fingers.

Suddenly, she was cresting, she was flying, she was coming. The orgasm surged within her and filled her entire body with its force. Colors burst in front of her eyes and they sounded like the ocean singing.

Tension coiled within her and made her body stiff beneath the rhythmic breaths and around his sliding fingers. Another burst of pleasure wracked her and she cried out. She hadn't thought she'd fallen until she rose again to ride another surge of climax.

At last her clit ceased its beating. Her heart slowed. The haze of Riordan's aura mingled with her own and cast a peach-colored light around them. She smoothed her hands on his shoulders and touched the top of his head resting on her belly.

"Don't ask me to move," she said. "For I don't think I can."

"I don't want you to move. I want to lay like this with you for a while."

Silence followed, broken only by the soft sound of their breathing. Noa closed her eyes and drifted for a short time in the first daze of sleep. Her limbs grew languid, and her breaths regular and slow. Dreams tickled her mind and she embraced them with a smile.

Riordan left her belly and came up to lay beside her. He tucked his head into the crook of her neck and shoulder. At the feeling of his erect cock against her thigh, Noa's eyes drifted open. She rolled to face him, to touch him. She held him in her fist and pumped him lightly up and down until his breath came faster.

With her own urge satisfied, it became easier to focus on the changes in Riordan as she stroked him. His cock filled her hand. She slid her fingers down to the base of it, and stroked the soft flesh covering his testicles. All at once the urge to taste him as he had tasted her made all vestiges of sleep vanish.

Noa moved down Riordan's body so swiftly she heard him make a startled noise. He gave another when she took him deep into her mouth and used her tongue to tease the ridge around the head of his penis. Still cupping his testicles with one hand, she used the other to stroke him as she sucked.

Within minutes his thighs began to tremble. His sac moved beneath her fingers as the jewels within swelled in response to her attention. She relaxed her throat to take him deeper, faster, harder.

With a groan, he lifted his hips to press himself further into her, and she took him. His hands tangled in her hair and pulled her away from him. With one smooth move, Riordan rolled her beneath him and entered her so quickly she gasped.

He thrust and filled her, and his pelvis ground on her clitoris. She rose again toward orgasm, faster this time even than before. The first shudders hit her just as she felt Riordan's cock begin to throb inside her. It sent her over the edge. They climaxed together in a tangle and tumble of limbs and sweat and flying hair.

When she could finally catch her breath, Noa began to laugh. "Sir, I fear you'll be the death of me with such passion."

"Never say that," came Riordan's reply. He kissed her, then wrapped her in his arms and held her tightly. "Not even in jest."

Kept safe by his warmth, Noa snuggled closer to him. "Tomorrow, will I wake alone?"

She felt the shake of his head. "Nay, love. I promise."

Chapter 5

Had he ever seen a day so bright, or smelled a wind so sweet? Caylen didn't think so. Whistling, he moved down the hall toward the common dining room where he planned to eat a quick breakfast and head out to the grounds to enjoy the fine Fivemonth sunshine. Today, not even the sight of Bragnon Hucka flirting with Solveig de Yourk, one of the prettiest girls in Somnus Keep, could blacken Cay's mood. Not even when he passed them and the pair turned their heads to whisper and giggle behind his back.

"Good morrow," was all he said and grinned.

Breakfast this morn was oatcakes with butter and syrup, and Cay helped himself to a large plate. He was ravenous. He walked toward one of the long trestle tables and concentrated on eating. While the food was delicious, he was anxious to get outside.

"You missed a spot."

A warm, feminine voice made him look up in surprise. "Good morning, Gabriana."

She reached out a finger to swipe a drop of syrup at the corner of his mouth, then tucked it into her own. "There. All better."

His heart thumped at her touch. He nodded toward the sideboard where the breakfast was being replenished by the students serving as staff. Gabri smiled and shook her head.

"It's sweeter when it comes from your lips, I'd wager." She leaned toward him and flicked the corner of his mouth, still sticky, with her tongue. "See?"

He was fully erect and straining the front of his breeches within seconds. "Gabri--"

"Shh." She shook her head. "Cay, forgive me. I overstep myself."

"No. It's all right." Cautiously, he looked around to see if anyone else had noticed her display. "I don't mind."

She linked her fingers through his and squeezed. "Caylen, what are your plans for today?"

"I was going to go outside for a while and practice summoning the thrall."

"Would you mind if I join you?"

"No!" He softened his voice. "Of course not. But...why?"

"Do you have to ask?" She bit at her lower lip and suddenly seemed shy. "I like you. I like being with you."

"You don't have to," he said. "You've given me enough already. I don't expect--"

"That's why I like you." Gabri gave a short shake of her head toward Bragnon now sauntering down the aisle toward them. "Men like him do expect."

"Had enough to eat, Cay?" Bragnon patted his stomach. "Stuffed yourself full to satisfy another sort of hunger?"

Bragnon's cruel laughter, which yesterday would have had Caylen leaving the table to avoid him, now only made Cay smile. Obviously, Bragnon didn't know things had changed. Caylen shrugged in response.

"I'm hungrier than normal, sure. I guess it's all the energy I've been expending."

Bragnon looked taken aback. His companion, Solveig, was shrewder than the handsome man. She gave Caylen a closer look, then looked at Gabriana.

"She's fucked him," she announced triumphantly. "Look at them. Can't you see it, Brag? He's got the high magic now."

Bragnon's brow furrowed. It would be too much for him to congratulate Caylen, not when it meant the he was losing his favorite whipping boy. Bragnon shrugged.

"It's about time," was all he said.

Solveig cast them a glance over her shoulder as she followed Bragnon. Gabri watched the pair go, then murmured, "Bragnon had better watch out. Solveig de Yourk is the most spoiled get I've ever known. If he steps on her toes one too many times, he'll find his soft bed and three squares a day not so easy to come by here at the Keep."

Cay took her hand. "Let's not talk about them, all right?"

Her fingers tightened on his. "All right."

Together, they left the dining hall and headed for the bright sunshine outdoors. Gabri watched Cay as he held the door open for. Though he was a few seasons younger than she, Gabri had been watching him for quite a while. First as a student in the class she'd helped teach, and then as a friend. Now, she watched him as a lover.

Gabri had never served as *ahavatara* for anyone before. The act required an amount of boldness she didn't often find within herself. She had offered herself one other time only--to a young man who had politely turned her down and waited for a wealthier and more accomplished sorceress to offer.

Gabri had tried not to be offended; young women got to choose their first lovers and young men had to wait to be chosen, but nobody was ever required to accept an offer. Being someone's bridge to the thrall was an important responsibility. It was more than initiating a young person into his or her sexuality, since most of them had experienced some form of sexual expression, just not intercourse. Being a magicreator's first lover meant taking a piece of them into yourself forever, and they a part of you. A tiny part, to be sure, but one that could mean nothing...or everything.

Still, being turned away the first time she'd offered meant Gabri hadn't offered again. Until Caylen. She'd had other lovers, of course. Few magicreators remained celibate once they'd come of age. There was no point in it. Magicreators didn't need to fear disease or unwanted pregnancy as unmagicked folk did. Sex was one of the Divine Creator's greatest gifts and meant to be shared. Of the other men she'd taken to her bed, however, none had pleased her as much as Caylen had.

"What are you thinking about with such a smile?" he asked her as they walked along the curving path toward the shimmering lake.

"You." She gave him an honest answer because he deserved one, and was rewarded with his own smile.

"You have a pretty smile, Gabri."

"Thank you." She had to stop if from spreading wider and breaking into laughter at the happiness she felt with him. After a moment, she didn't try to stop it any longer, and her joy bubbled out over her lips. "Come on, Cay. Let's run."

"Why?" He looked over his shoulder, as though expecting to see a foe approaching.

She took his hand and lifted her skirts with the other. "Because it feels good."

So they ran, down to the water's edge, where they collapsed on the soft grass in fits of laughter that looked like music and smelled like sunshine. She tucked the thrall back inside her, where it rightly belonged, and watched Cay try to do the same.

"It will come to you in time," she told him as his eyes cleared. "It doesn't always overtake you."

"I know." He grinned and stretched out with his hands behind his head. "But for now, I don't mind. I've waited a long time for the high magic to come when I call it. I don't mind if it comes when I don't."

She nodded. The low magic could be powerful, too. It was the magic most magicreators used for daily tasks. The high magic, though...was everything. All the time. A strange and overwhelming force with the fury and beauty of fire, wind, and water, thought and emotion and sensation all wrapped up in one package.

Gabriana shaded her eyes and looked out over the water to the small island in the center of the lake. "Have you ever gone out there?"

"To the fairies' grotto? No." He gave a mocking shudder. "I'd like to keep my eyes and my tongue, thanks."

"You wouldn't be much fun without your eyes or your tongue." She leaned forward and brushed her lips against his. "But I fear to disappoint you. There are no fairies in the fairies' grotto. They all died or moved away. There're only ruins there."

"How do you know that?" he asked suspiciously. "Hedavarius forbids students to go there."

"Cay, I'm not a student any more. I've been a teacher." She pointed. "Actually, Hedavarius would be hard pressed to call you student any longer, either, since you've gained the thrall. It's actually quite something to see. If you'd care to join me."

He sat up and looked across the water, then back at her. His blue eyes had gone dark with passion, and the sight made her stomach twist in anticipation.

"I'd like that."

She held out her hand to help him up. When he stood, the movement pulled her close to him. Their bodies touched. Her nipples hardened against his chest. His hand pressed on her back for a moment before he stepped away. Gabri knew she didn't imagine the flush rising on his dusky cheeks--and knew the color wasn't from the heat of the sun overhead. The day had become ripe with promise.

"How will we get there? Is there a boat?"

"Do you need a boat?"

Cay looked at the water, then down at his feet. "I don't know. Do I?"

She shook her head. "Not when you have the thrall to command. Do you want to try it?"

"Of course!"

She laughed at his exuberant answer and held out her hand. "This way."

She put her foot to the first gently lapping waves. They wet the toe of her slipper. Gabri closed her eyes for a moment and concentrated. The thrall, eager as a puppy, slipped beneath her feet and surrounded her. It was as easy and as comfortable as slipping into a soft pair of shoes. She sighed and looked down. The water still moved in its gentle pattern, but now her foot stayed atop it, not in it.

"You try."

Cay stood beside her and put his foot out. "I don't know the words for water walking."

"Look inside yourself, Cay. Do you need them?"

He took a deep breath and closed his eyes. When he opened them, she saw the thrall swirling in the depths of his pupils. "No."

"No. And this won't be water walking. Not quite. Water walking keeps you on top of the water, but you still get wet, and you can still be vulnerable to whatever is in the water. It's one reason why Hedavarius has made the island forbidden. Water walking might get you there...if you can get past the merfolk."

"And using the thrall protects us?"

Gabri nodded and let the high magic cover her like a cloak. "If you let it."

Cay took another step forward. His feet moved on the water without getting wet. He walked a few steps to where the water would have reached his shins, and looked back at her. "Are you coming?"

She had paused to watch him use his newfound power, but now she joined him. "You're doing well."

"I had a good teacher."

She blushed. They walked farther onto the lake's surface. Out here on the water, the breeze was stiffer. It rippled the water hard enough to thoroughly rock a small craft, if they'd been in one. As it was, the water occasionally splashed up onto their legs, but again did not wet them. The high magic protected them.

"Look here," she said, when they'd reached close to the lake's center. The deepest part. Here the water was as clear and still as glass, though they couldn't see even close to the bottom, only darkness. "Have you ever seen one?"

"Not this close." Caylen peered down past his feet to the mermaid swimming beneath them. "Not alive."

Gabri shook her head. "Hedavarius outlawed hunting them for sport, but they've never forgiven us. Beware, Cay, and keep the thrall about you. That bitch would harm you if she could."

"She looks like she'd like to eat me," Cay replied as the mermaid stretched her mouth into a wide, sharp-toothed grin.

"Mayhap that, too." Gabri shivered at the sight of the bare-breasted humanoid figure whose body ended in the thick, muscular tale of a fish. "Nasty creatures."

"Let's go."

The mermaid followed them, swimming on her back below the lake's surface. Her scaled tale moved the water with such force it lifted Gabri and Caylen as they walked. After a moment, she was joined by a merman. His powerful arms embraced the female, twisted her, turned her. The female bucked and fought, her face pulled into a grimace and her sharp teeth flashing.

The merman's penis rose from its concealed slit, and Gabri blushed to see it. The organ was long and ridged. It looked more like a weapon than an instrument of love. The merman gripped it with one hand and used the other hand to wrench his ladylove into position.

"Apparently merfolk do not make love face to face." Caylen sounded embarrassed, and when she turned to look, his eyes were wide. "If you can call that making love."

The water churned into foam around their feet as the merman thrust into the mermaid. The female flung out her arms, face down, and writhed as he impaled her. The merman humped against her rapidly, without grace. They turned in the water, so she was above him and he beneath. His tail beat the water as he pumped her.

It didn't look like an act of love, but the mermaid's nipples had become red and hard. Her face contorted in a scream they couldn't hear above the water's surface. Her tail bent forward to create better access to her lover behind her. His hands came around to caress her buoyant breasts and tweak the red, protruding nipples. They turned in the water, over and over as they fucked.

Gabri's own nipples tightened at the sight, which should not have aroused her but did. The raw, animal passion of it made her heart beat faster and her pulse pound in the spot between her legs. Those creatures were not completely animals, but they mated like beasts. It should have disgusted her...and yet, as she watched the mermaid's eyes glaze with unmistakable delight and saw the fishwoman's body tense and jerk in climax, her own body filled with a tension she couldn't ignore.

Again, the pair below them turned and Gabri saw the merman's face clench as he, too, climaxed. In another moment, they'd parted and swum away, leaving only a pattern of bubbles to show they'd been there at all.

She looked up with heat all over her cheeks and met Cay's gaze. He ran his tongue along his bottom lip, slowly, in a way she knew was unrehearsed. The sight shot a bolt of pure pleasure straight to her already swelling clitoris. He was incredibly attractive, mostly because he simply didn't realize it. She wanted to kiss him very much.

It seemed to take forever to get to the island, but once they were there, Gabriana bent and slipped off her shoes to wiggle her toes in the sun-warmed sand. The beach was tiny, miniscule really, and just inches away was the small stand of trees that sheltered the fairies' grotto.

She tilted her head up toward the sunshine, her eyes closed to see the bright pattern of red and gold against the back of her eyelids. She sensed Caylen beside her. The soft brush of his hand on hers, the puff of his breath on her cheek made her smile. If she were blind, she'd know it was him, and not only because she held a part of him inside her.

"Is it back there?" His voice broke her out of her silent thoughts.

Gabriana opened her eyes and looked into the trees. "Yes. Would you like to see it?"

He nodded and reached for her hand. "Show me."

She led him under the hanging tree limbs and through the undergrowth to the barely visible trail. Here, the sun was barely able to force its rays to the ground. The shade felt welcome after the brightness of the sun. She carried her shoes in the hand not holding

Caylen's and the ground was soft beneath her toes. In minutes, for the island was very small, they reached the grotto. Here the ferns and flowers grew more abundantly, once tended by the fairies who'd made this place their home.

Cay looked around. "Very pretty."

She could tell he wasn't much impressed. "This is just the outside of their homestead, Caylen. You have to go through that wall there to get to the ruins of their colony."

"A stone wall." He grinned. "With no door."

The wall had begun to crumble over time with nobody to care for it. Vines and weeds overgrew it. Gabri passed a hand over the stones and the thrall glimmered at the ends of her fingertips. The stones sparkled in response.

"Fairies don't have magic. They *are* magic. This wall is magic, too. It's not real. Put your hand through it and you'll see."

Looking doubtful, Caylen did so, then pulled back his hand when it slid through the wall with no resistance. "What happened to the fairies who used to live here?"

"Disease, I think. A plague killed them off quite some time ago. The rest moved away. I imagine it's better than having them here, kidnapping students for their dinner."

"Shall we go through?"

They stepped through together and came out inside the decrepit fairy colony. The buildings had long ago disappeared since they'd been made from organic materials. All that remained were the small stone columns that marked their wells and waste systems. The rest of the colony had been overgrown with flowers and plants that made what had been outside seem sterile in comparison. Sunshine glimmered with colored sparks that echoed the colors in the flowers. The ferns had multiplied like lacy banners and covered the entire earthen floor.

Gabri turned to point out the remains of one of the fairy circles where the creatures had their dances, but as she faced Caylen, the words died in her throat. The look of passion in his eyes had grown darker and more urgent, and she was speechless in response to the sight of it.

Without a word, but with infinite tenderness, Caylen laid her down on a bed of cool, soft ferns and kissed her. She opened beneath him, eager for his touch. He cupped her breast and her nipple nudged his thumb.

Caylen slid his mouth along her cheek to nuzzle at her ear, then went down the curve of her jaw to kiss the column of her throat. His fingers went to the line of buttons on the front of her gown, and he followed each one as he undid them. She was bare beneath the gown but for a thin pair of underdrawers. His mouth found her bare breasts, and he suckled gently on first one nipple, then the other. Sparks of pleasure tingled in her from his touch.

Gabri touched his hair as he used his hands to bring her breasts together and kiss them both. He palmed her nipples, then moved lower, down her belly. His mouth nipped at the curve of her hip and she wriggled at the tickling.

He looked up, as though to be certain she wasn't protesting, then bent back to her skin again. Gabri no longer felt like Cay's teacher, but instead had become his student. Though sexually she'd had more experience, none of her lovers had taken the time to so thoroughly explore her body and find the places that gave her the most pleasure.

The flowers around them perfumed the air with enough scent to make her feel nearly drunk from it. The thrall ebbed and flowed between them. She took what he gave, and he did the same with her. Caylen unlaced the front of her drawers, but did not pull them down.

Instead, he cupped her through the thin material, then drew his finger down across the small bump of her clitoris as it became more prominent in her arousal. He circled it gently. The pull and tug of the cloth against her flesh added to the sensation and had her biting her lip in seconds. He stroked downward and outlined her opening. Up again, over her nub, then down, until she would have cried with need had he not suddenly put his mouth to her and given her what she wanted.

His breath was hot through the cloth. He plucked at her button with his lips. He wet the material and used his hands to press it, transparent now, over her clitoris. He licked her firmly, stroke after stroke. Gabri began to shudder and he had, as yet, not even put his flesh to hers.

At last, Cay tugged on the waistband of her drawers and pulled them over hips, then off her legs. He paused at her feet to kiss her ankles, then up her calves. He kissed the tender spot behind her knees, which made her roll her hips helplessly. Up her thighs he pressed a line of kisses. When he reached her center at last, he used only the tip of his tongue to touch her clit.

"Caylen!"

The cry erupted from her mouth as her body tensed at his touch. She was close, so close. He slipped a finger inside her as his tongue stroked her from top to bottom, pausing at the top to swirl around the place she needed it most. Gabri spread her legs to let him in and lifted her buttocks to press herself against him. She gave herself to him completely.

She didn't know how Caylen had undressed himself while making love to her with his mouth, but when she looked down at him, he was as naked as she. The sight of him between her thighs, the sight of his tongue dancing on her aroused clit, nearly sent her over the edge. She gasped, she breathed, she sighed.

She put a hand into his hair and pulled, desperate to feel him inside her. He left her trembling center and moved up her body. He captured her mouth without hesitation. He was fierce in his passion, something she'd never have suspected of him, and that fierceness made her recall the merfolk's coupling. It made her gasp aloud as he entered her smoothly, without fumbling.

His body fit with hers like they'd been made for each other. His cock filled her completely. The hardness of his pelvic bone rubbed her exactly where she needed it most. Cay began to thrust, slowly at first, then faster, and with every movement, her clitoris throbbed anew.

Gabri clutched at his back and hooked her heels around his calves. Their eyes met and locked. In Cay's gaze, she saw a depth of emotion that touched her, moved her, sent her flying toward climax more swiftly even than their physical joining. She saw something she hadn't dared hope to see. Love.

His thrusts grew more ragged, along with his breathing. He slid a hand between them to press his thumb against her bud. The extra sensation was enough to send her over the edge. Her clitoris swelled and throbbed, then released. She brought his head down to kiss her again as she trembled beneath him.

His cock pounded inside her. He gave a low cry, first wordless, and then her name. Over and over as his orgasm rushed through him, he cried her name.

He gathered her into his arms, and they rocked together. Their hearts beat in time, fast and then slower. Finally, he grew soft inside her and rolled onto his side with her still held close to him.

"Gabriana."

She snuggled close to him, glad for his warmth against the cool ferns under them. "Yes, Caylen."

"I would like to say something to you, but I'm afraid you'll take it the wrong way."

That didn't sound good. Gabri sat up. "Yes?"

Cay sat up, too, and took her hand. "Gabri, we've known each other for a few seasons now. I want you to know I've always admired you."

This was getting worse and worse. Gabri looked down at their hands, the fingers linked, and thought of the passion they'd just shared. Perhaps she had been wrong about what she saw in his eyes. "Thank you."

"I know you can't possibly feel the same about me--"

"Caylen, stop." She took her hand from his and curled her knees to her chest. "You have no idea how I feel about you."

He looked surprised. "I don't?"

She sighed. "Oh, Caylen. Do you still think I'm doing this just as a favor?"

He looked. The high magic moved between them subtly and without force. He rubbed his face and shook his head. "I don't know."

Gabriana got to her feet and lifted her chin to keep herself from crying. She gathered her clothes about her. "I don't want to hear any more!"

"Gabriana--"

"Oh, stop!" she cried as she pulled her gown closed and did up the buttons with a swipe of her hand. "Is that what you think of me? That I just...just give myself away like that? To anyone? For pity?"

"No, no..."

"Then why do you think I asked you to come here with me today?" Gabri put her hands on her hips. "Why do you think I made love to you? For a favor?"

"I don't think that." Caylen held out his hands, but Gabri pushed them away.

"Then what?"

"I was hoping. I mean..." He gave a frustrated swipe through his hair, mussing it, before he looked at her. "I've liked you for a long time."

"Well, I should hope so." She gave a pointed glance down to the crushed foliage where they'd just made love.

"But I never thought you would ever like me in the same way."

She softened toward him...a little. "Why not? Wait. Don't bother to make a list."

He smiled and bit his lip. "Gabriana, I admire you greatly and would be honored if you would allow me to court you. Properly, I mean. Exclusively, I mean."

Her heart leapt. "You know I have to leave the Keep at the end of this term, Cay."

"I was hoping we might leave together."

She smoothed the front of her gown. "I would like that. I would like to be with you."

With no more hesitation, Caylen swept her into his arms and kissed her breathless.

"We should be getting back to the Keep." He kissed her again.

They stayed in a silent embrace for a few moments. Gabriana held him tightly, then let him go. "We should. Come on then. Back over the water."

When they came out of the grotto, she saw footsteps on the sand that hadn't been there before. Gabri looked around, curious. Who else could have decided to come to the deserted island today?

A few bent twigs and crushed ferns indicated someone had been there, and not long ago. Her cheeks heated as she thought of someone witnessing their lovemaking. Whoever it was had had quite a show.

Across the water, close to shore, she glimpsed a small craft. It was heading not toward the bank where she and Caylen had entered the lake, but instead moved steadily toward the high stone wall that kept the water from entering the subbasements of the Keep. Someone planned to enter the Keep unseen.

She shaded her eyes. "Who is that?"

Caylen put up a hand to keep the sun from blurring his vision. She sensed the shift of the thrall within him as he concentrated. "Bragnon. And that girl he was with this morn in the dining hall."

"Solveig de Yourk." Gabri looked, but too late. The boat had already entered the boathouse. "I wonder what they were doing out here?"

"Same thing as us, do you think?" he asked, and she had to look at him hard to see if he were teasing her.

He was. Gabri raised a brow at him. "They were much swifter about it than we, I'd say."

"Or maybe they changed their minds. She's still a maiden, isn't she? Maybe she decided against Bragnon as her *ahavatara* after all." Cay shrugged. "I couldn't care less actually."

"Me either," Gabri said, though she watched after them for a few more moments, even as she could see nothing. Then she shrugged, too, and followed Cay back across the water to shore.

Chapter 6

Noa hummed to herself as she hung her robe on the hook. She was looking forward to a long soak in the hot bath. Though the days had begun to warm in a prelude to summer, there was nothing like a nice soak in a heated pool, especially inside the cool stone walls of Somnus Keep.

Riordan had a private bathing chamber, but the tub there was purely utilitarian. She'd decided to visit the communal bath chamber instead, where she could not only soak, but also be massaged and pampered if she chose. She'd rarely used the facility in her time at the Keep, as she'd always had something better to spend her money on than extra privileges. Tonight, however, she'd decided to treat herself.

The pool itself was large enough to hold at least twenty young women. The stone steps did not reach to the pool's bottom, which was deep enough to make the water over Noa's head. A stone bench lined the pool's inner rim, and a flat, heated pallet rose from the pool's center for those who wished to lie above the water. Various lower flat stones were positioned just below the water's surface to accommodate those bathers who wished to recline while still being covered by the hot water, and Noa chose one of those. She grabbed a molded pillow of water-resistant rushes and stretched out, her head above water and her body nicely ensconced in the soothing warmth.

Her body ached, even between her legs, but she didn't mind the pain. In fact, it made her smile. She was sore because of the amount of lovemaking she and Riordan had been doing over the past few days. Every morn and every eve, and sometimes during the day if he caught her with a free moment.

He smiled more, and laughed more. He held her hand in the halls and kissed her shamelessly outside his office even when there were students in the halls. Somnus Keep was abuzz with the changes in the Instructor Primus, and Noa blushed at the rumors and stories abounding, but she didn't really mind.

He loved her, and she loved him, and it didn't really matter what anyone else thought. She knew most people were surprised he'd not only agreed to become her *ahavatara*, but her permanent lover as well. She knew there were those at the Keep who didn't believe their love would last long enough to reach the marriage canopy. Noa didn't care. Riordan had asked her to become his bride at the end of the summer term, and she had agreed. Whatever else anyone thought about it didn't matter, so long as she had him by her side.

Now she closed her eyes and drifted into waking dreams of Riordan and the plans they were making. The water covered her, stroked her, soothed and caressed her. She drifted, lazily, content to feel the firm stone beneath her back and the steaming water over the rest of her.

She heard the splashing of another bather, but ignored it. She'd chosen one of the pallets on the far end of the pool for privacy. The splashing grew closer.

"Hello, Noa."

Noa, surprised, opened her eyes. The girl who floated in the water next to her was a few seasons younger. Her face looked somewhat familiar, but Noa couldn't think of her name for a moment. "Solveig?"

A look of irritation flickered in the other girl's eyes, as though she was annoyed with Noa for not recognizing her right away. "Yes. You remember me. You helped with Instructor Chondley's class last season. I was his top student."

The Advanced Sexual Arts class. "Oh, yes. Solveig. How nice to see you again."

Noa recalled Solveig had been a vain and spoiled student. Not a girl she would have chosen for a friend. She gave the girl a strained smile and closed her eyes again. Solveig didn't swim away.

"I was wondering if I could ask your advice." The girl sounded concerned, and Noa looked at her. Solveig made a pretty pout. Her dark hair fanned out around her shoulders in the water. She put her hands, one holding a washcloth, on Noa's pallet to keep herself afloat. "I admire you so much, you being so much older and everything."

Noa looked at Solveig. To hear the younger girl admired her made her pause before answering. Solveig was pretty and rich, from what Noa remembered. She'd never paid Noa a second of attention before now.

"What sort of advice?" Noa asked carefully.

Solveig lifted herself onto Noa's pallet so quickly Noa had to sit up lest the other girl land on top of her. Solveig's naked skin brushed Noa's as she maneuvered. The contact was surprising and uncomfortable, but Solveig appeared not to notice.

"It's about a man." Unselfconsciously, Solveig pushed her hair from her face so it fell in dark sheets over her shoulders to reveal her breasts.

Though nudity in the bathing chamber was no new sight, Noa wished suddenly for a robe to wear. She usually wasn't shy or modest about her body, but the girl's closeness was making her so. She moved away as much as she could without being obvious.

"An older man?" Noa asked, making an assumption.

Solveig nodded, her eyes wide in a stare that seemed somehow contrived. "Yes."

"What happened?"

"He...he touched me."

Solveig's eyes filled with sudden tears and her shoulders began to hitch. Noa felt guilt for her initial distrust, for the girl's grief certainly seemed real enough. Awkwardly, she put her arm around the girl's shoulders. Solveig reacted immediately, bursting into further sobs and throwing her arms around Noa.

"Shh, hush." Noa tried to soothe the sobbing girl. "Tell me what happened."

Solveig sat back and swiped at her tears with the cloth. "He...he called me into his office. He asked to speak to me about something private. I thought he meant a grade or something. I went in and he locked the door. Then he told me to sit down. In a minute, he'd torn my gown open! And he put his hands on me, here! And here!"

As she cried out, Solveig clutched at Noa's breast with the hand holding the cloth, then thrust it between Noa's legs. "And he grabbed me!"

She'd retreated before Noa could protest or even try to move the girl's grip. Her skin tingled from Solveig's rough touch. Gooseflesh humped on her arms and legs, both from Solveig's words and from her grasp.

"And then he pushed me down and...he took me!"

"He raped you?" Noa's gasp echoed in the stone chamber. Rape was a crime of the common world, not of Somnus Keep. Men did not force women, especially not virgin magicreators whose power was tied to their maidenhead.

Solveig burst into fresh sobs. "Yes! He raped me! He said he'd grown a taste for cherries! I didn't know what he meant at first..."

But Noa understood the crude term. Cherry-picker was used to describe a man who actively pursued being asked to serve as a young woman's first lover. "Solveig, who did this awful thing to you?"

"You see, that's why I had to come to you for your advice." Solveig sniffled and turned her red-eyed gaze on Noa. "It was Riordan de Cimmerian."

Chapter 7

Riordan had never seen so many people in Judgment Hall. From his seat on the floor facing the multiple tiers of benches, he stared into the faces of what surely must be the entire population of Somnus Keep and some neighboring towns besides. He kept his face neutral, though he knew he was in some very serious trouble.

Hedavarius was head of the school itself, but he was not in charge of passing judgment. He had called a tribunal of Inquisitors. It had been difficult finding enough men and women who were Riordan's peers in the world of magic. Many of them lived far away from Somnus Keep. Some had refused to take part. Some who had had previous conflicts with Riordan had been ineligible. Finally, Hedavarius had gathered six men and three women to serve on the judgment board.

Riordan's eyes searched the crowd and saw many faces twisted into smug grins. He'd made enemies over the seasons. He'd been harsh to students and faculty, aloof, arrogant. And yes, he had been cruel. If he fell, there would be many who would applaud.

But not Noa. Please, by the Knight, he prayed. Not Noa. He searched the crowd for her, but did not see her. He hadn't seen her since the night she had come to his room to warn him of Solveig's story. He had tried to tell her then he'd never touched the girl, but the guards had come to take him away before he could tell her anything.

He had the power to destroy this place, but pride would have prevented him from doing it even if the Binding had not. It had taken the combined strength of nine other magicreators to Bind him, however, and he did take pride in that.

"Riordan de Cimmerian, Instructor Primus of Magical Theory and Practice, you are called to the table to answer for the crime of rape."

Riordan got up and walked toward the table behind which his prosecutors sat. He had worked with all but one, a woman who stared at him with implacable eyes. She was playing the role of First Inquisitor. He nodded to each in turn, but none of them returned the gesture.

"How do you plead?" said the First Inquisitor.

"I did not commit the crime."

"Bring forth the accuser."

Riordan sat in the high backed chair next to the table. Solveig de Yourk, wearing a far more demure dress than she'd worn to his office, her hair pulled back in a tight braid, face clean of any cosmetic, entered the room. She walked slowly and her eyes darted toward him, then away, as though she were afraid even to look at him. The act made him want to curl his lip, but mindful of the eyes upon him, he resisted.

"Have a seat, Mistress de Yourk."

She did and clasped her hands in her lap.

"Please tell the tribunal and these witnesses what transpired."

She went through her story. How he had called her into the office. How he had told her sit down. How finally, he had breached her maidenhead by force.

He'd heard her tale three times already, for she'd had to tell it thrice, convincingly and without discrepancy, in order to bring him to trial. Now, as she told her story a fourth time, even Riordan had to admit she sounded believable.

They went through her list of witnesses, the main one being the braggart Bragnon Hucka, who swore he'd seen Solveig enter Riordan's office and leave it weeping and disheveled a few minutes later. She had the bruises she claimed were from Riordan's touch. More damning, she could summon the thrall, which proved she had lost her maidenhead. At last came the final piece of evidence against him.

"This is the cloth you used to cleanse yourself?" The First Inquisitor indicated a white square of fabric, no different than any other of the Somnus Keep toweling.

"Yes." Solveig wiped at her face and put on what Riordan supposed was meant to be a brave smile. She was a good actress.

"Put it in the truthfire."

One of the men, Edward de Fenize, did so. The flames flared blue, then black before finally settling back to red and orange again. Solveig sat back in her chair and gave the audience a triumphant look.

"The truthfire says the mingled substances on this cloth do indeed belong to the two individuals in question." The First Inquisitor folded her arms across her chest. She looked at her fellow Inquisitors. Then she looked at Riordan. "Riordan de Cimmerian, the evidence which has been presented against you is very serious indeed.

You now have the chance to defend yourself and convince this tribunal of your innocence. If you cannot, you will be put to the final trial by fire."

Riordan stood and faced the crowd once more. He searched it for any sign of Noa, and though he refused to show it, his heart fell when he did not see her. He called on anger to chase away the pain inside. She had said she loved him...but she wasn't here to support him.

"I don't need to speak in my defense." The watching crowd murmured and Riordan met them all with a stony face to match his hardened heart. "Let the truthfire be my proof."

Chapter 8

"Where would you like to go?" Gabriana formed an orb that first took the shape of a ship, and then a bird. "Across the Sea of Days? To the Western Lands? Where, Cay?"

"I think I'd like to go someplace green." Caylen formed his own orb, which joined hers in flight across the room. "And flat. I confess I'm a bit tired of the mountains here."

He rolled atop her and kissed her again. She felt the press of his hardening cock between her thighs, and a surge of arousal made the thrall rise, humming, in her veins.

"I think I'd like to see the ocean," Gabri said. "Walk along real sand."

"I think I don't really care where we go," Caylen replied. "As long as I'm with you."

"Those are the nicest words I've ever heard." Gabriana kissed him.

Caylen pressed his erection between her thighs and a familiar heat flared. She spread her legs to let him settle closer against her. He tucked his head into the curve of her shoulder and held her for a time without speaking or moving. The past few days had changed them both.

"I love you, Gabriana."

"I love you, too, Cay."

He tilted his head to look up at her. "You know I can't offer you much."

"I don't need much."

He snuggled closer for another minute. His lips traced her neck as he reached up to cup her breast. He rolled her nipple under this thumb and the small pink bud tightened.

"I love touching you," he whispered.

He moved to the side and slid his hand lower to touch her center. She was already slick with desire for him. Caylen found her button and stroked it gently, then slid down and up to coat her with slickness. He kissed her mouth. His tongue swept inside her mouth, and she met it with her own while her hips lifted under his patient attention.

He was going to make her climax too soon. Gabri wanted this to last. She shifted herself away from him and pushed him until he rolled onto his back. Then she straddled his hips, his cock nestled between her thighs and nudging upward toward her belly. She gripped with her inner thigh muscles as she rocked back and forth. He hadn't entered her, but the position pressed his cock along her folds and her clit. It would take only a small shift to allow him to slide deep within her, but Gabri kept herself in place.

Cay put his hands on her hips to help her move. Soon his entire penis glistened with her juices. The shaft grew ever harder between her thighs as she rocked along its length. Gabri reached down between her legs and grasped his cock. She closed her fingers around the rim of the head and echoed the movement of her pelvis by twisting her palm on his sensitive flesh.

Cay moaned and throbbed in her hand. Gabriana's head fell back as pleasure overtook her. Her hair fell over her bare skin and across Cay's thighs. As the thrall filled her, her hair began to crackle and spark. The ends lifted. It surrounded and curtained them, and the colors of their mingled passion shone in every strand.

She felt the pulse of his balls between her legs and of his cock against her center. Her clit twitched in response. She was ready for him, more than ready, hot and wet for him.

"Yes," Caylen groaned as Gabriana lifted her hips to allow his penis to enter her slick passage. "By the Knight, Gabri, that's good."

He filled her so deeply he tapped the entrance to her womb. For a moment, Gabri didn't move. She held him inside her while she clenched and unclenched her inner muscles to bring him pleasure.

It worked. Cay's cock expanded inside her, and she felt the first ripples of his impending climax. Gabri wasn't ready to stop making love to him yet. Instead of lifting her hips to stroke herself on and off him, she continued to stay in one place and use her muscles to drive him closer to the edge.

It was working for her, too. Without so much movement to distract her, she found each sensation heightened. Each clench of her muscles tightened on Caylen, even while tugging on her hard button. She began to rock her hips, still not enough to finish him, but enough to draw out the pleasure even more.

Gabriana met Caylen's eyes, and they both smiled. The mingled threads of the high magic danced around them. Blue, red, green, gold. Every sense became stronger. She could hear his heart beat.

Caylen took one hand from her hip and brought it around to press his thumb against her clitoris. One touch, then one more, and she splintered and broke. She shattered and came back together. Her body shuddered with an ecstasy that did not fade but instead grew again, immediately, as he continued to circle her clit.

She could no longer keep herself from moving. Gabri lifted herself on Cay's cock, up and down, as she rolled her pelvis toward the delirious bliss of his thumb on her nub. She came again and bent forward to capture his mouth with hers while she continued to pump him.

A third time, her body shuddered and jerked. Gabri cried out. Caylen gripped both her hips and began to thrust inside her hard enough to crush her lips against him. Her hands found the pillow beneath his head and she gripped it. Her breasts pressed against his chest as he thrust harder and faster.

He slammed into her, his hands in a bruising grip on her hips, but the pain only made her pleasure flare higher. Caylen's cock leapt inside her as he buried himself as deeply as he could. Covered with the thrall, she heard the sound of his seed pulsing from him as she heard the blood flowing throughout her clit in its final surges of orgasm.

They rested there for a moment before she slid to his side to cuddle against him. The warmth of his seed coated her, and Gabri took a cloth from the bedside table to press between her legs.

"How do people without the thrall make love, do you think?" Cay asked her. "It can't possibly be as nice."

She laughed and kissed his shoulder. "Well, there are more people in the world who don't have magic than do, so I'd say their lovemaking must be at least adequate enough for them to keep doing it."

"Now that I have it, I can't imagine how I ever was before." Cay's heartbeat had begun to slow beneath her cheek. "The low magic seems like parlor tricks now."

Gabri yawned and pulled a sheet over their sweat-cooled bodies. "The low magic is just as useful as the high. More useful, sometimes, because it accomplishes the more menial tasks. You don't use the high magic to light a fire or to boil water. Most anything truly useful is done with the low magic."

"I know that. But the thrall...it fills me. It makes me see and hear and smell, taste, feel..."

"I know." Gabri rubbed his chest in slow circles and enjoyed the feeling of his smooth skin under her fingertips. "It's everything. But it can take everything, too. If you let it overcome you."

"I'd never do that," Cay scoffed. He kissed the top of her head. "You'd have to be pretty weak to allow that to happen."

Gabriana sat up to look into his face. "No. Just greedy. Or angry. If the thrall is a gift, it can also be a curse, Cay. Didn't you pay attention in History of the High Magic and Its Uses class?"

Cay looked embarrassed. "With Instructor Morgatine? Sorry. She put me to sleep nearly every time."

Gabri had to laugh at his honest answer. "If you'd stayed awake, you'd have learned some very important things."

"Maybe you can teach them to me." He kissed her.

Gone was the shy and awkward young man she'd known so well, Gabri thought fondly as Cay fondled her breast and nuzzled her cheek. Cay was confident. Eager. And a surprisingly accomplished lover.

"I studied in class, but it's you who've inspired me," he whispered, and took her aback.

"What?"

"You were thinking I'm changed," he said.

"Yes, but...the thrall?"

He nodded, then lifted his hand to show her the small orb he'd formed. He closed his fingers on it and it broke apart. The strands flowed over his arm and up his shoulder.

"Can you read thoughts, Gabri?"

She shook her head. "No, Cay. That's a very rare talent."

"It's faded now anyway." He showed her his palm and the vanishing sparks of magic. "But for a moment, I heard everything you thought."

"Do you think it's the tithe? That it's just me? Or can you do this with anyone?"

He lay back on his pillow, his blue eyes narrowed in concentration. "I don't know."

"Cay, if you can, you're destined for more than just casual accomplishments." Gabri felt a shudder trail her spine like a set of phantom fingers. "You'll have a great responsibility. You could be a Truthseer."

He gathered her close to him, and when he spoke, his voice was muffled. "I don't know if I want to be a Truthseer."

"Love," Gabri said. "You might not have a choice."

Chapter 9

Noa hadn't meant to avoid the judging. She had not seen Riordan since the guards had dragged him out of his chambers when she'd come to warn him of Solveig's accusations. She hadn't been allowed to follow.

Overnight, while Riordan languished in a cell, Noa had been struck with a fever that left her unable to get out of bed. Her stomach and bowels had rebelled against the mildest of broth, even water, and she'd spent most of her time on the privy chamber floor. With nearly the entire Keep in a frenzy over the scandal surrounding Riordan and Solveig, nobody had bothered to pay attention to Noa. The mysterious illness had laid her low.

Without Solveig's accusation ringing in her head, Noa would have assumed spoiled food had caused her sickness. Instead, every time her stomach heaved and her head spun, she saw the other's girl's face and felt her hands on her breasts and between her legs. This smacked of magic, bad magic.

She'd wasted an entire day wracked with chills and losing anything she ate or drank. She gathered her strength as night fell and forced herself to stand, to seek out the warmth of the bathing chamber, and to cleanse herself of the sickness that had overtaken her.

Sheer force of will kept the bowl of soup in her belly. Willpower helped her wrap herself in layers of winter robes that would normally have been too heavy for the Fivemonth weather. Her strength and the strength of her love for Riordan kept her on her feet when her vision doubled and tripled.

Noa made it through the night and greeted the morning from her window. She did not feel better; if anything, she felt worse. Her skin was red and blotchy, and heat rose all around her like flames even while she shivered and shuddered. She had to swallow convulsively, over and over, to quell the nausea. But she stood. She walked.

She'd never heard the Keep so silent, without the conversation and laughter of students in the halls. Even the cleaning staff had disappeared. Noa put a hand to the cool stone wall. Her head spun and she blinked away the dizziness. She needed to get to the Judging Hall.

Each step seemed to take the strength of three, but she made them. Head down, she concentrated. She summoned the thrall and felt it dance around her, but not even the high magic could keep the illness from her. It did, however, help her move her feet when she began to believe she couldn't take another step.

She had paused to catch her breath when her soul twisted. Noa doubled over, gasping. Blackness edged with crimson blinded her. She reached for the wall and her fingernails broke as she gripped the stone. The pain was intense, but far away as she fought to retain consciousness.

The tithe. When Riordan became her *ahavatara*, the act had tithed their souls to each other. What happened to him would affect any for whom he'd served as *ahavatara*...but not like this. Not this agony that ripped at her guts like a hand full of broken glass. This was not only because he had been her first lover. It was because he was her first love. Her only love.

Noa cried out as the pain grew. If she was feeling this agony, what must Riordan be feeling? She forced herself to take another step. She stumbled and went to her knees as the blackness made her blind.

A gust of a breeze on her cheek made her think she'd fallen in front of a door that opened. Noa opened her eyes. The blackness became gray.

"Noa? By the Knight, what happened to you?"

Hands lifted her. A hand cradled her head while another held her beneath the arms.

"Caylen?"

"It's me. And Gabriana. What's wrong? Are you sick?"

Slowly the gray left her vision, too, until she could see the man and woman who held her. " It's Riordan, Cay. They've taken him."

"What? Where?" Gabriana took a handkerchief from her pocket and wiped Noa's face. "Noa, you're burning with fever. What's going on?"

"Didn't you hear?" Noa licked her cracked lips with a tongue as dry as sand. "Solveig de Yourk has accused Riordan of rape."

Gabriana gasped. "No!"

Noa began to fall and Caylen picked her up. Her head fell against his chest. She wanted to say more, to tell them Solveig must be lying, but no words would come.

"He can't have done it." Caylen shifted Noa in his arms. "Not the Instructor Primus. He's mean, but he's not stupid."

"...not mean..." Noa breathed. "I love him..."

"Save your strength." Gabriana pushed Noa's hair from her face. "We know. We know this can't be true."

"This can't be right." Caylen carried Noa down the hall toward the Judging Hall. "Gabri, let's get Noa to the Judging Hall."

They got her there far more quickly than she'd have been able to by herself. By the time they entered the crowded room, some of her strength had returned. Caylen set her down, though he and Gabri kept hold of her elbows.

"Are we too late?" Noa asked from the doorway.

A woman she didn't recognize was speaking. "Riordan de Cimmerian, you have heard the accusation against you. You have seen the same evidence presented to this tribunal, and you have declined to offer your defense. This is your last chance to speak on your behalf. Do you have any proof of your innocence in this matter?"

Riordan's voice rang out clear and strong through the room. "There is nothing I can say to convince anyone in this room. There are many here who would be happy to judge me guilty no matter what proof I offer to the contrary. I will take my chances with the truthfire."

The woman, who must be the First Inquisitor, nodded. "Let it be so."

In front of Riordan, a column of blue flame shot up from the floor. It cast no heat, but its brilliance was so great all who looked at it had to shield their eyes.

"No!" Noa cried more loudly than she'd thought possible.

She felt the weight of many eyes upon her, but none heavier than Riordan's as he turned his head toward her and stepped into the column of flame.

Instant agony seared her. He went to his knees inside the column. His face twisted in a scream she could not hear. But she felt it. It ripped and tore at her, and she voiced it for him.

The flames did not change color. Riordan bent and put his head in his hands, and she could no longer see his face. More pain surged within her. Noa would have fallen if not for the hands of her friends.

"How long?" She heard Cay murmur. "How long do they wait to see if he speaks the truth? How long can he last in there?"

"You see?" Solveig cried triumphantly to the room. "It's staying blue! He's lying!"

"No," Noa whispered. "I can't believe it of him."

Beside her, Caylen touched his forehead as though to brush away a pain there. "No. I can't either."

He looked into the crowd. "Gabri, do you see Bragnon?"

Gabriana turned her head to look at the crowd. "No. Wait. Yes. Up there in the corner. He's doing something."

"He's working the thrall," Cay said.

Noa fought another wave of weakness. She lifted her head and sought the sight of the man Caylen had named. "Why? What's he doing?"

"Look." Cay used his head to point toward Solveig, who was smiling, her eyes locked on Bragnon's. "I didn't think he'd have it in him."

"He doesn't," Gabri said. "It's her. She's got the thrall now. That much is true. It's strong in her. But I don't think she got it from Riordan."

"That day at the lake!" Cay's grip on Noa's arm would have been painful, except for the pain already flooding her. "Solveig and Bragnon on the boat. He was her *ahavatara*. And they're lying about it to send Riordan down."

"But why isn't the truthfire changing color?" Noa felt stronger.

Caylen said, "Because maybe there's enough truth in Solveig's story to allow her to use the thrall, with Bragnon, to trick the fire."

Noa had never heard of anyone being able to trick the truthfire. "What is her story?"

The young woman sitting in the seat closest to the trio spoke up. "She says she went to his office, at his request, and that he forced himself on her there. She said she had cloth she used to clean herself after, and it proved to have both of their essences on it. And she's got the thrall." The young woman sounded convinced Solveig was telling the truth. "She couldn't get that without an *ahavatara*."

"But she could get it from anyone," said Gabri.

"The bathing pool." Noa stood suddenly so straight her friends no longer needed to support her. "She came to me in the bathing pool and tried to convince me of her story. She had a cloth, and she touched me with it. I thought she was just being dramatic, but she could have used that cloth to prove her story. Only she didn't get the essence from him. She got it from me."

"And she made you sick, so you couldn't come here and help defend him." Gabri's voice was grim. "By the Astria, she's a witch."

The blue column wavered. Riordan had stopped moving. Noa's soul twisted again.

"It's killing him," she said.

She didn't have to think twice about what to do. She would not stand by and allow Riordan to perish alone. She gathered every bit of strength she had left and ran into the truthfire.

Chapter 10

The room erupted into a cacophony of shouts. Caylen watched Noa dive into the column of blue. She cradled Riordan in her arms. He couldn't hear what she said to him, though he saw her mouth moving. Tears glittered on her cheeks.

"Why can't they see what she's doing?" Cay said.

"Nobody's ever tricked the truthfire." Gabri reached for his hand and their fingers linked. "Solveig must be very, very strong."

"Get her out of there!" Someone cried as Noa went to her knees with Riordan.

The First Inquisitor held up her hand. "She's chosen her path. If he dies, so will she."

Caylen watched Solveig watching Noa and Riordan. The younger woman's eyes had lit up with a joy so nasty it hurt him to see it. The thrall pulsed around her in waves, but even though Caylen knew she had somehow linked with Bragnon to fool the fire, he couldn't tell how. Nobody else would know either.

The high magic tickled the back of his neck, though he hadn't summoned it. "Maybe I can see."

"Caylen?"

He stepped toward Solveig and the table of Inquisitors. "Maybe I can see the truth she's blocking."

Gabri's fingers slipped from his. Caylen lifted his hands. The thrall crackled and snapped from hand to hand. An orb formed in each palm. Both splintered and merged, then formed again as he walked. He'd never done this before, not on purpose, and he wasn't sure how to urge the thrall toward his goal.

"Stand back!" cried one of the Inquisitors as Cay approached Solveig's chair.

Caylen heard the questions.

"What's he doing?"

"Who is that?"

"Caylen de Marque!"

Caylen waited until Solveig turned to look at him. The smile on her pretty face became a frown. Caylen held out his hands.

"Go sit back down, chum." She glanced back toward the truthfire, but not for long before her eyes turned back to Cay as though she couldn't help herself.

She was strong. She was hiding how much of the thrall she commanded, and he understood why. Just the ability to hide her strength indicated exactly how much power she could wield. Solveig gripped the arms of her chair and fixed him with a steady glare.

Go sit down.

The words echoed inside his head, and Cay actually turned to do as she said before he broke the command. He turned back. Surprise flickered in her eyes before it was quickly replaced by cunning.

"State your name and your business," said the First Inquisitor.

"I am Caylen de Marque. And I can prove this woman is lying."

The room rippled with outrage and shock. Caylen didn't buckle beneath the wave of disbelief around him. Behind him, he felt Gabriana's presence. She didn't have to touch him to give him the benefit of her strength.

"How do you propose to do this?" said an Inquisitor. "The accuser has provided sufficient evidence to convince this tribunal she speaks true, and the truthfire concurs."

"She's lying." Caylen watched Solveig's face crinkle with a fury she fought to conceal. His gaze flicked to the crowd. Bragnon had vanished.

"The truthfire doesn't lie." The First Inquisitor looked at Caylen calmly. "How can you prove otherwise?"

"He can't!" Solveig's voice was harsh. She looked toward Hedavarius. "I'm not lying! I'm not! That man forced me!"

She burst into loud, braying sobs that moved Hedavarius to take her into his arms. "Hasn't she been through enough?"

Inside the truthfire, Noa and Riordan clutched each other. Cay couldn't tell if they were still conscious. The blue didn't waver.

He held up his hands again, and with a subtle shift in his mind, he opened himself to the thrall. It flooded him with more force than he'd ever felt. It rocked him, but Gabri's hand upon his back helped him stand straight.

Light exploded around him, then drew together and formed a large orb over his outstretched hands. The orb beat in time to his heart. Caylen was vaguely aware his cock had hardened into an erection so stiff it was nearly painful. He ignored it and focused on Solveig.

Get out!

Gabri's thoughts had come to him unbidden on the island. He had to work to get to Solveig's.

You're a liar, Solveig.

Get out of my head! Get out, you common-born mongrel!

Everything else faded away as he faced her. He was aware of Gabri behind him and the Inquisitors watching, of the crowd in the room babbling, but none of that mattered. He faced the sorceress without flinching.

I know what you did.

You don't know anything!

I just don't know why.

An image came to him of Solveig sitting in an office. Riordan's office. The Instructor Primus was shaking his head while Solveig gave him a simpering smile. Solveig spoke and Riordan reached for her. That much of her story was true.

You offered yourself to him, and he refused.

He took that common-born slut to his bed. He should have begged to have me!

But he didn't, and you took Bragnon instead.

Solveig sneered around Hedavarius' arms.

I have more power in my little finger than that bitch will ever have! And even though I took that imbecile Bragnon for my ahavatara, it gave me what I needed!

The thrall.

And now Riordan and his haggard slut are both going to die, and I'll be the most powerful magicreator this realm has ever seen! Now get out of my head!

Caylen staggered from the sudden force of Solveig's will. Her expression didn't change, even as she hammered him. Gabri's touch fueled him further and Caylen spoke the truth.

The orb above his hands formed the pictures he'd taken from Solveig's head. Hedavarius stepped away from her as Solveig straightened. Her hands clenched into fists. She lifted them and formed an orb of her own.

Caylen had trained to control the thrall when it should come to him, but like lovemaking, a text could only hint at what the experience was actually like. Solveig already had more control of the high magic than Caylen did. He couldn't hope to match her. He could only hope to do his best.

228

"What is this?" the First Inquisitor asked. She stood, followed by the others. "Caylen de Marque, are you a Truthseer?"

"He is, Inquisitor." Gabri answered for him, since he could not.

Get out of my head!

Pain exploded in Cay's skull. Blood began to flow from his nose. It smelled like the sound of drums and tasted like midnight. He went to his knees, but kept his hands upraised. His orb didn't flicker.

More truth poured out of him. The vision swirled above them. Solveig, riding Bragnon. The two of them, head to head, making plans. Finally, Solveig with Noa in the bathing pool, and the cloth she'd used to condemn Riordan.

"Solveig de Yourk," said the First Inquisitor. "You have been proven a liar."

"No!" Hedavarius cried.

Solveig said nothing. She raised her fists to the sky and the room rocked. The Inquisitor's table fell over. Hedavarius was flung back. Some of the benches holding the spectators cracked and spilled them to the floor.

As screams and cried filled the air, the room rocked again. Harder this time. Hard enough to crack the stone floor of the Judging Hall.

Solveig spat on the floor next to Caylen. She clasped her hands together and looked up to the ceiling.

Then she disappeared.

Chapter 11

"You don't have to leave, you know." The woman who'd served as First Inquisitor said to Riordan. Her name, Noa had learned, was Felicita de Quaya. "You've been cleared of all charges. And you, Caylen de Marque. Somnus Keep could use a talented Truthseer."

"So could many other places," Caylen replied. He and Gabriana had packed their things and planned to leave the Keep at the same time as Noa and Riordan, though their destination was different.

Riordan didn't answer at first. His time in the truthfire had weakened him. At last he said, "I served Somnus Keep for a long time. But I can't stay in a place which would allow such a travesty to take place."

Felicita nodded. "We understand. You won't be easy to replace. But we understand."

Hedavarius had not come to see any of them off. Noa didn't care. As far as she was concerned, the sooner they left Somnus Keep, the better.

"The Keep won't be the same after this," Riordan said to Felicita. "Its reputation is as cracked as the floor in the Judging Hall."

Felicita nodded again. "We understand that, too. And we've taken pains to assure something like this never happens again."

"Too bad you hadn't taken the time to assure it couldn't happen at all." Riordan turned and reached for Noa's hand. "Come, love. Let's quit this place."

Chapter 12

And quit they did. Riordan took her to his ancestral home, in the land of Grimearth, to the house of Cimmerian. The manse was more a castle than a house, but Noa didn't mind. Not as long as she could share it with Riordan.

The days grew long with summer and they spent them together. They had a simple ceremony beneath the wedding canopy with only Caylen and Gabriana to attend them. They lived, and they loved, and they tried to put the past behind them.

Word spread quickly to the surrounding realm that Riordan was once again in attendance at Cimmerian. Every Granting Day, people came from miles around to have the two magicreators listen to their wishes for healthy babes, fertile fields and successful journeys. In exchange for a coin or two, the wishes were usually granted.

"I'm glad this day has ended," Noa said after one full day of listening to petitioners. "My ears are fair weary from hearing all those pleas."

"But you do it so well," Riordan told her. He kissed her as she bent to slip off her shoes. He helped her pull her gown off over her head, then led her to their large, soft bed. "The people love you."

"The ladies love you," she replied wryly as he stretched out beside her. "Why do I only get the old crones, the fat merchants, the lovesick, young boys? While you get the simpering, eye-fluttering maidens and busty housewives?"

"Do I? I've barely noticed."

She laughed and held him close to her while he nuzzled her nipples. "You know you do."

"I only have eyes for you, dear Noa."

She sighed as his tongue traced a pattern on her skin. "Riordan, have you ever been tempted to grant the request of someone who wishes for evil?"

He paused. "Yes. Of course I have."

She thought of Solveig whose power had been mighty despite her youth. "What stopped you from giving in?"

"The more evil you grant, the more you receive."

She didn't ask him about the girl who had accused him falsely. Instead, Noa pulled his head back to her breast. She was determined to put the witch from her mind. Wherever she was in this world, she was far from them.

Riordan made his way down to the soft curls between her legs, and Noa arched to meet his kiss there. He brought her to the edge of climax with his hands and his tongue, then moved up her body and filled her with his cock until she cried his name as she burst with pleasure.

He loved her hard, and he loved her sweetly, and when it was over, they slept in each other's arms without bad dreams to disturb them.

About the Author

Megan Hart is a USA Today, Publisher's Weekly and New York Times bestselling author who writes in many genres including mainstream fiction, erotic fiction, science fiction, romance, fantasy and horror. If you liked this book, please tell everyone you love to buy it. If you hated it, please tell everyone you hate to buy it.

Connect with me…

Twitter.com/Megan_Hart
Facebook.com/READINBED
MeganHart.com

The Morningstar
　　　　Parts 1 & 2

Originally published as two novellas, Ride with the Devil and Dance with the Devil

Ride with the Devil

If you take enough rides with the devil, pretty soon he'll drive. Jake learns this the hard way when the devil sets him a task he thinks he can't finish...or can he?

Dance with the Devil

When the devil starts the music, you'd better get ready to dance. Kathleen Murphy has sold her soul to the devil. Fame, fortune, success...everything she's ever dreamed of is hers, and all she has to do is the devil's bidding. When love comes knocking, the last thing in the world she wants to do is involve Jake in her twisted world, but the devil's started up the jukebox and Kathleen has no choice but to learn the steps.

Excerpt from:

Dance with the Devil

It was quite possibly the best book she'd ever written.

Kathleen had been asked many times which book was her favorite. She always said it was Walk With Me, because that was the one that had been made into a movie. It had paid for her flat in Manhattan and would pay for Callie to attend any college she wanted. It was the book that had the best reviews, but it wasn't really her favorite.

She would always have the fondest spot in her heart for Ride With the Devil. Her first sale, her first hit on all the lists. It was the book that had made her famous and everything that had come since then might've surpassed it in sales and acclaim, but nothing could compare to how it had felt to write that book. Sitting in the coffee shop's front window for hours on end, writing from her heart.

It was different, now.

Now she wrote to market, or to contract when someone approached her about participating in an anthology or some other special project. Now she wrote knowing about the criticism — and there was plenty, because for every reader who loved and raved about her work, there were equal numbers who hated every word she'd ever written. They continued to buy and read the books, though, something Kathleen had never understood. In a life too short as it was, why waste any precious second of it on something you hated? But who knew, maybe that was their devil's task.

The document she'd just closed and saved, backing up to an online storage site as well as several external hard drives, was due in two weeks. It was a closer skate to her deadline than she was used to. It was always a point of pride with her that she met her professional commitments on time, if not early. But this project had been stalled several times by self doubt and having to take time away from writing so that she could do the devil's bidding.

She'd finished it now, though. A hundred thousand words and seven sets of revisions, including a complete rewrite of a third of the book. Three months of her life, give or take.

There was always a moment of hesitation before she hit send on the email submitting the manuscript to her editor and agent. That final moment when she could still change her mind, take it back. Tinker with the book some more. She could drive herself mad with the tweaking, though, so with a deep breath, Kathleen moved her finger on the computer's trackpad, intending to stab "send."

"Wait," said the Morningstar. "Don't."

Kathleen whirled in her chair with a yelp. Her elbow knocked the cold mug of coffee onto the floor, where it splattered her bare ankles. "What the!"

"Hell?"

Her heartbeat slowed. "Surely you can find a less startling way of showing up."

"Not my style," the devil said without so much as the hint of a smile. "You would do better to address me more respectfully."

Kathleen froze. Then nodded. "Yes. I'm sorry."

"Don't send that manuscript."

"But…it's finished," she began.

He was on her in a second, a hand at her throat and the slavering, snapping jaws of a wolf grazing her cheek. Only a second, before the devil stepped back looking as calm and serene as a summer sky. Not a hair out of place. If you'd asked her to describe him in that moment, though, all Kathleen would've been able to say was that he looked like a man.

"You're going to be late with this book. Very late. Four, five months late. No. Six."

Her voice shook when she answered. "If I'm that late with this book, their entire publishing schedule is going to be messed up. I have four books scheduled with them —"

"Your choice," Satan told her in that silky caramel voice.

She curled her fingers into fists in her lap. "Fine. I won't send it now."

It would be the first time she was ever late on a deadline. It would be all right. She could make it all right, she thought as the devil vanished and left her alone in front of the computer.